PRINCE ANDY
AND THE
MISFITS

To: Kim,

Best wishes,

Karen Gammons

PRINCE ANDY
AND THE
MISFITS

EPIDEMIC
IN THE
DARK LANDS

KAREN GAMMONS

Map Art: Randi Gammons and Caleb Gammons
Cover design: Elizabeth E. Little, Hyliian Design, www.hyliian.deviantart.com
Interior design: Ellen C. Maze, The Author's Mentor, www.ellencmaze.com
Published in the United States of America
ISBN-13: 978-1470073046
ISBN-10: 1470073048

Fiction / Fantasy / General 2. Juvenile Fiction / Fantasy & Magic

DEDICATION

For Melissa
My littlest, best friend.

ACKNOWLEDGMENTS

I would like my readers to know that even though I have written a secular book, I am a Christian. I believe that Jesus died for me, and that He is the Son of God. All the credit and thanks for my imagination go to Him.

My best friend and love of my life, Troy is the best supporter a wife and author can have. I love you very much and thank you for taking this journey with me.

My three children: Caleb, Randi and Haylee are such an inspiration. I don't know what I would do without you. All three of you have worked hard and contributed to my books, book trailers, and websites. A huge heart of thanks goes out to you.

A heartfelt thanks goes out to Lenda Selph, for helping me proofread my book and making it the best possible. I don't think my book would be as wonderful without you.

I would like to recognize the wonderful lady that helped this book become published, Ellen C. Maze from The Author's Mentor.

Gerald Whitaker keeps my computer running smoothly. Kudos to him.

A nice big thank you goes out to Clint Brown, the winner of my Dragon Kingdom name contest. He came up with the name of Eldfjall, which means volcano in Icelandic.

I used some of my friends' names in the books and I wanted to say thank you to them: Hannah Thornburg, Taylor Castle, Amanda Brown, Jennifer Brown and Lauren Telford.

A huge thanks goes to my beautiful mother, Winnie, my brother Gary Tucker, my sister Cindy Cain, my wonderful mother-in-law, Sue, friends Temple Thornburg, Evelynn Skinner, and Ken and Kay Monroe, for reading the book and giving me their opinion.

And to everyone who loves reading Prince Andy and the Misfits books, thank you for your support. It means everything to me.

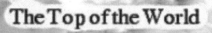

The Top of the World

Loombria

River Birch
Forest

The Bitter Plains

The Golden River

Hamamelis
Prison

Dingy
Mountains

The Black
Mountains

Land
of the
Fitful

Ogre
Cave

Troll
Cave

Ant
Realm

The Labyrinth

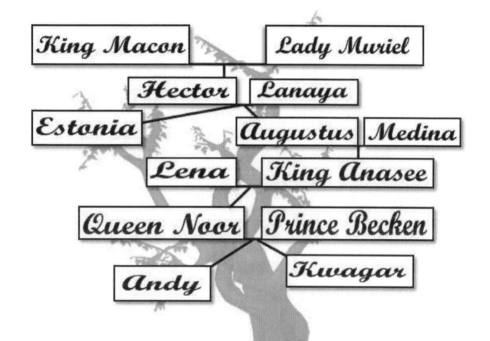

King Macon   Lady Muriel

Hector   Lanaya

Estonia   Augustus   Medina

Lena   King Anasee

Queen Noor   Prince Becken

Andy   Kwagar

Andy's Family Tree

TABLE OF CONTENTS

PROLOGUE

T he cold water from the swift, rushing river cooled Morgan's aching throat. He had been walking for quite a while beside his horse-drawn cart. The market had been a success that morning! He sold almost all of the produce he had grown in his garden that summer. Morgan felt good knowing that his pockets were full of money and that the shelves in his pantry at home were lined with enough food for the winter months.

The elves were a delightful sight as usual. They had brought entertainment with them to the market and there had been a huge feast to celebrate the end of the season. The elves had a life that most envied. It made Morgan smile as he remembered some of them. He even got to see his most cherished friend Thane, nephew of King Silverthorne.

As he watched the sparkling water rush by,

Morgan thought about his life in the Dark Lands. Sometimes it could be so rigid and lonesome. Even though the Shadow People fervently accepted their own kind when a newcomer came to the Dark Lands, the loss of one's own family and friends was heart-wrenching.

Morgan had a wonderful life as a child. His father, an elf, had fallen in love with a human woman. He had seen her pass through his forest quite often on her way to visit her uncle and his family in Filligrim. Morgan's father was smitten from the very beginning and had pursued her with love songs and flowers and long walks in the moonlight. They married despite what their families had thought. Where Morgan's mother lived, they didn't have any laws about marriages of different races and they felt it would be safe to have a family. Morgan and his twin sister had been born a year after the marriage. His parents had brought up his sister and him in a magnificent home and gave them everything their hearts desired.

Morgan had been a good-looking kid, with wavy brown hair, and dark brown eyes and the sharp features of an elf. His happy life ended, however, when he became a teenager. He began changing—slowly fading into what he was now: a shadow. His sister showed no signs of changing. His parents brought him to the edge of the Dark Lands when he turned eighteen. The Dark Lands were a refuge for the Shadow People, created just for them by the Shadow Queen. They gave him money to buy a home, food and enough clothes to last him through the winter. They wished him luck, and then left him standing there, heartbroken. Morgan knew it had been hard for his parents as well. His mother had suffered deep depression. She begged his father not to leave him. But there was nothing his father could do. The whole town had voted that Morgan be sent to the Dark Lands. Morgan's father couldn't go against the elders of their settlement. His sister, like her mother, had nearly died of a broken heart, knowing she would never see her twin again.

With the money his father had given him, Morgan bought a run-down farmhouse on thirty acres. With the skills acquired from his father, Morgan had fixed up the house, built a fine barn and plowed ten acres for a garden. He was what most called in the Dark Lands, "a farming success."

Morgan finished drinking from the river, then sat down by a large boulder. It was so quiet in the Dark Lands. No birds or crickets chirping. No wildlife scampering around, just stillness and silence. His thoughts turned to an elf that had passed through his farm almost two months ago. The elf looked so desperate to find information about his young friend. All Morgan could give him was bad news. Morgan was at the castle delivering produce and stopped to visit his friend, Marcella the Sheely. She lived under one of the bridges close to the castle. The Sheeleys were a special type of mermaids from the Crystal Sea. As they visited, she told him all the latest gossip she had heard from the castle. She got very excited when she talked about seeing Saber, a Shadow Man who lived in the castle with the queen. She had seen him coming home one night with a boy draped over the back of his saddle. The boy looked as though he were dead. After Morgan told the elf this information, the elf walked a few paces away and began crying. In all of Morgan's life he had never seen an elf cry. It just wasn't in their nature. Sorrow filled Morgan's heart just watching the grieving elf. He wished he could have helped him in some way. The elf had left his farm and that was the last that Morgan had seen of him.

At market that morning, he overheard a group of old Shadow Men talking about a young boy up at the castle. One of the old men worked for the queen in the dungeon, where he brought food to the prisoners. The old man complained about his wages and the slop he had to feed to the creatures and the young boy in the jail, but he had said nothing except that the boy was alive. Morgan breathed a sigh of relief. He wished he knew where to get in touch with the elf, so he could tell him the good news. Morgan only hoped that the elf had heard the good news as well.

Morgan looked at the large tree near where he sat and noticed a huge gash in it, as if someone had started to take an ax to it, and then changed his mind. He reached out and ran his hand along the gash, touching the sticky sap that seeped from the lesion. It seemed so awful to damage a tree and not use every bit of its resources. Morgan was part elf, and trees were an elf's passion.

After examining the tree, his eyes came to rest on a smaller tree growing just a few feet away. It was only three feet tall and already had fruit growing on the branches. The fruit was golden and looked temptingly delicious. Morgan got up and walked over to the tree, picked one of the fruits and smelled it. It was like nothing he had ever smelled before, rich and fruity with a hint of almonds. His mouth watered just looking at the fruit. He bit deep into it. It tasted as good as it smelled. Morgan sat back down against the large tree, closed his eyes and enjoyed chewing and savoring the fruit. When he raised the piece of fruit to take another bite, he noticed the flesh of the fruit was solid black inside, with dark red seeds. It looked rotten. Morgan threw the fruit to the ground. He felt sick for having taken a bite of it.

A rumbling overhead from an oncoming storm made Morgan rise to his feet. Rain would be there soon. He gathered the horse's tether in his hand. As he took one more look at the little tree, fear clenched him, like he was in the grasp of a giant intent on eating him. The sight of the little tree reminded him of deep sorrow and tragedy, as though his life had been stolen and he was now a slave to it.

He began feeling a strange sensation. Then pain began to burn, first in his stomach, then spreading to his chest. Morgan gasped and fell down on his hands and knees. He couldn't catch his breath. The sensation expanded further through his body, reaching into his limbs, and finally his fingers and toes.

"What's happening to me?" he breathed to the stillness of the forest. No one was there to answer him back.

The pain was so severe he collapsed and rolled onto his back. The last thing he saw as he blacked out was his horse standing over him, his hand still holding the reins. His hand was turning green.

CATCHING UP

A cloaked figure stood in the shadows of a group of trees, scanning the perimeter around the little cottage; he had been watching for the past ten minutes. He had to make sure he had not been followed. Just the slightest of movements from any of the trees or perhaps an animal, would suggest that he was not alone. He stood stock still until he was sure that no one was around, and then he moved forward. Taking his time and with careful steps he reached the cottage and took one last look around; another safe trip under his belt.

The aged, ramshackle cottage was a haven to those who needed sanctuary in the brewing storm around the land of Filligrim. It stood resolute as if it were thumbing its walls, roof, doors and windows to the world, almost daring to a point. Faded, the peeling yellow paint was a reminder to its charm of long ago. The stranger knocked softly on the rickety door and waited.

The scraping noises of chairs dragging across the floor could be faintly heard from within, and then whispers. Deliberate footsteps walked to the door and paused.

"Who is it?" asked a raspy voice, as a door shut quietly somewhere in the house.

"Elsfur," the cloaked figured whispered back. He grinned as a short, grotesque creature opened the door, dwarfed in size, yet with extremities that were very large in proportion to the rest of his body. He had a huge, bulbous nose, large yellow eyes that looked like moons, two small antennas on top of his head for ears and protuberances on the side of his head that were shaped like lips. They flapped and slobbered when he spoke.

The door opened a crack, just enough for the person to identify the newcomer as an elf. The elf was very impressive-looking, with a slender build that was very muscular, a chiseled face with straight flowing blond hair, and pointed ears.

Then with sighs of relief, the person inside threw open the door and welcomed the cloaked figure with open arms. Snollygob showered Elsfur with tears and slobber as the two embraced once more.

"It has been so long, Elsfur. I didn't know if you would ever return," Snollygob slobbered as he poured a cup of tea, then placed it in front of the now-seated elf.

"Two and a half months is a long time. I didn't know if I would return as well," Elsfur said, sipping the hot tea.

"What have you discovered?"

Elsfur paused and drew a deep breath before answering. "Not much. The Dark Lands are so immense, not to mention what lives there. I had a hard time finding any information. I'm very worried about Andy."

"What about Kwagar?" Snollygob said, spraying slobber. "Did you find what has become of him?"

"The goblins have moved him to their prison in the Dingy Mountains beyond River Birch Forest." He sighed hard. "I tracked them for three weeks. I was able to get a glimpse of him in chains as they were taking him into the prison. He looked as if he was being treated well enough."

"You went all the way to the Dingy Mountains and back?" Snollygob said in amazement. "You must be exhausted!"

"Not to mention the Dark Lands, and yes, I am very tired. I could sleep for a week." Elsfur looked around. "I thought I heard voices when I approached the door or am I going mad?"

Snollygob smiled at Elsfur. He got up and went to a door just off the kitchen and opened it.

The slight figure of a girl, who looked as if she had been immersed in a sea of ice-blue glitter, stepped through the door. She had on a dark blue robe tied with a gold belt. Her shiny black hair hung to her feet and was pulled back in a ponytail. Her deep blue eyes came to rest on Elsfur.

"Shimmer!" Elsfur said in surprise. "How good it is to see you again." They embraced awkwardly and then sat down at the table.

"So, you've been to the Dingy Mountains and the Dark Lands. Did you find Andy?" she said, slightly breathless from the embrace.

"I spoke with a farmer in the Dark Lands. He takes his food from his garden and sells it to the cook up at Charlock Castle. He has to pass over the Golden River where Marcella the Sheely lives. He gives her culls from his garden and she gives him information on who to sell to, to make the most money. They have become good friends over the last year."

Elsfur stopped speaking, leaving the two listeners to wait while he sipped the piping hot tea. He gathered his thoughts for a moment, reflecting on the conversation that he had with the farmer. Shimmer and Snollygob looked at each other and then back at Elsfur in anticipation, waiting for him to finish telling them the story.

"What information did he receive from the Sheely?" Snollygob asked, trying to act casual.

"She told the farmer that a huge Shadow Man, who works for the Charlock Castle in the Dark Lands, came riding in on an enormous horse very late one night. Draped over the back of the horse behind the rider was a boy." Elsfur took another sip of his tea and sat quietly staring into his cup.

"Oh, for crying out loud Elsfur, get on with the story!" Snollygob shouted, causing an abnormal amount of slobber from his lips on each side of his head, to dislodge and fly all over the table. Then he mumbled, "You do that on purpose so that everyone will be on the edge of their seats."

"I'm sorry old friend," Elsfur smiled wearily. "I'm very tired."

"It's okay, Elsfur," Shimmer said, sympathetically. "Why don't you go and lie down for a while. You can finish your story later. Meanwhile, Snollygob and I will prepare a nice hot meal for when you wake up."

"That would be wonderful." Elsfur yawned. "I just need a few winks, then I'll be right as rain. Where should I sleep?"

Snollygob pointed out a room down a long hall. He left Shimmer and Snollygob at the table. Shimmer stood up, went to the sink and began peeling potatoes.

"I saw the way you looked at him when you came into the room a while ago," Snollygob whispered. "Still got the old embers burning, do ya?"

"You know that I care for someone else now," Shimmer said, watching her hands rhythmically peeling the potatoes.

"I don't think you do. I think that Elsfur will always be the one you love."

"All that is changed, Snollygob. I do care for Elsfur. But those lovesick feelings are gone. Andy has filled my heart and thoughts now. I just wish we could find him. You know I would rescue him in a minute if I could."

"We'll find him," Snollygob said, patting her on the back. "Don't you worry, we'll find him."

"I do worry. It has been nearly three months

11

and not a word about where he is and now we find out that he's in Charlock Castle. You know what happens to people who go into that castle," she said, stifling a sob.

"I know. But we have to hope for the best. Andy is very strong-willed. He also has the dragon blood in him, so you know that will give him some protection."

"Well, just remember this conversation is just between us," Shimmer warned. "I don't want anyone else to know."

"You can count on me."

The conversation lulled into a lapsed silence with only a word or two spoken every now and then while they worked to put together a meal. Thirty minutes later a piping hot stew simmered over a fire, while Shimmer and Snollygob sat sipping hot tea at the kitchen table. They both were deep in thought, worrying about Andy, Kwagar and the whole Kingdom of Filligrim. So much so, they didn't hear the tiny rap at the door the first time. When the rap came again, they jumped from their thoughts and looked at one another.

"Are you expecting anyone else?" Shimmer whispered.

Snollygob shook his head. They both turned when the door just down the hallway creaked open and Elsfur stepped through with his sword drawn. He nodded to Shimmer to open the door. Shimmer rose and slowly walked to the door and placed her hand upon the knob. She looked back at Elsfur for one more confirmation. He nodded again and she opened the door a crack.

A woman cloaked in a fine forest-green velvet robe with the hood up, shadowing her face, stood before the door. A tiny light hovered near her shoulder.

"May I help you?" Shimmer asked, eyeing the woman suspiciously.

"You can get some old friends some of that fine stew that is boiling over your fire," she said, taking the hood off her head.

Shimmer gasped. There before her stood a beautiful elf. Her face looked as if it were chiseled from fine porcelain. She had long, raven black hair, twinkling blue eyes, rosy cheeks and pointed ears. The only trace of what was left of her appearance from the other world was the gray streaks that still speckled her hair. The pixie that hovered at her shoulder stood about three inches tall, when she wasn't flying, with beautiful silver wings and long, braided golden hair. Tiny purple flower petals made up her skirt and bodice, and tiny purple slippers adorned her feet.

"Gladdy," Shimmer said faintly, and then she embraced the elf. "Oh…and Daisy, I'm so glad to see both of you."

"Shimmer, it's so good to see you," she said stepping into the cottage. "Well, look who else is here."

Gladdy gave both Elsfur and Snollygob extra-long hugs. It had been quite a long time since they had last seen one another. Gladdy took off her traveling cloak and pulled a bag from her shoulder. She reached inside the bag and carefully took out a little mole that usually accompanied Gladdy everywhere she went nowadays. She placed the mole on the floor and everyone in the room watched as the mole turned into a beautiful, rainbow-colored dryad named Grandmother Muckernut.

"Well, everyone," Grandmother Muckernut said. "What a pleasure it is to see all of you again." She looked at Elsfur. "I see you made it back from your travels. Did you just return or have you been back for a while?"

"I returned a few hours ago. These two were kind enough to allow me to get some rest."

"The last time we saw you, you were leaving Mystic's cavern with Flopsy, in search of Andy and Kwagar. Did you find them?" Gladdy asked, desperately.

"We found Flipsy," Elsfur said quietly. "He was at the edge of the Bitter Plains, up against the Dark Lands. Flopsy stayed with Flipsy, while I went into the Dark Lands to find Andy and the Shadow Man. I followed the trail of footprints for a ways and then the footprints turned into horseshoe prints. I went farther in, but I knew that Flipsy wouldn't last much longer. So I retreated and helped Flopsy get Flipsy back to the castle."

"How is Flipsy now?" Daisy asked, apprehensively.

"He is doing better. He told me how he swooped in to save Andy and Kwagar, but the goblins swarmed them. Flipsy said that he felt Andy get on, and about four goblins as well. Kwagar jumped, but he guessed that Kwagar either fell or the goblins pulled him back because Kwagar wasn't with them. Flipsy also said that one of the goblins had a dagger and continually stabbed him in the neck. Two of the other goblins fell off." Elsfur stopped and looked at his hands. When he looked back up he had tears in his eyes. "Flipsy said that the goblin Andy was fighting stabbed Andy in the stomach."

"NO!" Shimmer shouted. "How would Flipsy know this? He was flying and was hurt himself."

"Flipsy said that he saw Andy holding his stomach and that he was completely covered in— blood. I also found human blood where we found Flipsy, and a trail of it leading into the Dark Lands."

"My poor child," Gladdy gasped and began crying. She wiped tears from her eyes. "What about Kwagar?"

"Kwagar is now in the Dingy Mountains as I told the other two earlier. I followed the goblins to the prison that they have there. Kwagar looked in good enough shape. However, I have heard stories about what goes on in that prison and I don't know if Kwagar will hold up."

"Elsfur told us that he spoke to a farmer in the Dark Lands," Snollygob said. "Finish telling us about the farmer's encounter with Marcella the Sheely."

"As I was telling Shimmer and Snollygob, I met a farmer in the Dark Lands who had befriended Marcella the Sheely--"

"Why is Marcella the Sheely in the Dark Lands?" Gladdy interrupted.

"She told the farmer that the goblins were

hunting her for their own use and that she followed the Golden River into the Dark Lands to get away from them. She ended up in a drainage pipe not far from the Charlock Castle. A bridge leading into the back of the castle is right next to her drainage pipe. She only comes out at night to find food and that is when she saw the Shadow Man and a boy ride in on a horse."

"Did she say if Andy was alive?" Grandmother Muckernut asked.

"She told the farmer that the boy was draped over the horse like a blanket and that he looked dead to her." He looked at the faces staring back at him. They were horrified by the news. "It was just something I heard from the farmer. I feel in my heart—that Andy is just fine."

They all sat staring at Elsfur, trying to comprehend all of the information. He looked worn from the trip and dispirited. Elsfur looked back at all the faces staring at him, with his eyes coming to rest on Gladdy. She had put her faith in him to bring Andy back safely, and he had let her down. He felt as though he had let them all down.

The night crept on through the sky, finally reaching the windows of the little cottage. The wind had begun to blow, bringing with it a storm. Heavy rains poured down on the cottage, while lightning streaked the sky and thunder boomed. The Misfits took to their beds, too tired to think of what to do to save their loved ones from certain doom. They hoped with a good night's sleep and the rhythmic beating of the rain on the roof, their heads would be clearer and they would be able to get a better perspective on the situation in the morning. One by one they got up from the table and wandered into the various rooms where they would sleep. Not one of them said a word.

However, halfway through the dark, stormy night another figure appeared a distance away from the little cottage. He stood with rain pelting his head, trying to make up his mind about going up to the door. It could mean danger for the inhabitants within. About a half hour after he had arrived there, he made a move toward the door, but stopped. He could have sworn that he had seen something stir near a group of bushes to the right of the cottage. He stared hard for a time, but nothing ever moved again.

Knowing that he had been followed when he had left the Dingy Mountains, he had zigzagged and backtracked as best he could, hoping to lose whoever was following him along the way. The large figure decided to take a chance under the cover of the darkness and the heavy rain and go into the cottage. If he didn't, he would probably be very sick from being so wet and cold, and he needed his strength for the days ahead.

He stepped from his cover and hurriedly ran to the door of the cottage and rapped hard on it. At first no one answered and he began beating on the door. A light came on and traveled from room to room until it shone from beneath the front door. A latch clicked and the door inched open.

"Who's there and what do you want?" Snollygob growled. "It's late and if you hadn't noticed, it's pouring down rain!"

"I have noticed," a booming voice growled back. "I happen to be standing out in it. Now let me in, Snollygob, before I catch my death."

"Timmynog, is that you?"

"Yeah, now let me in, you gross, disgusting excuse for a creature." Timmynog pushed in past the little Killmoulis, nearly knocking him over.

"Oh, Timmynog," Snollygob said as he lunged for Timmynog's leg, that looked more like a huge tree trunk than a leg.

"Get off of me! I'm wet and I need to warm by the fire," Timmynog said, dragging Snollygob towards the fire.

"Snollygob," Gladdy said coming into the room wearing her nightgown. "Let the giant get warm. You can hug him later."

Snollygob let go of Timmynog's leg and landed hard on the floor.

"Hello Gladdy," Timmynog said, beaming. "I see you're back to your old self."

"Yes, I am. It happened shortly after Andy was taken. So where have you been, Timmynog?"

"Well," he said, scratching his head and looking around as everyone else came into the room. "I really don't know where to begin. When I last saw you, I was going out with the giants to help find any stray ogres and goblins that had gotten away. Then, we fixed up the giants that were hurt really badly. I knew that Elsfur had left to find Andy, so I felt that since Kwagar had been my charge, I needed to find out where they had taken him. I, like Elsfur, found out that Kwagar had been taken to the Dingy Mountains to the goblin prison."

"How did you know that I had left for the Dingy Mountains?" Elsfur asked.

"I saw King Foxglove, Shade and Meadow down on the Bitter Plains heading back to River Birch Forest. He explained that the goblins had overrun the elves as they came out of Phantom Road and into the Bitter Plains. A huge fight had occurred and left a lot of the elves and goblins either injured or dead. Most of the goblins headed for the Dingy Mountains. He said that he saw you from a distance riding a horse in that direction as well. I just naturally assumed that you had found out what had happened to Kwagar."

Timmynog shrugged. "Since I didn't have a horse or a dragon, it took me quite a while to make it to the Dingy Mountains."

Rain pelted the windows and the wind howled through the trees, making the night feel eerie to the Misfits inside the cottage. So much had happened to their peaceful life in such a short time.

"Did you find out how we could go about trying to rescue Kwagar?" Snollygob asked. "We can't just leave him there to rot."

"That prison is a fortress. I don't see any of us making it past the guards that are stationed in front of its gates," Timmynog said.

"Yes, I saw the guards as well. Gargoyles from the Luna Peelo Caves in the Dingy Mountains." Elsfur sighed. "Slaves of the goblin king."

"Couldn't we send Shimmer in to bring him out?" Gladdy asked.

"No. The Gargoyles can smell up to a quarter mile. They have been trained to recognize the smell of every race. And let's not forget their razor sharp talons and fangs that are both tipped with poison. Shimmer would be dead before she ever got near the gates. Besides, we could never put her at such a risk." Elsfur looked longingly at Shimmer, and then glanced away.

"What about sending me into the Charlock Castle? I could find Andy and bring him out safely," Shimmer said, brightening.

"I don't know much about the Charlock Castle, but it's worth a try," Elsfur said. "I need my rest first though. I am very weary, and we also need a plan. From here on out no one goes anywhere alone. I think I was followed here."

"I know that I was followed!" Timmynog said. "I don't know what it is that followed me, but I could feel something almost evil near me all the time."

"But we need to rescue Andy as soon as possible!" Shimmer said, slamming her hand down on the table. "I think we should go tomorrow."

"Shimmer, that's not possible. But we will start planning his rescue tomorrow," Elsfur said, with finality in his voice.

Shimmer looked at Daisy and Daisy nodded back. They could tell that the same thought was going through their minds. They were going to rescue Andy with or without everyone else.

"Tell us what you two were doing, while we were off on our mission," Gladdy said, as she looked back and forth from Snollygob to Shimmer.

"We went to see the Fairy Godmother at the Hall of Records," said Shimmer. "We thought we would help out by trying to find some information about the Crown of the Races."

"Did you find out anything?" asked Elsfur.

"Not one blooming thing," bellowed Snollygob. "I just knew there would be something about it there. By the way," Snollygob said, to Gladdy, Daisy and Grandmother Muckernut, trying to change the subject, "where have the three of you been?"

Gladdy smiled mischievously at Grandmother Muckernut.

"We helped Portumus and some of the guard take Queen Noor, Mystic and Cobblefoot back to Filligrim castle. Once they were resting comfortably and in the care of the surgeon, we left and went back to Hemlock Forest to see what was going on there. It took us a while to get there as well, because we decided to walk and stay under the cover of the trees. When we got to Hemlock Forest we found that the seal which protects its woods had been removed and nearly all of the dryads had left. The ones that did remain told us how Lady Apricot and most of the dryads had set off for the Dark Lands." Grandmother Muckernut swallowed hard and dabbed her eyes. "They killed some of my very good friends. They also destroyed some of the precious forest in their wake. I was sick to see my home in ruins. I raised a lot of the trees that surrounded it. They are all rotting and bug infested now. How could a dryad, whose only duty in life was to care for the forest, kill the very thing they have sworn to protect? It's just beyond my comprehension," she ended sadly.

"The handful of dryads that stayed said they had to run for their lives," Gladdy went on, finishing Grandmother Muckernut's story. "Lady Apricot told them that if they weren't on her side, they would be on no one's side and she ordered them to be killed. We helped bury the unfortunate ones and stayed to help clean up the forest and nurture some of the trees and animals back to health. So, I guess that Lady Apricot is not only in league with Mosaic, she's also in league with this Shadow Man."

"There is something I don't understand," said Shimmer. "Is the cat that we have come to know as Theodius, really the true Theodius? You knew him best, Gladdy. What do you think?"

"That cat is not the true Theodius," said Gladdy. "The Theodius I knew would never have betrayed his friends or the Kingdom of Filligrim."

"Well, there is one thing we know for sure," Elsfur said, staring at the fire. "Theodius the cat has left the country. I spoke with Caleb, the hired hand who runs the stable. He told me that Theodius hasn't been seen since the battle in the Dark Lands." He yawned and stretched. "I think that all of us should try to get a little more sleep. In the morning we'll begin the plans for rescuing the two captives and try to figure out where the jewel and crown are. Also, we need to figure out how we're going to capture the imposter Theodius. He needs to pay for what he has done."

KWAGAR

oblins in heavy armor marched back and forth under the glare of four enormous gray creatures that were perched on pillars just outside the Iron Gate leading to the Hamamelis Goblin Prison. King Vulgaree's great, great, great grandfather King Hamamelis had the prison built to house the enemies of the goblin race. The goblins had dug deep into the Dingy Mountains to build the prison five stories below ground. Passages lit with torches were guarded with two goblins in every hallway, patrolling constantly. Prisoners were chained in their cells and fed morsels of food through a small slot in the lower part of their heavy wooden cell doors. The worst of the prisoners were housed in the deepest parts, where the torture chambers were located, so that the goblins that worked there wouldn't have to walk very far for their next victim.

Most of the prisoner goblins were mole goblins and they had special acid glands in their mouths, that when mixed with saliva could liquefy rock, making it easy for the mole goblins to escape. These goblins were put into special cells that were designed to prevent them from escaping. They were usually treated worse than the other prisoners, mostly because the other goblins felt as though the prisoner goblins were traitors to their king and race.

A long tunnel going south along the mountains separated the second goblin palace from the prison. Unlike the Goblin Palace built by dwarves, this palace was dark and damp and showed none of the grandeur of the palace in the Black Mountains. Although the quarters were cramped, it still housed a huge amount of goblins from the other palace. Trickles of light filtered through the skinny slits in the heavy wooden door, barely illuminating the dark, damp cell that Kwagar now called home. Shrieks and cries of some unknown tormented being would ring out and reverberate throughout the prison for about twenty minutes at a time and then fade away into silence until the next poor soul found it to be his turn. Kwagar would shake with fear until the cries were gone.

Kwagar knew he had been in the Hamamelis Prison for quite some time. When he first arrived he had found a small rock and had scratched marks on the wall to keep up with the days. Days had turned into weeks and then into months as he wondered where his faithful Timmynog was or where any of the Misfits were for that matter. He had quit marking a few days ago. His spirit was breaking.

He sat with his back against a nasty dungeon wall, pondering in the silence. What had become of everyone he had ever known? He knew that his mother had been taken to safety, but still did not know her fate. Had she made it or was she dead? He remembered how she was tied to the pole of the goblin's cart, looking as if death were upon her door. And what had happened to Andy? Kwagar had watched as Andy fought the goblins on Flipsy's back, but the goblins whisked Kwagar off the dragon's back so fast that he had lost sight of his brother and Flipsy.

Mosaic had not been kind to Kwagar. He had Kwagar tied and whipped just because the queen had been taken to safety. The wounds on his back were just now healing. They had starved him as they marched him all the way up the mountains, not letting him eat for five days. Only when it looked as if he might die did they give him bread to eat and water to drink.

Mosaic told Kwagar that when his spirit was broken and when he was ready to give valuable information that would help Mosaic, then he would be set free. Mosaic had asked him about a crown and a jewel, of which Kwagar pretended to have no knowledge. The result was that Mosaic had choked him into unconsciousness. Kwagar knew it was only a matter of time before Mosaic came to the prison, demanding his questions answered.

Kwagar wondered about Timmynog as he dozed off. Were he and the others planning some sort of rescue? He hoped once again that it would be soon. However, seeing the gargoyles outside of the prison made Kwagar think that any hope of a rescue or escape was impossible. In school he had been instructed about the different creatures that roamed the lands around his home. He knew that the gargoyles were deadly.

He jumped, bumping his head as the wooden door creaked open. Dread treaded upon his heart as a huge goblin in armor strode in and stood in the doorway, staring in his direction. The goblin didn't move for a long time, then he stepped to the side, grunted, and two other goblins holding a fourth goblin in-between them, entered the cell. They threw the goblin to the ground against the wall and then proceeded to shackle him.

"You special cell. Can't run way," the big goblin said in terrible English. Then he smacked the goblin on the head with a heavy hammer. The little goblin crumpled to the ground and didn't move anymore.

"Your time is-s coming," a smaller goblin stuttered, leering at Kwagar. "King Mosaic s-sent word by messenger of his-s arrival." The goblin pressed his nose into Kwagar's face and whispered, "And I'm the one who will be working on you in the torture room. If I were you I would come up with s-something convincing for the King or I might just have to mess-s up that pretty face."

Kwagar just glared at the goblin. He was not about to let the goblin see fear in his eyes. The large goblin grunted again and all three of the goblins left the cell. The large wooden door shut with a booming thud. The bolt slid into place, leaving Kwagar in the darkness once more.

Squinting, he looked over at his new cellmate and he could see blood running down the little goblin's face. Kwagar hoped that he wasn't dead. Even a goblin would be better company than any he'd had over the past couple of months. The only creature he had seen, apart from the hand that slipped his meal through the slot every day, was the occasional small mouse that found its way through a tiny hole in the wall.

From all the gashes on his back and legs, Kwagar could tell that the goblin had spent quite a lot of time in the torture chamber and it made him shiver. He had not yet had the privilege of the torture chamber, but he knew it was only a matter of time. The goblin's skin hung in drapes all over his body from being dehydrated and his ribs stuck out from being starved. Kwagar knew how the goblin felt. He had lost a lot of weight and his clothes hung on his body. Both his facial hair and the hair on his head were getting pretty long. He imagined that if he were to look in a mirror he would no longer recognize himself. He would probably look more like a beggar on the street than a Prince from the land of Filligrim.

A while later, the goblin stirred and then gingerly sat up. He looked around the cell, still wincing from the pain in his head. His eyes came to rest on Kwagar.

"Well, at least I'll have someone to talk to," he said, rubbing the blood off his face. Kwagar said nothing. "You do talk don't you, or do I have the privilege of being put in a cell with an idiot?"

"I speak. I just didn't really have anything to say."

The goblin tried to stand but the chains on his feet tripped him and he fell to the ground. He hissed and muttered things about big, stupid goblins and then sat with his back against the wall.

"How long have I been here?" he asked, looking at Kwagar.

"I think it's only been a few hours."

"How long have you been here?"

"Months, I guess. I don't know. I quit counting." Kwagar sighed and looked at the marks he had made on the cell wall. "I came here right after the battle in the Black Mountains."

"Oh yeah, the battle Prince Idiot started. I remember that very well. He threw me into the dungeon in Goblin City just because I questioned whether he should start a war or not. After the battle they decided to clean out Goblin City, so they brought me here."

"You know Prince Mosaic?" Kwagar asked.

"I was his right hand goblin, or at least I thought I was. I did everything for him. Does he appreciate it? NO!" the Goblin shouted, making Kwagar jump.

"What is your name?" Kwagar eyed the goblin cautiously.

"My name is Mucous. What's yours?"

"Kwagar, Prince of Filligrim." Kwagar mumbled, not sure why he felt it necessary to state his title to this pitiful goblin. Then he felt regret in doing so.

"Q—Queen Noor is your mother?"

"Yes," Kwagar said, sadly. "I hope she is okay. The last time I saw her was during the battle."

"Let me guess. She was tied to a pole and was being used as a pin cushion."

"Yes, she was. How—did you know that, if you weren't in the battle?" Kwagar asked, eyeing the goblin distrustfully.

"Because, Mosaic told me that was what he was going to do with her, right before he threw me into the dungeon," Mucous said. He looked down at the chains bound to his feet. "I was responsible for your mother being in Mosaic's possession. He promised me riches and glory if I would capture the queen from Mystic and bring her back to him. But instead I was chained and thrown into a dungeon. I am very ashamed of what I did."

"You should be, you filthy goblin!" Kwagar tried to lunge at Mucous, but his chains pulled him back.

"I know, I know..." Mucous began crying. "I have had to live with what I've done for these past months. I have paid dearly for it too."

Mucous pointed to all of his wounds.

"I—I'm sorry you were tortured. But you should have gone against what Mosaic wanted. You should have fought him," Kwagar said, looking sickeningly at Mucous' wounds.

"I am a weak and pathetic fool," Mucous whimpered more to himself than to Kwagar.

"I don't think that," Kwagar said sympathetically. "It took courage to tell me what you have done. I admire honesty in a person. At least my mother was taken to safety by my dragon, Flopsy."

Mucous slowly raised his head and looked into Kwagar eyes. He couldn't comprehend how Kwagar could be so nice to him after what he, Mucous, had done to Queen Noor. Kwagar's attitude toward him reminded Mucous of King Foxglove and the kindness that he had always bestowed on Mucous.

"No one has ever admired me for anything before." Mucous wiped the tears from his face with the back of his filthy sleeve, then half-heartedly smiled at Kwagar. "Thank you."

Kwagar looked away, not wanting to acknowledge Mucous' thanks. In some ways he felt pity for the creature, but mostly he felt rage that his mother had been put through such an ordeal.

Kwagar sighed and stared at the filthy floor. After a moment he asked, "Do you think there is a way out of here?"

"I doubt it."

"But aren't you a mole goblin?"

"Yes, I am a mole goblin. I have acid glands in my throat and mouth that when mixed with my spit, can cause a great hole to appear." He said this as if he had said it a thousand times.

"That's wonderful! We can get—"

"However," Mucous said, cutting off the elated Kwagar. "We are in a special section of the prison, made just for mole goblins. The floors and walls are treated with a solution that neutralizes the acid, making it useless for escape."

"Oh," was all Kwagar managed to say, and

then they both fell silent again. The slot in the large, wooden door opened and two plates of food slid in. They both reached for the plates and examined the food. Kwagar almost lost his appetite just looking at the moldy bread and the gray lump that was supposed to resemble gruel. He looked at the goblin who was eating with enthusiasm.

"I can't live much longer on this garbage they call food. I'm half-starved now!" he whined, throwing the plate on the floor, and then sat back against the wall. "How can you eat that stuff?"

"It's wonderful when you've had nothing but dirty water for a week," Mucous said, with his mouth full.

"I guess that's true," Kwagar said, with disappointment in his voice. He picked the mold off the hard, crusty bread and began eating. Chewing was becoming difficult. His teeth and gums were red and swollen from lack of brushing and they usually bled when he ate, giving his meal a whole new flavor. He had to drink a lot of water with the gray gruel, just to be able to swallow it down.

They passed the rest of the day by insulting Prince Mosaic, talking about the battle, and finishing with Kwagar telling Mucous about his new brother. It felt wonderful to Kwagar just to have someone to talk to. He knew some subjects probably shouldn't be talked about, but he couldn't help himself. He needed to talk to someone about his bottled up feelings and the little goblin was his only outlet.

"Andy is older than me, so I guess he will

become king."

"What was your mother doing with Mystic?"

"Seeking help. She was hoping that either the goblins or Mystic would help her find out who the traitor in the castle was. That traitor turned out to be Theodius the Wizard. The scum pretended to be my friend and even my mentor. He betrayed the Kingdom of Filligrim. I hope they catch him and give him the punishment that he deserves," Kwagar said bitterly. "I told my mother several months ago that I didn't really want to become king. I had different ideas for my future." He stopped as if remembering his talk with his mother, and then went on. "She said she had a plan that involved Mystic training me and that I would be pleasantly surprised with the outcome."

"I can't imagine any kind of involvement with that old bat would be pleasant in any way. She almost killed me!"

"What did she do to you?" Kwagar said with a smile.

"She opened that floor in the cavern and it swallowed me up. Thank goodness it was a kind of rock that my acid glands could dissolve or I would have become a petrified goblin fossil."

"She's not so bad," Kwagar said. "She is the mother to Prince Becken...my father."

"That means Mystic is..." Mucous said in astonishment.

"My grandmother. My mother told me about her years ago."

"Mystic is Prince Becken's mother?" Mucous said, not comprehending. Why didn't Mystic raise your father?"

"She had been banished from the land of Filligrim for helping the goblin king. I think she wanted my father to have the type of home she felt that she couldn't provide and that is why she did it. My mother found out that my father was Mystic's son shortly after she and my father were first married. He did something that was pretty amazing."

"What was that?" Mucous asked, enthralled.

"He took my mother to the Crystal Sea Palace so that they could have a picnic by the ocean. My father made a tree grow an apple for my mother just by touching it. It wasn't even an apple tree."

"No!"

"Yes. My mother was very amazed and that was when she realized that my father was from the Asrai tribe. My father then went on to explain to her how he came to live with King Renauldee and his wife Arianna, my grandparents on my father's side." He stopped and swallowed some water. "Mystic had traveled to the Crystal Sea right before he was born. She was devastated over being exiled from Filligrim. Even though she had the cavern, Mystic knew that it was no place to raise a child. So she went to visit King Renauldee to see what he could advise her to do."

"What did he say?"

"He told her that Queen Arianna was barren and that she longed for a child. He asked if he could have the child and raise it as his own. No one would ever know anything different."

"And Mystic just let them have her baby?

Wow! There's a lot more to Mystic than I would have ever guessed," Mucous said, shaking his head. "Was she able to see your father after that?"

"Mystic would go to the Crystal Sea Palace to see my father, though he always knew her as Auntie Mystic. At first she visited often. Then her visits dwindled until she didn't come to see him at all anymore. My father asked my grandfather about her one day and my grandfather told him everything. He told my father never to tell anyone because of the promise that my grandfather had made to Mystic." Kwagar looked up. "I guess my father felt it was his duty to his wife to let her know who she was married to, even though he had made the promise to his father, King Renauldee."

"How was he killed?" Mucous asked, enthralled with the tale.

"My mother told me that he died fighting in a war. But—" Kwagar hesitated before going on. "As I learn about my family, I'm not so sure."

"Wow, quite the family history," Mucous said mockingly and then he paused. "That would make your father very old, wouldn't it? I mean they banished Mystic quite a while ago."

"I haven't thought much about it, but yes I think that he would be several hundred years old, if he were still alive. I know he was much older than my mother, even though he didn't look like it."

"But what about King Renauldee and Queen Arianna, how could they be so old? They are still living aren't they?" Mucous asked, looking astonished.

"Yes, but I haven't been to see them in several

years. I'm sure they are very old now. They aren't fully human you know. They both have mermaid blood in them."

"Wait a minute," Mucous shouted, making Kwagar jump. "If your father was Asrai, then you're part Asrai as well!"

"I don't think that is possible. That was why Mystic was supposed to train me. I'm different from ordinary Asrai people. My powers are like Mystic's powers. I can control nature, but I need an instructor or I could do something really bad. If I don't watch what I'm doing, power will surge uncontrollably." Kwagar looked at the ceiling. "I could hurt someone, or even bring this prison down on our heads."

"You shouldn't give up so easily," said Mucous.

"You don't understand," Kwagar said, putting his face in his hands. "It's scary not being able to control yourself. It makes me feel like I'm a child."

"You've fought in a battle and slain many goblins, so that would put you in the category of a man, wouldn't it?"

"I guess so," Kwagar said slowly. He looked around at the cell and muttered, "But I sure don't feel like a man, being in here."

"Well, you are," Mucous said, encouragingly. "Let's get you and me out of here. I have a few scores to settle."

"I suppose I could try. If Mystic were training me, she would probably have me start out on something small and work my way up. Maybe that is the approach I should take. If I do well enough, I might just get us out of here." Kwagar laughed nervously. "Or kill us, one of the two!"

"I prefer that you don't kill us," mused Mucous.

"Well, since we do have all the time in the world to work on my gifts," Kwagar said, looking around again at the four walls and then at his cell companion. With a little hesitation he continued, "Do you think I should give it a try?"

"You bet I do! I'm willing to help you in whatever way I can. I want out of this place as fast as possible. You get me a good-sized crack in that floor and I'll do the rest."

Kwagar had never purposefully used his power before. It had always come as a result of his temper or by accident. However, he was willing to try anything to avoid living in prison for the rest of his life, or worse—certain death.

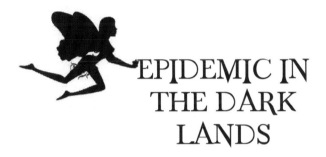

EPIDEMIC IN THE DARK LANDS

Morgan awoke in the early light of the morning to find himself drenched and muddy. Water from the rainstorm was still dripping from the leaves all through the forest. He pulled himself upright and looked around, still unclear as to why he had been lying on the ground. He was feeling faint and like he had a fever. His horse and wagon still stood in the same place. When he got to his knees preparing to stand, he saw his hands and arms were sickly green with large pustules all over them. Then he remembered. Fear encased him as he stumbled toward the river. He had to see his face. Bending over, he stared at his reflection. At first, he thought it was someone else's reflection he was seeing. He spun around, but there was no one there. Morgan turned around and peered back at the water. It was his disgusting face he was seeing. It was the same color as his hands and arms, and it had even more pustules on it. A scream stuck in his throat. Trembling violently, he scrambled backwards from the water, falling down hard and hitting his back against a tree. He sat there a moment trying to think of what to do. Deciding, he jumped to his feet, running wildly back the way he had come earlier that day. As if running away would help rid his body of this horrible infection. He had to get to town and find someone who would help him.

It took Morgan about an hour to reach the town. Charlock castle, perched on a hill, loomed like a dark beacon over the settlement. The apothecary's shop was close to the castle gates. If Morgan could make it there, the apothecary might be able to help him. The street was still bustling with people who had been to market that morning. Morgan bumped into several of the Shadow People as he made his way down the street. They backed away from him in horror and disgust. He recognized a group of men who were gossiping about the goods they had sold at the bazaar, standing close to where the apothecary's shop stood. They didn't see Morgan approach until they heard a woman screaming nearby.

Exhausted from running and from whatever was wrong with him, Morgan fell into the arms of a large, beefy Shadow Man wearing a butcher's apron. The man laid Morgan down on the ground and backed away from him.

"Morgan, is that you?" asked the large man, not sure of what he was seeing. It looked like his friend Morgan, but not the Morgan who had been to the festivities that morning. "What's the matter with you? Did you get stung by a logger beetle?"

But Morgan couldn't answer the man. He didn't know what had happened to him. Morgan reached out to touch the man, seeking help. That's when he saw with horror that the Shadow Man had begun to change. At first he doubled over and began shaking fiercely. Then he stood up, rigid. Next, green streaks started running up the man's arms toward his face, followed by large, nasty pustules that bubbled up all over his skin, disfiguring him even more.

Morgan got to his feet and watched as the man collapsed. The other men, who had been looking on in horror, began to change as well. Morgan looked around wildly at the men convulsing on the ground. His breath caught in his throat. He heard noises behind him and looked back to where he had entered the town. The seen was surreal. Shadow People were collapsing everywhere with the same green streaks and the same nasty pustules covering their bodies as well. Morgan realized with revulsion that he had brought a plague of some kind into the town. He couldn't think of what to do, to bring an end to the madness.

He rushed to different people to see if he could help them, but it was as if they weren't human anymore. They couldn't talk to him. They only screeched like some kind of large, green shadow monkey covered in sores. Morgan noticed that they would stand erect, sniff the air as if catching a scent, and then run toward the scent. The scent, Morgan realized, was uninfected Shadow People. All the infected had to do was touch the uninfected, and then the uninfected would collapse and the process would begin all over again. Morgan knew that if the progression kept going, all of the lands would be contaminated in a matter of days. In what seemed like minutes, the Shadow People had cleared the town and were running toward the forest. Morgan stood alone in the eerie silence, as he watched the backs of the Shadow People, running toward the plains.

The scene played over and over in Morgan's mind. The town swirled around Morgan like a gyrating whirlpool. Morgan had to find out how to stop the plague. He thought of going to the castle, but knew Queen Estonia could do nothing for her people and he might infect her and all that were in the castle as well. Instead, the little tree came to mind. Maybe it held the answers he was looking for. This plague had started as a result of eating the fruit from that tree. He couldn't think of anything else that would have caused this devastation.

As he ran out of town, a loud wailing sound followed Morgan. He was halfway back to the little tree when he stopped to catch his breath. That's when he realized the howling sound was coming from his own mouth. Tears blurred his eyes and ran down his green, pustule-covered face. He gulped air like he would never breathe again. The sickness was beginning to take its toll on him. He was

growing weaker. His sight began to grow dark. As
he passed out again, he had a vision of a beautiful
jewel, sparkling brightly, with three blood-red
stripes on it, set in a beautiful, delicate silver
crown.

THREE TAKE A TRIP WITH SOME UNEXPECTED COMPANY

Pink tendrils spread their way like a wild vine across the still dark morning, as the sun began its ascent into the sky. One small light from a candle moved its way through the little cottage and to the front door, where it was quickly snuffed out. A cloaked figure opened the door as quietly as possible, and then stepped out into the fresh morning air.

Shimmer hurried down the path through the forest, thankful that the night's rain had dampened the leaves, making her retreat as quiet as possible. Only when she was some distance from the cottage did she unveil her companion from under her cloak.

Daisy flitted out beside her.

"That was easy enough," she whispered close to Shimmer's ear. "How long do you think it will take us to get to the Dark Lands?"

"We'll go to the stables at the castle and borrow a horse." Shimmer bit her lip in concentration as she stepped over a small log. "I really think we should go around the Black Mountains though, and through the Mulberry Forest. Then we can go on to the Land of Chaldeon, where Gladdy is from, since it's located next to the Dark Lands. I'm afraid if we go through the Black Mountains there might still be stray goblins and the Bitter Plains are so vast, we would have to carry large amounts of water, which would slow us down. Perhaps the elves of Mulberry Forest will give us shelter for a night."

"I don't know about that, Shimmer," Daisy looked concerned. "They aren't fond of strangers in their forest."

"I know. But we'll just have to take that chance. It's a much quicker way to the Dark Lands and we need to get to Andy as quickly as possible."

"Elsfur is not going to like what we're doing. I bet you all the gold in the land of Filligrim he sends someone after us, or worse, he comes himself."

"I'm not really worried about what Elsfur or anyone else has to say. I only care about saving the future King of Filligrim."

"Is that all?" Daisy said in a teasing tone.

"Just what is that supposed to mean?" Shimmer asked, her face becoming a deeper shade of blue.

"Oh, I don't know. Andy is a very handsome

young man."

"You're right about the young man part. He's definitely too young for me," Shimmer said purposefully, avoiding Daisy's eyes. "We better stop talking or someone will hear us."

They walked in silence for some time, as the sun climbed higher into the sky. Water leftover from the rain dripped from the trees, making their clothing damp. They glanced backward often, and even backtracked to make sure they weren't being followed. At strategic points Daisy would sit in trees watching the trail to make sure the coast was clear, while Shimmer would walk on ahead. Taking great effort to ensure no one was following them, they finally made it to the stables near the castle.

They moved twenty yards off the path and hid in a clump of bushes. Shimmer had a clear view of the path, and of the stables.

"I still think we were followed. I couldn't see anything and neither could you, but I sense something is out there," Shimmer whispered uneasily. "Let's stay here for a while. Maybe we'll be able to spot whatever it is."

They settled themselves down on the soft earth and peered through the bushes, listening and watching intently for any signs of life. Hours passed and their stomachs began to rumble.

"I sure hope you brought something to eat. I'm starved!" whispered Daisy.

"You can get something at the Filligrim castle if you want. I'm sure they have plenty," said a deep voice behind them. Shimmer jumped so hard she lost her balance and fell through the bushes, landing in a mud puddle. Slowly she pushed herself up and wiped the mud out of her eyes. When her vision cleared she was staring at Daisy and a beautiful, powder blue colored unicorn. They both were laughing.

"Windsor! You scared me out of my skin!" Shimmer said heatedly. Then she began to laugh. "I bet I look a sight."

"You definitely blend in with the woods," Windsor whinnied. "Now maybe you'll catch whatever you and Daisy were looking for."

"Oh, ha, ha!" snapped Shimmer. "Don't you have a herd of nags to look after? O great and mighty leader of the unicorns."

Windsor stopped laughing and became very serious. "I wouldn't call a female unicorn a nag to her face, Shimmer. She might turn you into something really nasty. Besides, I take offense to your comment. Unicorns are the most majestic of all the races."

"I'm sorry, Windsor." Shimmer wiped more mud from her face. "Where did you come from? My hearing is excellent and I didn't even hear you come up from behind me."

"I have been following you for quite some time. You need to look around a lot more. Also," he paused and looked back through the woods, "I don't think I was the only one following you. I sense there is something else out there."

"We have felt the same way ever since we left Snollygob's cottage." She looked down at her clothes. "I better get extra clothes in case this happens again."

"Where are you two headed?"

"We're going to the Dark Lands."

Windsor looked at her quizzically and then he smiled his best horsey smile. "Andy?"

"Yes. Elsfur told us that Andy has been taken to Charlock Castle," Shimmer said. "Tell me something, Windsor. If you have the sight of the future, how come you couldn't see Theodius becoming the bad guy?"

"Shimmer!" Daisy said, shocked.

"It's a fair question, Daisy. I am a unicorn and we do have special sight. However, that sight is only for seeing the good in things, not the bad. Sorry I couldn't have been more help to Filligrim's present situation. It grieves me to my very core."

"That's okay, Windsor. I'm sorry I asked."

Windsor stared at her for a moment as if contemplating something and then said, "I am going with you. I will meet you on the west side of the castle at noon." He turned and cantered off before Shimmer could object.

"Great! Now, we are practically a crowd with him going along."

"I don't think that an Asrai warrior, a pixie and a unicorn classify as a crowd," Daisy pointed out. "Besides, Windsor can move through the forest and not even you can see him."

"I guess he might come in handy. But I sure don't want to put up with all those stupid, dumb, annoying horse jokes of his."

"You better stop calling him a horse. He might turn you into something you'd regret."

"Yes, Mother," Shimmer said acerbically,

under her breath. "Let's try to sneak into the castle without any more interruptions. We need to go to my room for a change of clothes and get blankets from the hall cupboard. Also, we need to stop by the kitchen for some food to take with us." She looked around to make sure the coast was clear and then said, "Let's go."

The cook, Mrs. Plumthistle, was taking a nap with her head down on an old wooden table in the kitchen when Shimmer and Daisy peeked into the open kitchen door. The kitchen was balmy from the fire burning and food cooking on the stove. Shimmer raised her hand then slowly lowered it from the top of her head down towards her feet, turning into a blue mist. While Shimmer was the blue mist she could do all sorts of things. Her favorite was going through impossible little cracks. Her blue mist form floated up toward the ceiling of the kitchen and moved along it until she was in the main dining hall. Shimmer stopped and contemplated on what to do next. Seated at the head of the long dining table was Mystic, Andy and Kwagar's grandmother. Mystic was very old. Her silver hair hung in limp strands over her hunched back. Her green eyes were faded and dull. Also seated at the table was Portumus, Captain of the Filligrim Guard, a large black man with a bald head.

Without so much as looking up from his meal Portumus said, "Well Shimmer, are you going to join us?"

The blue mist stopped and then floated down, settling beside the table.

Droning like a thousand bees the mist asked, "How did you know I was there?"

"I have seen you turn into that blue mist at least a thousand times," he said. "You also have a slight humming sound that is very annoying to human ears."

Shimmer reappeared in front of them.

"I just love to see you do that," Mystic said admiringly. "I would give anything if that were my talent."

"I think you're dangerous enough with the talents you already have, Mystic. You don't need any more abilities," Portumus teased.

Shimmer smiled.

"So, how are you feeling, Mystic? You look really good," Shimmer said, hoping to keep the conversation away from what she was doing and what she had been up to.

"I'm fine. Never felt better," she said in an ancient voice. The cracks deepened in her face as she smiled at Shimmer. "What have you been up to? You're filthy."

"Oh," Shimmer's face went deep blue. "I fell in a mud puddle on the way back from Snollygob's cottage."

"Portumus has been on the edge of his seat wondering where everyone has been." She eyed him musingly.

"Well, Portumus, what's on your mind?" Shimmer asked, gawking at Mystic. She and Portumus were certainly getting along well.

"I had a little talk with Queen Noor this morning. She asked me if I would find you and the others, so that we could have dinner this evening. You wouldn't by chance happen to know where Elsfur, Gladdy, Snollygob, and Timmynog are, would you? We haven't seen anyone for ages."

"I guess they're here and there. I haven't seen much of them myself." Shimmer was telling the truth after all. She hadn't seen a great deal of any of her friends for months.

"You haven't said what you have been up to."

"I—I have been with Snollygob at his house in the forest."

"Really?" Portumus said, questioningly. "I went to Snollygob's cottage and found no one home."

"Um...I—I mean we—that is," she laughed nervously. "We must have been out gathering some herbs and plants for Snollygob to sell in the market," Shimmer said, feeling uncomfortable about lying. "Well, I better be getting along. See you both later."

As she turned to go, Portumus stopped her.

"Shimmer," he said with a sudden coldness. "It looked to me as if you were sneaking into the castle."

"I like to practice sneaking around. It keeps me sharp." She laughed nervously again. She needed to hurry.

Portumus continued to stare at her, making her more nervous. She had never been edgy around him and she didn't like the feeling. She caught Daisy's eye. Daisy shrugged at her as if to say, "What's wrong with him?"

"I hope you all aren't doing anything foolish

that would jeopardize the rescue of our beloved princes," Portumus warned.

"I—don't think anyone of—us would…what I mean to say is we would never—go against anything that—you and the Filligrim Army have put together in—in order to save Andy or Kwagar," Shimmer said, stumbling over her words.

"Good," Portumus said slowly. "Like I said, Queen Noor wants all of you here for dinner. Is that understood? I'm sure the queen would like to know what Elsfur and Timmynog have found out about Andy and Kwagar. Also, I will debrief you on what the secondary guard is doing and where they have stationed themselves."

"Aren't Elsfur and Timmynog here?" Shimmer said, trying to act innocent. "I thought they would come straight here to give a full account to Her Majesty."

"Well, they haven't," growled Portumus.

Shimmer jumped.

"I really don't think that was necessary, Portumus," Mystic said, putting a bite of food into her mouth.

"It's really none of your business!" declared Portumus rather loudly.

Mystic stared at him and said threateningly, "If I were you, I would remember to whom you are speaking."

Portumus cleared his throat, glared at Mystic for a moment, and then looked at Shimmer.

"I apologize for my behavior," Portumus said, his tone softening. "Please, be here for dinner. I will have Mrs. Plumthistle cook up something wonderful. I hope that I won't have to take drastic measures if you and the others don't show up. Queen Noor just might have me hunt you down." He smiled, but the smile didn't reach his eyes.

"I hope not either," Shimmer said, looking at Portumus and feeling very confused by the conversation. "I'm not sure what you mean by drastic measures, but I'm pretty sure the others will show up."

"I'm sure it won't come to that," Portumus said, staring at her with the strange smile still on his face.

"Okay. Well, I have some things that I have to do, so I…" Shimmer looked at Mystic, who was looking curiously at Portumus. Then Shimmer looked back at Portumus. "I'll see you later."

Shimmer turned and walked very fast out of the room with Daisy following her, wondering what had gotten into Portumus. She knew she would be in a lot of trouble if she didn't show up for dinner but that was a chance she had to take.

"What was that all about?" Daisy asked after they were on the second landing of the stairs.

"I don't know," Shimmer said, looking back over her shoulder. "Maybe he's just worried about Andy and Kwagar and that's his way of showing it."

"I guess. I don't know him very well, but I get the impression there's a lot more going on there."

"I got that same impression when he was looking at me." Shimmer smiled at Daisy. "Oh well, we don't have time to worry about Portumus. We have to get changed, grab some blankets, get some food and meet up with the nag."

"You just keep on saying that word, Shimmer. Windsor is going to hear you and then you'll be in for it," warned the small pixie, wagging her finger. "Let's try not to run into anyone else we know, or we'll never get out of this castle."

Shimmer and Daisy got cleaned up, filled their satchel with food, found blankets and water skins, and managed to get out of the castle without being noticed. In the barn, munching on some oats, they found Mistletoe, a beautiful black mare that Shimmer was partial to riding. The mare was in a stall next to a griffin, a creature that was half eagle and half lion.

"Hello, Mistletoe," Shimmer said softly to the mare, trying to avoid being heard.

"You know," said Daisy, staring at the griffin. "If we were smart, we would fly that griffin all the way to the Dark Lands."

"Yes, that would be a way," said Shimmer. "Of course we would be hunted down by the royal guard. Those creatures are for the queen only."

"Oh."

Shimmer took the mare out of the stall, bridled and saddled her, and then led her away from the barn toward the west side of the castle.

It was a glorious day. The birds in their nests sang sweet songs, while white puffy clouds floated across a bright blue sky. The rushing waters from the river could be heard as if it were shouting that it too had a destination it needed to reach. From the flower gardens, fragrance filled the air and wafted on breezes, filling the whole forest with its perfume. Everything in that moment made Daisy and Shimmer feel good about the start to their journey.

They met up with Windsor in the woods on the west side of the castle. Windsor was lying in some soft grass. As they approached, Mistletoe bowed down to Windsor and whinnied. Windsor stood.

"Mistletoe!" he exclaimed. "It has been a while. You are looking well."

"Yeah, yeah, yeah," Shimmer said in an annoyed tone, while getting up on the horse. "Enough with the chit chat. We have a long trip ahead of us and we don't need to waste precious energy on talking." She sat on the horse for a second and looked from Windsor to Daisy and then down at Mistletoe, and then said under her breath, "Geez, we're practically a herd!"

"I heard that, Shimmer!" Windsor said in an aggravated tone. "Let's get a move on. I would like to travel quite far before sunset."

"You!" Shimmer exclaimed. "Why is it all of a sudden you think you're in charge. No one even asked you to come along, and now you think you're the boss. I don't think so! We go when I say we go."

Windsor stared at Shimmer with soulful eyes, not knowing what to say. Shimmer had never talked this way to him before and he found it very offensive.

"I apologize," he said hurtfully. "I never wanted to interfere. I—I just wanted to help get Andy back. I like the boy a lot. And I see by the expression on your face that you have a fondness for him as well." He paused. "Shimmer, I know you've grown attached to Andy. And...." He stopped her from speaking. "Before you say anything further, remember that I am a unicorn."

That said it all. Shimmer knew that unicorns had special powers to see into a person's heart.

"You're right, Windsor. I have grown very fond of Andy and I should be the one to apologize for my behavior, not you. I am very anxious to get to Charlock Castle and see how he is doing. Since you have lived in these woods longer than I, I think you should lead the way." She smiled sincerely at him and he whinnied back. All was forgiven.

They traveled the rest of the day hardly exchanging a single word. Windsor did know the woods very well, and if he had not been along, it would have proven a very tricky trip for Shimmer, Daisy and Mistletoe. The sun was barely visible in an ever-darkening sky, and the gloomy clouds brought turbulent winds with them.

Windsor stopped and sniffed the air, then said, "A storm is brewing. We better find shelter."

They found three boulders sitting in a u-shape. The gap in the middle of the boulders was more than wide enough for all of them to fit into. The trees that grew around the huge rocks bent inward, forming a canopy-like roof. Shimmer stood there wrinkling her nose as she looked at the inside of the dark gap. It smelled as if bears had hibernated in it all winter.

"If you would prefer, we could go farther and find something else," Windsor said, seeing the expression on her face.

"Never let it be said that an Asrai warrior couldn't sleep in a damp, smelly hole with two horses and a pixie," she retorted.

"I am not a horse!" Windsor growled.

"Oh—sorry, Windsor." She half laughed and then ventured into the gap, followed by everyone else.

The evening went well. Shimmer made herself and Daisy a nice soft bed with pine boughs and the blankets she brought from the castle. The rain had cleared the air leaving a wonderful fresh scent. A fire just outside the entrance made Shimmer feel a lot safer about spending the night in a dark hole. She had tried to build the fire inside the gap, but the smoke lingered, causing everyone to cough.

They hadn't been asleep very long when noises from some distance down the trail woke them. Windsor nickered at Shimmer warning her that there were quite a few people traveling toward them. Shimmer grabbed her sword, poured dirt on the fire, and found a bush to hide in. From her position she could see the strangers' progress. She didn't have to watch for long. Trampling through the woods was a short, slobbering person, an elf, and a slightly small version of a giant. She sighed hard, and stepped out from her hiding place.

"Well," she muttered under her breath, "we've just officially become a herd."

Timmynog walked up to Shimmer, smiled at her and then gave her a big bear hug. After he set her on the ground he said, "I was worried about you, little one. You have been a very naughty, blue girl."

"Oh, you big oaf," she said, a little embarrassed, "I thought by now you would know that I can take care of myself."

"I know you can. However, I still have the right to worry. After all, you're like a little sister to me, and I would feel horrible if something happened to you."

"Thank you, Timmynog. I'm very fond of you too."

"I would be careful, Shimmer. Elsfur is not in a good mood," Timmynog said, pointing his thumb in the direction of Elsfur.

"Don't worry about him," Shimmer said, resolutely. "He is one part of my life that I can handle."

"Well, if it isn't the disappearing magician and her companions," Elsfur said sardonically, as he approached her.

"Hello to you, Elsfur. How's the whole wedding planning going? Or did you tell your beloved that you had to come and rescue me, and that the wedding would have to wait!" Shimmer laughed haughtily. "I bet that went over real well."

"Let's get one thing straight, Shimmer…"

"No, Elsfur, you get something straight," she said, cutting him off, "You are not the boss of me, nor do you have any authority over me. As I recall, I am the head of weapons department. You have no official title, other than Mr. Interference! So why don't you run along back to the castle and your precious bride to be."

Elsfur swallowed hard, trying to hold his emotions in check and not say something that would injure their relationship for good. He couldn't understand why Shimmer was so antagonistic.

"Shimmer, I will not interfere with this mission," he said in a very controlled voice. "However, I'm Andy's true protector. Theodius put me in charge of protecting Andy when we first went to the other world and I mean to be the one to do so. You will just have to get over the fact that I'm coming on this rescue mission."

"Oh, you mean the impostor, wizard cat that was traitor to the Kingdom of Filligrim. The same cat that is also known as 'the Shadow Man.' I really don't think he had the authority to assign positions to anyone."

Elsfur stared at her, his jaw flexing.

"Fine!" she said, giving in, trying to control her temper. She bit her lip hard, and blinked away her unbidden tears. "Just fine. You can come, but I'm in charge."

Elsfur's hand reached toward her as if to caress her face and they looked into each other's eyes for a brief, awkward moment. His hand dropped in defeat and he walked away, before Shimmer could say another word. How would Elsfur feel when he found out the real reason behind her actions—that she had grown a heart for Andy.

Shimmer looked at his retreating back, swallowed the lump in her throat and whispered, "It will break his heart."

CHARLOCK CASTLE

S hades of white and gray, interspersed with black, seemed to flicker in and out of Andy's blurry vision. He wondered how long he had been unconscious? Where was he? He tried to remember the very last thing he had been doing before the weird, shadowy darkness fell on him, but it was no use. He just couldn't remember. He felt his head. He did remember that there had been a huge knot on it, but he couldn't remember how it had happened. Then there was the white, almost ashen face that disturbed his dreams, or were they dreams? He knew the face belonged to a woman, but like no woman he had ever seen before. She was different; like a ghost. One minute her face was in plain view and the next it was blurry. He knew one thing and that was when her face was recognizable, she was beautiful. She had soulful green eyes, and white grayish hair that framed her face and fell down below her shoulders.

Andy heard a scraping noise in the room and he turned his head. He blinked, trying to focus his eyes. An old man came into view. He had an ancient, lined face that broke into a black-toothed smile, and his blue eyes twinkled beneath long, gray, bushy eyebrows. His face wore a gray beard that hung down to just below his belt.

"Hello, young man." His voice was craggy, as if he hadn't drunk anything in a long time. "I didn't think you would ever wake up."

"How long have I been asleep?" Andy said, groggily.

"I've watched you sleep for nearly three months now. I have never seen anyone sleep that long in my life." He cackled. "Is your name Rip Van Winkle?"

"No—it's…" Andy couldn't think of who he was, causing confusion and fear. "I—I don't remember who I am."

"Oh, you've been given a potion. The evil that runs this castle loves to drug people." The old man shook his head in a knowing fashion as if he knew some big secret. "It will wear off."

"How do you know it will?"

"Because for a long time they did the exact same thing to me. Then when they thought I was no longer a threat, they stopped giving it to me. They must not think you're a threat anymore."

"Who are they?" Andy tried to sit up but his

body felt like it weighed a ton.

"I don't know. Ghost-like beings come and take you away. Then about two or three hours later they bring you back." He gestured his hand in a sweeping motion towards the door and then towards the bed that Andy was lying on.

"Do you know what they do with me?"

"I don't know, but you usually have burns on different places on your body and sometimes you come back with lots of bandages."

"What! What do you mean I come back with lots of bandages?" Andy shouted at the old man.

"Well, just look at yourself. Your leg has a bandage and so does your hand." The man pointed at Andy's leg and then looked at him in an apologetic way. "I'm sorry, young man. I wish they hadn't hurt you."

Andy looked at the bandage covering his hand. He felt bile fight its way towards his mouth. Then he felt his leg. It was covered with bandages from his ankle all the way to his hip. He started tearing at the bandage on his hand, revealing a repulsive wound. It looked like they had been cutting him. But why?

"Who would do such a thing?" he asked, horrified. Tears threatened to spill down his face. "Why me? I've never harmed anyone."

"There, there now, little man." The old man hobbled over to Andy on very crooked legs. "Don't cry. I think they're done working on you, or you wouldn't have come out of your sleep."

"Are—are you sure?" Andy hiccupped.

"Yes, yes, I'm sure." The old man patted Andy

on the shoulder. "You lie there and relax. Old Theodius will help you get better."

"Theodius?" Andy said, not sure why that name sounded so familiar.

"Yes, that's my name. No, wait." The old man stopped as if not sure of himself and scratched his head, "Yes, I'm positive that's my name. I've been here so long, I'm beginning to doubt myself."

"How long have you been here?" Andy asked.

"Well now, let me think for a moment." He stuck his finger on the end of his nose and pushed it straight up to where Andy could see the man's boogers inside. Andy looked at the peculiar man in disgust. The old man sat that way for a while just thinking and then said, "I believe I have been here about, about sixteen years. Give or take a year."

"Sixteen years, REALLY!" Andy said, disbelievingly. "Why did they put you in the dungeon?"

"Now that is something I can't for the life of me remember. I was drugged like you for a very long time, and I also remember coming out of my drugged state with bandages as well. They had done some awful things to me. That's one of the reasons I walk with a limp," he said somewhat proudly, while pulling up his trouser and showing Andy his leg. It looked as though it had been badly broken and then never put in a cast.

"Well, we've got to get out of here," Andy said, with determination. "I'll go crazy if I have to stay in here for sixteen years."

"Oh, it's not so bad. I haven't gone crazy," Theodius said, as he watched a bug crawl across the floor. He smacked the bug with his shoe, then began licking the contents off the bottom of the shoe.

"That's it!" Andy said, appalled. "We're definitely getting out of here."

He sat up as best he could and then gingerly put his feet on the floor. He swayed as the room swam in front of his eyes. He lay back down on the bed.

"Maybe you can try after you take a nap, little man," Theodius said, smiling at him. Andy could see a bug leg sticking out of his teeth.

Holding back bile he said, "Yeah, I guess I better wait. You've got a little something sticking out of your teeth that you might want to remove."

"Oh," the old man said, then he started sucking his front teeth. After the remains were gone from his teeth, he laughed and said, "Them bugs don't like to go down all at once. Sometimes it takes two or three swallows."

"That's good information. I'll try to remember that if I ever decide to crunch on a few bugs."

"I'm positive before it's all over, you will to want to eat a bug or two yourself. They don't feed us on a regular basis around here."

"Oh, that's just great! Torture and starvation. I'm liking this place more and more." Andy closed his eyes. He felt that if he could rest for a while, his head would be clearer and then he could think of how to escape. He would have to take the old man with him. He couldn't believe that Theodius had been here for sixteen years. Andy thought about the old man for a moment. Why had his name sounded so familiar, and why was it that Andy couldn't remember his own name?

Sleep enveloped him, with bad dreams as a bonus. Andy dreamed that bugs were chasing him down a long road, toward an old, dilapidated two-story house, while a cat with spectacles sat on a fence staring at him. Surrounding the cat were different creatures: an elf, a girl with blue skin, and a boy that looked like him, but just a little different, and a giant with an axe. Andy woke with a start; he was covered in sweat.

"That must have been some dream, little man. You were yelling at me in your sleep." The old man was standing next to a table that Andy hadn't seen before. There was a pitcher and cups on the table and a plate with bread on it.

"What do you mean, I was yelling at you in my sleep?" Andy asked, confused. He sat up.

"You were yelling, 'Theodius, help me!'" he garbled through a mouth full of bread.

It was like a light switched on in Andy's head. Memories came flooding back of Filligrim, his Aunt Gladdy, Theodius, Shimmer, Snollygob, Elsfur and Timmynog. Even the Shadow Man who had captured Andy in the Dark Lands. He remembered that Flipsy had been injured and that Andy had been trying to find help, and that he had drunk from the stream and nearly died from its poisoned waters. Andy lifted his shirt, remembering the wound he had received from the goblin. There was no puncture hole, not even a scar. Then he looked at his clothes. They still had blood all over them, so he knew that the fight between the goblin and himself had really happened.

"I remember who I am," Andy said, slowly rubbing his chest.

"Who are you?" the old man replied, losing interest in his bread.

"I'm Andy." He stopped and his heart swelled. "No, I'm Prince Andrew Misfit and my mother is Queen Noor, of Filligrim Castle. However, most people call me by my nickname, which is Andy."

"That's nice," Theodius said. "I guess I don't know who Queen Noor is, but at least you have a name I can call you."

Andy's head swirled with questions. Did Flipsy live? Where was everyone else? Did his mother make it back to the castle? What had happened to Kwagar? Was Shimmer safe? What had happened at the castle? Was Theodius named as the traitor after all? Last but not least, were they planning to come and rescue him?

"I was supposed to find out something very important at the castle that would affect the future of Filligrim and all the other kingdoms. How am I to do that, now that I'm in here?"

"I don't know. However, you have a lot of time to think about your situation. Well, I better get back to work," Theodius said. He put his bread and water down on the table and sat down on the hard stone floor next to the wall. He began shoving on the table with his feet. When the table moved out of the way, Andy could see an opening in the wall just big enough for the old man to struggle through and disappear. Andy's mouth fell open in amazement.

"Hello, what's this?" he asked the empty room as he eased himself off the bed and onto the floor. His leg wound burned as it touched the cold ground, and he bit his tongue to prevent a scream escaping. After the pain subsided, he scooted toward the opening and found light trickling from deep within. He poked his head through the hole and gasped. The old man had dug a tunnel so far that he had disappeared. Andy couldn't even hear the old man working. He wondered how far it was from being finished. Andy sat back against the wall and waited for hours, dozing and waking every now and then. Finally, Theodius' head poked out and he smiled a black toothy grin at Andy that made Andy smile back.

"Well," he said, as he pulled himself back through the hole, "I have some very good news."

"Yeah, what's that?" Andy said, enthusiastically.

"I'm almost through."

"You mean we can get out of here? How long until you're through?" Andy could have jumped for joy.

"I would say about a month or two and we will be out of here," Theodius said proudly.

Andy's good mood deflated like a balloon. "One or two months! You've got to be kidding me!"

"You need to keep your voice down. The creatures that guard us might hear you," Theodius chided. "Yes, one or two months. I've been working on that tunnel ever since they put me in here. For sixteen years, give or take a year, I have been digging in that tunnel. So don't be so ungrateful. At least I haven't just started digging. Why, with you here the work will go much faster. We'll be done in no time at all."

"You're right. I'm not being very grateful," Andy admitted, ashamedly. "I apologize...I will help you dig. We'll dig in shifts."

"I still think you need to rest. A few days won't matter much."

"I guess. I had to crawl just to get over here," Andy replied, looking at his leg.

"I'll help you get back into bed and then I'm going to get some rest myself. It's hard work on an old man, down in that tunnel."

Theodius helped Andy to stand and get back into the bed. After he covered Andy with blankets he said, "A word of caution. If those ghost creatures start to come in here, pretend that you have never woken up. That way they'll think the drug they gave you hasn't worn off yet. Then they won't give you more."

"Thank you, Theodius," Andy answered as he watched the old man hobble over to his bed. "Hey, maybe when we wake up, you can try to tell me a little about yourself."

"I hope I can remember. I've been in here so long I don't recall much about my life before this place. Those drugs they gave me were very bad." He lay down and pulled the covers over himself. Then he pulled a little chain that Andy hadn't noticed before and the light in the ceiling went out. In the dark Andy heard the old man's croaky voice, "Goodnight, Andy."

"Goodnight, Theodius." Andy smiled to himself, then said, "Hey, you have the same name as a friend of mine back in Filligrim. It's kind of funny that I have never heard the name Theodius before in my life, and in just a few months I have met two of you."

Andy lay listening in the dark to the sounds echoing from somewhere in the castle. Water was dripping, doors were opening or closing, something was growling, people were crying, and others were talking. However, Andy couldn't understand what they were saying. He wished with all his heart that he were back in Filligrim sleeping in his nice soft bed, knowing that his mother was safe, that his aunt Gladdy was in her bed in the next room, and that everything was right in the world. But it wasn't. He had been taken by that horrible Shadow Man. Andy thought hard about the Shadow Man. How had he known who Andy was? No one, outside the small group of people that Andy was associated with, knew who he was.

Another thing came to Andy's mind. When he was in the Dark Land Forest, he had seen an image of Mystic's face in the tree. She said something to him that seemed to be important, right before the Shadow Man had arrived. But he couldn't remember what it was.

Andy closed his eyes and relaxed. He hoped that tomorrow his mind would be even clearer and that he would be able to think about digging in tunnels, and figure out who the Shadow Man was and how Theodius the Cat was connected to him. Sleep drifted into his mind like a welcome guest and this time it was peaceful. Dreams of a beautiful blue girl, who shimmered like the sun shining on the sea, filled his happy sleep.

KING RENAULDEE

A castle set by the sea stood as a place of protection for the mermaids that lived in the adjoining ocean, and the half-mermaids that lived in the adjacent village. It was a beautiful castle known as the Crystal Sea Palace. It was so called because of the brick work it was crafted from. The rock, quarried from the Crystal Sea, contained flakes of gemstones embedded in the granite, which gave the castle a crystal effect. Atop the walls of the palace were stunning, multi-colored coral arrangements made by the mermaids, beautifying the palace even more. Also, there were arches leading into the palace made from seaweed, decorated with shells and starfish.

The village that surrounded the castle was made up of half-humans, half-mermaids. They lived in little cottages along the coast, where fishing was their main livelihood. The full-blood mermaids made up the rest of the population. They lived in homes on the ocean floor, built from coral not far from the sandy shore. Having both human and mermaid blood, King Renauldee and Queen Arianna built their kingdom so that both half-mermaids and pure-mermaids could benefit from the safety the castle provided. The sea creatures kept enemy ships away and the magical woods surrounding the village kept any advancing adversaries from approaching. The woods were full of creatures that had once lived in the sea, but now preferred the freedom of being able to walk on dry land. They were fierce creatures that hungered for hearts that had evil in them.

In the Crystal Sea Palace, a soft ocean breeze blew through an open window, and ever so slightly stirred King Renauldee's hair as he sat staring at a closed door across the room. A small, yellow cat rubbed against the king's leg and felt a little rejected when the king did not return the affection. The cat looked at the king with indifference, then went over to bathe himself on a rug by the fireplace.

King Renauldee sat up a little straighter with anticipation when he heard footsteps echoing down the hall. He hoped that this was the much expected news he had been waiting for. Tidbits of information about a war with Filligrim and the goblins of the Black Mountains had reached his ears a couple of weeks ago, but he had not heard anything since. He feared that something tragic had happened.

The door across the room slowly opened and a tall, slender man who was part merman and part human entered, looking disheveled and very tired. He crossed the room and bowed before the king.

"I rode night and day to get back to you, my king," the man said, lowering himself into a chair.

"What news have you heard, Darius?" King Renauldee anxiously asked.

"Filligrim did go to war as you had heard. However," Darius hesitated before continuing the rest of his sentence, "it was three months ago that it occurred."

"Three months!" King Renauldee shouted. His eyes morphed into the eyes of a merman. So black, the whites of his eyes were no longer showing. The patch of scales on both sides of his face turned from their normal color of light blue to a deep sea blue. He sat back in his chair and placed his face in his hands, sighing hard.

"Yes, King Renauldee," Darius almost whispered the three words. "There's something else that you should know."

King Renauldee sat with his face in his hands for quite some time before looking up at Darius. He took a drink of water and swallowed hard before asking, "What would that be?"

"My informant at the Filligrim Castle told me that apparently..." Darius knew how hard it would be for the king to accept the next piece of news, but he had to tell him. "Queen Noor had twins."

"What do you mean she had twins?" the king asked, confused. "You mean she has recently had twins? Who is the father?"

"No, your majesty. Prince Kwagar has a twin brother."

"A—a twin?" King Renauldee stammered, not comprehending. "How could that be? I have never laid eyes on another baby, much less been told about one!"

"I don't know any details about the other twin, Sire."

"Then maybe it's not true."

"Maybe." Darius stared at the king who had now stood and walked to the open window.

"What about my grandson, Kwagar?"

"He—he," Darius faltered, "he is in Hamamelis Prison, in the Dingy Mountains."

"What! King Vulgaree will answer for taking my grandson, a prince, from Filligrim," growled King Renauldee.

"No, my lord, it will be his son, Prince Mosaic."

King Renauldee looked at Darius with a puzzled look on his face.

"Prince Mosaic?" King Renauldee questioned.

"Yes. My informant told me that he has done something to his father, and has taken King Vulgaree's throne."

"I don't understand all this lunacy. What would make Prince Mosaic commit all of these atrocities?" King Renauldee said, shaking his head.

"My informant said that there have been whispers of a traitor from the Dark Lands, and

74

something about a crown and a jewel. If you can make any sense of that," Darius said, shrugging.

"Do you mean, '*The crown and jewel*'?" King Renauldee asked, turning to Darius.

"I don't know what crown or jewel they were talking about, Sire."

"How very interesting." King Renauldee sat back down and rubbed his chin.

"What do you mean, Sire?" Darius asked, genuinely interested as well.

"Hmm, oh never mind what I mean," King Renauldee said flippantly. He sat there for a moment and then commanded, "Darius, saddle my horse and have fifty soldiers ready to ride with me. I'm going to Filligrim Castle. I must speak with Queen Noor."

"But your majesty, what about Queen Arianna? She will not want you going to Filligrim with the Mermaid Festival about to start," Darius warned.

"She will have to understand that the future of our kingdom is in danger. I can't believe my grandson is in prison," King Renauldee said, shaking his head. "He is the future ruler of Crystal Sea Palace and of Filligrim. That filthy prince goblin will pay for this. Hurry, Darius. I must help him if I can."

"I will ready the horse and guard, your majesty," Darius said, bowing deep with understanding. Kwagar would be next in line if King Renauldee were to die. They would have to do all they could to ensure that Kwagar would be safe.

King Renauldee watched Darius leave the

room. He walked to the open window and looked out at the ocean that lay before him. Small whitecaps dotted the water as far as the eye could see, while a flock of seagulls hovered around some dead fish, down near the shore. A group of mermaid children played with a ball in the water not far from the coast, while fishing boats returned from their day's work. They would be providing for the town's supper that night.

However, King Renauldee wasn't really concentrating on what was going on in his kingdom. He had more serious things to think about, like a certain crown and jewel.

The Crown of the Races had been made with the sole purpose of uniting the races. But war broke out among the races before they could pick a ruler, dividing them forever. That was when it was discovered that the jewel was evil. If it had been placed in the crown, and the crown placed on the wearer's head, the person wearing the crown would inherit the evil and rule all the lands, till the end of time. Two parties were chosen by a council, one to hide the jewel and one to hide the crown. The jewel in the crown was worth more than anything in all the lands around. It was created from the tears of a thousand fairies, the sweat from a hundred dwarves, the warts from ten goblins, a hair from a unicorn's tail, the scale of a dragon's hide, the tooth of an ogre, the fingernail of a giant, the venom of an ant, and a single drop of blood from a man. To make the jewel enchanted, a pixie gave up all her fairy dust, which ended her life. King Renauldee had been privy to the tale because of his ancestry. His forbearer had been on the council that had been responsible for hiding the jewel and crown.

Renauldee's ancestor had been found wandering the lands in a stupor. His people had taken him to Mermaid Island, to be cared for by an ancient mermaid sea herbalist. Even though his memory had been wiped, he was still able to record some bits and pieces of what had happened to him and the crown. It was written in a diary in the king's secret study that Renauldee's father had showed him right before he had died. When King Renauldee took over the throne, he had read through the papers, taking in every word. After Renauldee's ancestor recovered, a messenger had delivered a note to him. The note told him that the crown was hidden in his kingdom and that he would be responsible for its safety. It also stated the whereabouts of the crown. The note had no signature and had been written in a very elegant script.

Renauldee remembered how clever he had thought the council had been, hiding the crown in Renauldee's ancestor's kingdom. No one would ever think of looking for the crown in the ocean.

Why was the secret of the jewel and crown coming out now, so many years after they had been hidden away? What did Queen Noor have to do with it? There were so many questions with no one to answer them. However, he would have his answer. He would ride to Filligrim, and he and his daughter-in-law would have a sit down talk. She would tell him everything, including the reason why his grandson was in the hands of the goblins.

The queen's handmaiden spoke quietly to him, pulling him from his deliberation. The king jumped, never hearing her knock or come in. He looked into the girl's face and smiled. She was like the daughter he had never had. Half mermaid, her pale skin was adorned with soft pink scales that glittered on her cheeks. Her golden hair flowed around her beautiful oval face, as it would under deep water. Her light gray eyes sparkled as she smiled back at him.

"Your majesty," she said bowing low, "forgive the intrusion. I would have waited until you acknowledged me, but my lady...."

"I know, Lauren," he said in understanding. "My exquisite queen is requesting my presence. You don't have to apologize for entering my study. You are like a daughter to me, and when you marry Kwagar, you truly will be."

"Thank you, your majesty," she said curtsying this time, "that's kind of you. But the other servants wouldn't like hearing that, Sire."

"Bosh, who cares what they think. I'm king. I take that back, they should be caring what *I* think." He winked at her and then smiled. He was proud of his grandson's decision. Lauren would make him a fine wife. He thought briefly about telling her about Kwagar, but decided to keep the information to himself, until he talked with Queen Noor.

Lauren laughed at his teasing. He was a good king and all of his subjects loved him. Most times they vied for his acknowledgment and praise. He moved toward her, picking up his traveling cloak as he went.

"Are you going somewhere, Sire?" Lauren asked, eyeing the cloak.

"Yes. I'm leaving for Filligrim as soon as possible. I have to speak with Queen Noor about a delicate matter."

"Her majesty will be disappointed that you are leaving the castle. The Mermaid Festival is only three days away," she said smiling at him.

"I will miss being here for the festival. It is my favorite, after all. However, my precious, sweet queen will have to do without me." He touched Lauren's shoulder, and grinned heartily at her. "Don't worry, I'll speak with her about being grumpy while I'm gone. I know she tends to take out my absence on everyone around her." He laughed a little and then said, "She just can't live without me, can she?"

"You two have a bond as I have never seen in any other mermaid couple, Sire."

King Renauldee left Lauren standing in the doorway and headed in the direction of the royal quarters. He found Queen Arianna working on some knitting, while another handmaiden read poems to her. The handmaiden rose as King Renauldee entered the room, and then bowed.

"You can take a break, Martha. Why don't you go and have some tea and fish pie in the kitchen," Queen Arianna said, smiling at the pretty girl and then at the king. "My dear husband, something has reached my ears that...."

"I know what you have heard my sweet queen, but I have no choice in the matter. Kwagar needs my help," King Renauldee said, cutting her off.

"That was not what I was going to say at all. What do you mean, Kwagar needs your help?" she asked.

"Oh," was all King Renauldee could say.

"Should I ask again, husband?"

"No, I heard you. I just have this horrible habit of sticking my foot in my mouth. When will I learn," he said, turning a little red.

"Once more, Renauldee, what is the matter with our grandson?" she asked a little more impatiently.

He sat down in a chair next to Arianna and looked deep into her lovely gray eyes that reminded him of storm clouds, then spoke slowly, "Some news has reached my ears about a war with Filligrim and the goblins of the Black Mountains. Apparently, Kwagar has been taken to Hamamelis Prison as a prisoner of the goblins."

Queen Arianna's quick mermaid temper flared. Her eyes flashed dangerously and the larger scales that adorned her cheeks and neck turned a deep shade of crimson. She stood and without thinking, pointed one of her knitting needles at a nearby vase. A white light shot from the end of the needle, shattering the glass. "Why would King Vulgaree risk the wrath of the Crystal Sea Palace, might I ask?" Arianna fumed.

"Please calm yourself, Arianna." King Renauldee took his wife's hand in his. "It's not King Vulgaree that has done this. It's his son, Prince Mosaic. I must go to Filligrim and find out for myself if this news is true. I will also find out

what our daughter-in-law is going to do about it."
He paused a moment before going on, "What I'm
about to tell you next, my dear, will shock you. So
prepare yourself." He paused. "Apparently, Queen
Noor didn't just have Kwagar."

"You mean someone else had him for her and
he is adopted!" she shouted. Her normally light
blue hair turned flaming red.

"No, no, no, my dear," King Renauldee
calmed, pulling her back down into her chair. He
smoothed her hair and watched as it turned several
different colors before turning blue again. "You
misunderstand me. I didn't really know how to say
it. Let me put it another way. Noor had twins."

"Are you trying to tell me that Kwagar has a
twin brother?" she said slowly. "But how can that
be?"

"I don't know any of the answers. That is why
I am going to Filligrim to find out for myself."

"Then you must go at once, and I will come
with you!" she practically demanded. This time her
beautiful, pale-colored skin turned into thousands
of tiny multicolored scales and her human eyes
morphed into eyes like a sea serpent.

"I don't think that would be wise, my dear.
What would our subjects say with the Mermaid
Festival only three days away? One of us must be
here to start the festivities. The mermaids will be
counting on you. I will send word back with Darius
straight away when I find out everything from
Queen Noor about our grandson Kwagar, and the
other twin. I will also send word about what my
plans are in rescuing Kwagar. Who knows, I might

be able to make it back for the festival."

"What of my other grandson?" She asked in such a way that it caught Renauldee off guard.

"What—do—you—mean, my dear?" he asked, slowly.

"If I have another grandson, I want you to bring him here so that I can meet him. I already know that I love him just as much as I do Kwagar."

"Let's take things as they come, Precious. I want to meet our grandson's twin as well. However, I don't want to be hasty. Is that okay?" He knew his wife could be a very impatient person.

"All right dear, if that is what you want," she said, smiling. He watched as she turned back into her beautiful human form. "Just think, Renauldee—twins!

King Renauldee leaned into his wife and kissed her perfect rose-colored lips. She was the love of his life and he didn't know what he would ever do without her. Darius knocked, and then entered the room. He waited until the kissing stopped and the king waved him forward.

"Your horse is ready, Sire," Darius said, bowing. "Also, the men that you requested are assembled."

"Darius," Queen Arianna said, still staring at her husband.

"Yes, my Lady?"

"You must make sure that this gentleman comes back to me in one piece, understand?" she said, turning to smile at Darius.

"You can count on me, my Lady. I would give my life for my king."

Renauldee kissed her once more, very deeply and then started for the door. He stopped and turned around, "My dear, please be nice to all of the staff. They love you so."

"You know how I am when you're away. But I will try to behave just for you, dear."

"Thank you, my sweet. Take care." He closed the door and then sighed with relief. That conversation had gone a lot better than he thought it was going to.

ONE TAKES FLIGHT

The Filligrim castle in the land of the Misfits was in a flurry as Gladdy walked through the front door. People were running here and there, with Portumus shouting at everyone who came near him. The pageboy, Bogart, walked past Gladdy and she stopped him.

"Bogart dear, what is going on?"

"Oh, well…" Bogart whimpered as he looked toward Portumus, who had now stopped shouting and was in deep conversation with Theodius the cat.

"You can tell me. I'll protect you," Gladdy said, while staring at the man and cat.

"Theodius is back and has issued a warrant for the arrest of Elsfur, Timmynog, Snollygob, Shimmer, and…" He hesitated before saying anything else, then almost whispered, "and you."

"ME!" Gladdy practically shouted. She looked at the stricken boy and said, "I'm sorry, Bogart. I wasn't shouting at you. You can run along. I have a few words that I want to say to a certain cat," she said, as she started toward Theodius. However, she stopped and turned toward the young boy. "You might want to go and hide. This could get ugly."

Gladdy turned back around and continued walking purposefully toward Portumus and Theodius. Theodius spotted Gladdy and stopped talking.

"Well," he said, smiling under his mustache. "At least we won't have to go looking for one of our prisoners."

"Prisoner," Gladdy said through gritted teeth. "How dare you try to arrest me! For what?"

"For aiding the enemy," Theodius said calmly. "I have had reports that you authorized Elsfur and Timmynog to go the Dingy Mountains. Also, I heard reports that you and a certain old twig were in Hemlock Forest aiding the dryads, so they could go and help the goblins."

"That, Theodius, is preposterous! If anyone needs to be arrested, it's you! You are a traitor to the Kingdom of Filligrim," Gladdy shouted at him. There came a similar shriek from Gladdy's bag. Gladdy reached inside the bag and pulled Grandmother Muckernut out and set her on the floor. Everyone in the main hall of the castle stopped what they were doing, and watched as Grandmother Muckernut transformed into her beautiful, rainbow-colored dryad self. She pulled up to her full height, walked over to Theodius, bent down, wrapped her fingers around his throat and pulled him off the floor as she stood up. He began trying to meow, and then started choking. Portumus drew his sword, but Grandmother Muckernut ignored him.

"Listen to me, Theodius, you good for nothing magician," Grandmother Muckernut spat. "Don't you ever insult me again, or you will spend your days as a Milk Thistle weed in an overgrown pasture with cows dropping dung on your head. Do I make myself clear? If I were you, I wouldn't go around talking about other people being traitors. You have a lot of explaining to do about your traitorous acts."

Before he could respond, she opened her fingers and let him fall to the floor, where he landed on all fours sputtering and coughing. Portumus looked down at Theodius and then stared at the rainbow-colored woman in awe. He had known that dryads were fearsome warriors and he believed the woman would do just what she said she would, if Theodius were to say one more wrong word.

Grandmother Muckernut looked back at Portumus and then down at his sword. Portumus put his sword away immediately.

"I don't think you understand," Theodius said, hoarsely. "If you are in this castle then you are a prisoner. Portumus, my friend, arrest these dear ladies and escort them to the tower. They won't give you any problems."

"Portumus, you lay one finger on me and I will have your head!" Gladdy threatened. Gladdy began to say more, but stopped. Suddenly, her body started withering as if she were at the end of her time. Her skin sagged and wrinkled, her back hunched and her hair became solid white and some of it even fell out. She turned to Grandmother Muckernut, her eyes shining with tears and confusion. Grandmother Muckernut was changing as well. She was old and bent.

"What are you doing to us?" Gladdy's voice strained and crackled.

"It's a side effect that the enchantment has," Theodius chuckled. "Go ahead, Portumus, they can't hurt you," Theodius said, nonchalantly. "You see, I have placed spells on the castle. While you are in this castle, you and Grandmother Muckernut can no longer do magic, and since you are magical creatures, you have been weakened by the spells as well."

Gladdy stepped back and tried using her magic, but nothing happened. When she saw that Gladdy's did nothing, Grandmother Muckernut tried hers as well, only to find herself in an even more weakened state.

Portumus took Gladdy by the arm, while a guard stationed nearby stepped forward and took Grandmother Muckernut by her arm.

"Where is Andy? What have you done with him?" Gladdy demanded breathlessly. "I want answers, Theodius!"

"My name is Saber," the cat answered. "Not Theodius. The Theodius that you knew no longer exists."

"What are you talking about?" Gladdy exclaimed in surprise. "Where is my Theodius?"

"He died years ago. Right after he came to the

Dark Lands. I took his place in this form, and came here to complete my goal in life."

Gladdy was so shocked by the news she couldn't speak.

"What goal would that be?" Grandmother Muckernut asked.

"Total domination. I think that the Crown of the Races will look good on my brow, don't you?"

"Never," Gladdy said defiantly. "You will never find the crown or the jewel."

"Oh, but I will, Gladdy. You see, I have something that will motivate you into finding it. You can guess by now, I'm sure, what that motivation is."

"Andy," whispered Gladdy.

"That's right," Saber said, smoothly.

"I will rot before I help you do anything."

"Are you willing to let Andy do the same? It's funny what a vacation in the Dark Lands will do for a person. Why, even as we speak, Andy has started to turn into a Shadow Person. Is that what you want for him?"

Gladdy stared at Saber.

"Why are you doing this? Locking me away in a tower won't help you succeed in getting the crown and the jewel."

"It's only temporary. I will be taking you to the Dark Lands. Once you have seen Andy and how much he likes torture, I'm sure you will help me find what I'm looking for. As for the others, I think death will be in order for them. Now, I'm sure that you will be very comfortable sharing a cell with Shimmer and Elsfur.

"But Shimmer and Elsfur are on their way to rescue Andy," Gladdy accidentally blurted out.

"Thank you for that information," Saber said, chuckling; "Now I will know where to find Shimmer and Elsfur and the others. Being cooperative might help you in the long run. It might help you to stay alive."

"Saber, let us go!" Grandmother Muckernut said, with as much strength as she could muster.

"I'm afraid I can't do that. You two are traitors to the Kingdom of Filligrim."

"Queen Noor will have your head on a platter, Saber. You just wait and see," said Gladdy, threateningly. She pointed a long, gnarled finger at him. "I want to see Queen Noor, now!"

"I can't do that, my dear," Saber said with a sickeningly sweet voice. "You see, it was dear Queen Noor that ordered all of your arrests."

Saber held up a piece of parchment with his paw. Gladdy and Grandmother Muckernut both mouthed the words as they read the names of all to be arrested, and then Queen Noor's signature. They looked horrified at one another, and then back at Saber.

"What have you done with Queen Noor?" Gladdy shouted.

"Queen Noor is resting comfortably. Of course she doesn't know that she has signed this warrant. You see, she still thinks I'm Theodius and that I'm on her side." Gladdy and Grandmother Muckernut looked at each other. "Now, you can take them away, Portumus. They are so confused, weak, and old that they won't give you a moment's problem."

Portumus and the guard took the two women by the elbows and escorted them to a smaller, winding staircase across the room from the main flight of steps. They climbed until Gladdy thought she wouldn't be able to climb any longer. She had forgotten just how tall the prison tower was. She was in such shock that she didn't even pay attention to where Portumus was leading them.

"I'm sorry about this, Gladdy," he lamented, as they stopped in front of a prison door. "Saber told me that if I helped, I would be head of security for him. It was either that, or prison."

She just stared at him in disbelief, speechless.

Portumus helped Gladdy to one of the cots in the room and the other guard did the same for Grandmother Muckernut. A table and two chairs stood under the only window in the cell. It held a pitcher of water and two glasses.

"I'll make sure that you are properly fed and that you have enough water and blankets. It gets cold at night this far up in the tower." He poured two glasses of water and handed them to the women. "I want you to know that I will go very slowly about searching for the others. Maybe they'll be able to rescue Prince Kwagar and your son Andy before I get to them."

He turned back to the table and did something the others couldn't see, and then he and the guard left the cell, locking the door behind them. Gladdy thought about Portumus' last words. Her son, Andy. Queen Noor may have been his birth mother, but Gladdy was his true mother. How could she have brought him here to this situation?

How could she have taken him from the only home he had ever known? Andy had been safe back in the other world. Now he was in prison in one of the darkest parts of the land. Gladdy felt such horrible helplessness. She couldn't help him, not locked up in this room and not without being able to use the power that had been passed down by the generations of elf females before her. Her only hope was that the other Misfits would find Andy before they became prisoners themselves.

The enchantments that had been placed on the castle were taking their toll on her. Gladdy felt as limp as a wash rag. She rolled her head to look at Grandmother Muckernut. Gladdy remembered the first time she had met the beautiful dryad in Hemlock Forest. Her mother had taken her there when she was just a little elfin girl. It was traditional for the females in Gladdy's family to go to the forest and take oaths in the ancient dryad language, to protect the secret of the crown and jewel, and the whereabouts of Grandmother Muckernut.

Gladdy could almost smell the woods and the exotic flowers that grew in the forest. She remembered the dryads as they danced around her in a whirl of color singing beautiful sweet songs to her. She ran and played with the dryad and dormer children until her little legs couldn't run anymore. Gladdy remembered when it had been time to leave, that Grandmother Muckernut had kissed her on the forehead and told her that they would become great friends. And that is what had happened. They were great friends and would be so until they passed away.

Gladdy was pulled from her reflection by an ancient, craggy voice coming from somewhere nearby. She looked up at the small window in the door that had bars across it.

"Gladdy," the weak, feeble voice said again.

With great effort, Gladdy willed her body to move off the bed and stand. She wobbled as the room spun for a moment, then stopped. She stepped toward the door and grabbed one of the bars to steady herself. She peered through the bars into the hall and found no one there.

"Who's there?" she asked, faintly.

"Gladdy, it's me. I'm in the cell across from you."

Gladdy peered into the dimness of the cell window across the hall from her, and saw two eyes, black as coal, staring back.

"Mystic, is that you?" Gladdy said, shocked.

"Yes, it's me," Mystic said, almost crying. "Gladdy, I've lost all my power. I'm so frightened. Is—is there anything you can do to help me?"

"How did that cat take you captive?" Gladdy asked, confused.

"I assume he placed the enchantments on the castle last night," Mystic said, bitterly. "The cat is calling himself Saber."

"Mystic, do you know where Queen Noor is?"

"Saber said she was in her wing of the castle. He also told me that she was not to know of his plans until everything was in place."

"Did he tell you about Theodius?"

"Yes," said Mystic sadly.

Gladdy was torn between relief that Theodius the cat was not her Theodius, and at the same time heartbroken that her Theodius was dead. She had loved him all her life. He had been her closest friend and companion. They had even thought about marriage right before Theodius had left for the Dark Lands. Then Gladdy had to leave with Andy for the other world and their dream of love died.

"Are you still there?" Mystic asked, when Gladdy didn't respond.

"Yes, I'm still here. Mystic, are you sure that you have no powers? Your powers are so much greater than mine. I just can't believe that Saber would be able to do this to you."

"Are you admitting that I'm stronger than you, Gladiola?" Mystic said mockingly.

"Mystic, this is not the time or the place for that!" Gladdy reprimanded her. "Just answer the question!"

"My power is gone. It's like…it's like…" She couldn't bring herself to say what it was.

"It's like you're human," Gladdy answered softly.

"Yes," Mystic whimpered.

"It's going to be all right, Mystic. I'll think of a way to get us out of here. Just rest for now."

Gladdy got back on her bed and looked at the sky through the window. Clouds drifted lazily by in an azure sky, not caring where they were being blown. Not caring that an elf, a dryad and an Asrai were locked up in cells with no one with whom they could depend on to rescue them.

Just as Gladdy began to drift off to sleep, a bird landed on the windowsill. Gladdy looked at the bird and wondered where it had come from and where it was going. It was a beautiful bird with dark blue feathers on its back and a solid ruby red chest. Tufts of tiny feathers stuck out of its head and rustled in the breeze coming through the window. Gladdy looked at the bird and then at Grandmother Muckernut. Then she looked at the bird again, and then looked back at Grandmother Muckernut.

Gladdy sat bolt upright. She had an idea. "Vinca," Gladdy said, calling Grandmother Muckernut by her birth name. Grandmother Muckernut rolled her head and looked at Gladdy.

"I had the strangest dream," Grandmother Muckernut said wearily to Gladdy. "I dreamed that I could hear Mystic crying, but I couldn't find her."

"Well, I can tell you where you'll find her," Gladdy said, pointing to the door. "She's in a cell across the hall. Apparently, Saber took it upon himself to take her as a prisoner as well."

"What for? Did she steal his catnip or something?" Grandmother Muckernut snickered at her little joke, which Gladdy didn't find amusing at all. Gladdy told Grandmother Muckernut everything that Mystic had said.

"Very clever, getting rid of the more powerful beings in the kingdom. I wonder what he's going to do with Queen Noor."

"I don't know," Gladdy said in a tearful whisper.

Grandmother Muckernut looked

sympathetically at her friend. "So, how do we get out of here?"

Melancholy began seeping into the very core of Gladdy's bones. She felt such a responsibility to all those who had depended on her. All of her very dear friends were about to be imprisoned and there was nothing she could do about it. Andy and Kwagar were in prison, and who knew how they were being treated. And to top it off, one of the people whom she loved and trusted most in this life, the person she could have married, had been murdered by Saber.

Gladdy lay back on her pillow and began to cry.

"Gladdy," Grandmother Muckernut said, a little hesitantly. When she didn't get a response, she said it a little louder. Gladdy still did not respond. Grandmother Muckernut felt she had no other choice but to yell. So she took in a deep breath, opened her mouth and yelled, "Gladdy!"

Gladdy stopped crying and looked very pitifully at Grandmother Muckernut. She sniffed a little and then looked at the window. Tears still fell unbidden down her cheeks, but she didn't make any more noise.

"Are you okay? I have never seen you cry before, and it's very alarming," Grandmother Muckernut said.

Gladdy looked down at the covers on her bed. "I'll be all right. I just can't believe that I left a world where Andy was safe, even with all its craziness. My life as his mother was great. I could have seen him graduate, get married and be the grandmother to his children. Look at what my selfishness has got him."

"It wasn't selfish to want to come home and see the land of your birth. And it's not your fault that Saber, the Shadow Man, decided he needed to rule the world. And as for the other, you're not Andy's mother," Grandmother Muckernut said tenderly, coming over to her and wrapping her arms around Gladdy's shoulder.

"I may not have been his birth mother, Vinca, but I'm his mother in every other way and I have let him down."

"You have not let him down. You have raised him to be a wonderful, responsible person. Now he's grown into a man who will take this kingdom by the hand someday, and rule it the way King Macon envisioned it to be," Grandmother Muckernut said, reassuringly.

Gladdy sat in silence for a moment, mulling over Grandmother Muckernut's words. "You're right, Vinca. He is great, and we're going to save him."

"You bet we are!" Grandmother Muckernut said, patting Gladdy on the shoulder. "Now, what was your plan of escape?"

"Well, Saber told us that we could no longer use our magic inside the castle. I think that if I help you get through the window and I hold onto you, you could transform into the shape of a bird and fly away. You could find Shimmer and the others and warn them before Portumus finds them. They probably went toward the Mulberry Forest. That's the way I would go if I were Shimmer. I just hope that my people will allow them to pass that way."

Grandmother Muckernut slapped her hands together. "Why didn't I think of transforming into something like that? You really are an amazing elf, you know that? You're also right about Shimmer and Elsfur. That is the only logical way to go without being noticed. I don't think even Saber will think of that."

"I wouldn't put anything past Saber right now, especially since he knows that's where I am from. He just might think of Mulberry Forest." Gladdy's eyebrows were almost touching as she thought about Saber. Then she said, "I want to forget about him for the time being. Let's try to walk over to the window and then I will help you up on the windowsill. Then you can transform. Okay?"

It was harder than either of them thought it would be. What would have been easy for a normal person, tired them out tremendously. They had to hold onto one another as they went. Once the two of them almost fell over, but were able to steady themselves. Gladdy helped Vinca crawl onto the table and then pushed her up toward the window. As Gladdy pushed, she accidentally knocked over the pitcher of water. Ignoring the mess, she continued helping Grandmother Muckernut and was relieved when Grandmother Muckernut finally swung herself onto the window ledge and stuck her legs out the window. Gladdy gasped as Grandmother Muckernut's body began to turn back into her old self.

"Well, I guess I'm up high enough away from the enchantments, since I'm back to my old self.

Now to transform into a bird. Wish me luck," she said as she closed her eyes and slowed her breathing. Gladdy watched her turn into a beautiful white dove with a ring of rainbow colors around her neck.

"I like the ring of rainbow colors around your neck. It's very fashionable," Gladdy laughed. She stepped onto a chair by the window and gently slid her hand down the back of the bird.

Grandmother Muckernut flapped her wings for a bit, and looked at Gladdy with her large, round bird eyes. She nodded at Gladdy, and then Grandmother Muckernut jumped from the window ledge, soaring on the wind. Finally, she began flapping her wings, turning back toward the castle. When she was close to the window she turned her little bird head so that she could see Gladdy in the window and gave a loud coo of encouragement before flying off in the clouds.

Gladdy felt a little envious of Grandmother Muckernut and wished that she could fly away as well. Then a thought occurred to her and she whispered to herself, "I hope that Saber doesn't come in here while Grandmother Muckernut is gone, or I'm in big trouble."

Gladdy looked down at the overturned pitcher and noticed something shiny sticking out from underneath it. She bent over and pushed the pitcher aside. There staring up at her was her own reflection. A small mirror in a gold frame lay on the floor. It dawned on Gladdy what Portumus must have been doing before he left their cell. Portumus had given her a way to escape.

SHADOW QUEEN

Andy opened his eyes and yawned, trying to wake up. It was dark except for the faint glow of a lantern on the table in the cell. He rolled over and was startled to see that Theodius was not in the room with him, but someone else was there. He tried to focus on who it was, and found that the person was more shadow than human. Fear enveloped his heart momentarily as he thought of the Shadow Man. But this shape was smaller and looked more feminine.

"Hello, Prince Andrew," the dark figure said. Her voice was sweet and calming like a little child's.

"Hello," Andy said in return, feeling very comforted all of a sudden.

The dark, shadowy form rose and walked toward the table. She turned the lamp up, brightening the room. Andy could see it was actually a woman. Though, she almost didn't look human. She drifted in and out of shape, darkening and lightening like she had a light inside her and someone kept turning her on and off. Then Andy saw the green eyes, and he recognized the woman. She was the woman in his dreams. Now that he had a chance to see her without being drugged, she was even more beautiful than he remembered.

"I'm glad to see you are awake and healing well. I hope you weren't in too much discomfort," she said, sitting back down on Theodius' bed.

Andy looked once more around the small cell that had become his temporary home and asked, "Who are you and where is Theodius?"

"You always answer questions with questions," she laughed. "Why is that?"

"I didn't realize that I did," Andy answered wearily. "Have I been asking a lot of questions?"

"Obviously so, you just asked another one. I've hardly said two words and you've already asked three questions," she said, matter-of-factly.

"I don't mean to ask so many questions. Maybe if you would tell me where I am and what I'm doing here and where Theodius is, I will stop asking so many questions."

The woman faded and then came back in full form several times before saying anything. Then, as if she had made up her mind she said, "You're here because Saber brought you here. This is my home, Charlock Castle, in the Dark Lands. Don't worry about Theodius. He's in a room down the hall with a nice meal and a cold drink. I even let him have some playing cards to entertain himself."

"Saber?" Andy ran the name over his lips. "Is that the Shadow Man who found me in the woods?"

"Yes," her tongue clicked. "He is a very powerful man in my kingdom."

"May I ask who you are?" Andy asked cautiously.

"I am the Shadow Queen," she said smiling. Then she bent closer to Andy and whispered, "but you can call me Aunt Estonia."

Andy laughed, "Why on earth would I want to do that?"

"Because silly, I am your aunt," she said again, patiently.

"Well, I happen to know that neither of my parents had siblings, so you couldn't be my aunt. So just go away and bother someone else." Andy waved her away and rolled over onto his other side.

"You know Andy, there are other ways to have aunts."

Andy slowly rolled back over and looked at the woman with such a quizzical look she started to laugh.

"Just how could you be my aunt?" he asked, a little annoyed at her amusement of him.

"I think I should tell you your family history first. Then you will understand who I am," she said, her laughing coming to a halt. "I think I will go as far back as King Macon. He is the one who saw a future in Filligrim. He saw that valley and instantly knew that it would be a fine kingdom one day. He gladly welcomed the different races to come and live in his realm, and that is how it became known as the Valley of the Misfits. He married a woman from his former land by the name of Lady Katalyn. Her beauty was talked about throughout the kingdoms. She was a caring and wise queen. They had a son whom they named Hector. Hector grew to be great in everything he did. He was a powerful hunter..." Estonia stopped talking and walked over to the door. Andy thought she was just going to leave and not say anything else, but she turned around and looked at him. Andy was astonished to see that she had tears on her face.

"Hector was my father," she said, in a barely audible whisper. "He was out hunting one day for a beautiful stag in River Birch Forest. He loved the elves and they loved him. He was always welcome to hunt in that forest as much as he wanted. That is where he met and fell in love with my mother, Lanaya."

"Your mother was an elf?" Andy said, thunderstruck. "But what about the law?""

My father disobeyed the law and married my mother in secret. He kept it from my grandparents. When they died he declared the law banished and placed my mother on the throne in the Filligrim Castle. They were so in love that everyone figured it would be okay. They had twins, my brother and me, only a year after my mother became the official queen. We grew up in a very happy home." Estonia sat down at the end of Andy's bed and looked straight at him and in a very serious voice she said, "Until I started to go bad. This is the result of their carelessness!" she said, pointing to herself.

She began to cry and turned very dark. Andy couldn't even see her face anymore. She stayed that way for a while and then finally turned a lighter shade of gray.

"I'm sorry that happened to you," Andy said, "but what has that got to do with me?"

"I'm getting to it!" she snapped. Then she smiled at him and said, "When I was older, I left Filligrim and wandered the lands. I came here and lived like a hermit in a hut in the forest for quite some time. The longer I lived alone the more I started to become a shadow of my former self. My father would come and visit me, but after a while I forbade him to come. I began to do magic even though I didn't want to and everything in the forest started dying as a result. I couldn't even begin to tell you why. I tried for the longest time to be a good person, but the darkness was inside of me. Hatred grew for my family. I couldn't see them anymore without something bad happening to them. I wouldn't even do anything and the magic would come. It was like there was someone else living in me, making it all happen."

"What happened to your family?" Andy asked, absorbed in her tale.

"I accidentally killed my father," she said sadly, staring at the floor. Black tears fell from her cheeks and splashed onto the sleeve of her dress. "He came to tell me that my mother was ill. She wanted to see me one last time before she died. I never wanted her to see me like this and it enraged me that I couldn't go to her." Estonia looked down at her gray hands. "I don't know what happened. It was like I blacked out and when I came to, my father lay in my arms, dead. You cannot fathom my grief for what I had done. I cried until my black tears became a small stream. I tore my clothes and laid myself in ashes for days. Finally, I sent his body back to the castle with a letter explaining— no, pleading my case to my mother and my brother. I told them how sorry I was."

"Did they understand?"

"My brother was infuriated. He sent a small army of soldiers to kill me. However, when they stepped onto this land they all died. The land had become infected with whatever was infecting me. I found that if you came on this land with bad intentions you would die. But if you came with good intentions, the land would let you live and almost take care of you."

"Is that what happened to my stab wound?" Andy pulled up his shirt and looked at his now perfect stomach.

"The water has healing powers. It pulls power from the Shadow People that have come to live here." She touched Andy's stomach with her ice cold, shadow-like hand. Andy felt as if ice water had been thrown on his stomach and he jumped.

"Then how come I felt like I was dying?" he asked, pulling his shirt back down to warm his stomach.

"That's the way it works. It has infected you as well. The longer you're here, the more shadow-like you will become."

"Then I have to leave!" Andy said, becoming

frightened. "Why didn't the land just let me leave that day? I could have gone and saved Flipsy, my dragon!"

"The land was holding you here until Saber could come and get you. It alerted him that someone had come onto the land, but that you were here with good intentions."

"Does this mean the land will never let me leave?"

"No, it will let you leave...someday." She smiled at him. "When I allow it to."

Andy felt his joy over finding that Theodius was making a way to escape, drain from his heart.

"What happened with your brother and your mother?" he asked, trying not to think of the hole in the wall just a few feet from him.

"My mother passed away without me ever seeing her again." She stifled a small cry and sat there a moment longer before continuing. "I heard that Augustus, my brother, married Medina, one of the ladies from the court. They had your grandfather, King Anasee."

"If his parents were both human, then why did my grandfather turn evil?" Andy said a little perplexed.

"I didn't know that he was evil," Estonia said. She looked as if this was news to her. "From what I understand he was a good king. He married an elfin girl as well. Her name was Lena. She was King Foxglove's sister. She was from the Land of Chaldeon and she often visited her brother during harvest time. She had been visiting her brother when she saw King Anasee come riding into the forest. She fell in love instantly and the rest they say… is history."

"King Foxglove is my uncle!" Andy shouted in surprise.

"Yes, he is actually your great uncle," Estonia said, amused. "Your mother turned out just fine from what I hear, and so did you and your brother. It's amazing how it hits some and not others."

"I don't understand how you can be so old and your age doesn't show. I mean," Andy blushed and then went on, "other than looking like a dark shadow, you look as if you could be twenty years old."

"That's another side effect of the magic. It has kept me young all this time."

"Wow. That's amazing!"

"Any more questions?" Queen Estonia asked, very amused by her nephew.

"How did you come to live in a palace?" Andy asked, wondering about this strange woman.

"I built this palace and I became queen of it. Other people who had the misfortune to have mixed parents came to live in this land also. We are all shadows of our former selves. I welcomed them with open arms. It felt so good to have people around me again, people who understood what it felt like to be shunned by the ones who were supposed to love you most in this world. However, I'm the only one here that is powerful. Other Shadow People have some powers but not as great as mine."

That explained a lot to Andy. Now he knew why the Shadow Man wanted the crown and the jewel so badly. He wanted the type of power that the Shadow Queen had and the only way to get it was to acquire the Crown of the Races. The queen went on, "I also started a rumor about the Shadow People that helped keep unwanted and innocent people from coming onto the land. We are known to most as a horrible, evil people. The elves however know differently, and keep our secret."

"I still don't understand why you feel a need to keep me here," Andy said a little more hotly than he should have.

"Saber wants to keep you here. He says you're an asset to me."

"How would I be an asset to you?" Andy asked with irritation.

"I don't know. However, I trust him as my advisor and I'm going to keep you here until he is done with you." She held up her hand when Andy began to protest. "I will hear nothing more about it. I will get you something good to eat. I might even let you come and stay up in the palace with me. But you have to promise me you will be good."

Andy's eyes darted toward the wall behind the table. He had to take the chance of getting out that way. He knew that she would be watching his every move if he were to go up to the palace.

"I want to stay here and keep Theodius company," he said, coming up with an excuse. "He's old and I think he needs a friend."

She sighed hard and looked at him, "Very well, you can stay down here. However, I will call you up to the palace from time to time. I would like to get to know my great, great nephew better, and I don't want to come down here to do so." As she said this, the queen rubbed her palms together like they were dirty and looked around the cell in disgust.

"I—I would like to get to know you better as well," Andy said, thinking the information might help him in some way.

She stood, walked toward the door, and put her hand on the doorknob. She then turned back to Andy. "I think that tomorrow night will be a good night for you to come and dine with me. I will have my servant Claude retrieve you and make sure that you receive a bath and nice clothes. Good day, Andy."

She left the room and Andy heard the door being locked, leaving him in silence. His head hurt from all the information the Shadow Queen had told him.

Andy thought about Saber. He wants the jewel and crown and will probably stop at nothing to get it.

Andy worried about how much information he had given the Shadow Man while he was drugged. Had the Misfits found the crown? Was that why it was taking them so long to rescue him? But if the Misfits came to Charlock Castle with the thought of retrieving Andy, would they all die just to try and save him? Maybe the land would think it was good intentions and not hurt his friends. Then he thought about the jewel. He had buried it in the woods when he thought he was dying. How would he ever find it again? He looked down at his sheets where the queen had been sitting. Black dust was covering the spot. He brushed it off his bed and felt shivers run through him. He felt like he was brushing off a part of Queen Estonia.

While Andy sat mulling things over, they brought a very happy Theodius back into the cell. He carried a small basket of fruit and cheese, with a loaf of bread placed on top of it. The old man smiled a black, toothy grin at Andy as he set the basket on the table. Then he pulled a deck of cards out of his pocket and held them up for Andy to see. Andy smiled back.

Then Theodius said, "Wanna play?"

ESCAPING

Sitting in his cell in Hamamelis Prison, Kwagar focused, as much as his food-deprived brain would allow, on the small hole in the wall in the opposite corner of his cell. It was about an inch off the floor. If he could get the crack to spread down onto the floor, the goblin promised he would do the rest. He had been trying for hours, and had only succeeded in making a half-inch fracture below the hole.

He sighed hard and sat back against the wall, exhausted.

"It's no use," he said. "It's like I've forgotten how."

"Maybe it's because you never really used your power on purpose," Mucous said, staring at the wall.

"That's probably it. When Mystic finds out that her grandson can't even make a crack in the floor, she'll probably send me packing. That's if I ever get out of here so she can send me packing!" Kwagar threw up his hands in frustration.

Thunderous footsteps could be heard outside of their cell door. Wide-eyed, both of them looked at each other and then back at the door. Kwagar could hear Mucous mumbling under his breath, along with rapid breathing. Metal clanked against the door, as rattling keys were inserted into the lock. The large wooden door swung inward, revealing a lizard goblin. The goblin entered and then stepped to one side. There in the doorway stood Prince Mosaic and two other mole goblin guards.

Mosaic's eyes darted in their eye sockets, taking in the dreary cell, coming to rest on Kwagar's face. He smiled, revealing nasty, yellow, pointed teeth. His pale skin was stretched very thin over his bony face, showing blue, spidery veins beneath. He wore a purple robe and a small gold crown perched cockeyed on his bald head. He pushed the crown back with his index finger, like a cowboy would his cowboy hat, and strode forward, stopping in front of Kwagar and Mucous.

With his greasiest voice he said, "Well, well, well, what do we have here? A couple of miscreants sharing a cell together and no one told me. I hope you two have gotten well acquainted. Mucous, has Kwagar told you anything that I might use against him?"

Kwagar's eyes opened wide and he shot a look at the little frightened goblin. The trembling goblin looked at Kwagar in fear and then at Mosaic.

"N-n-no, your majesty, he barely says anything

to me." Mucous looked as if he was about to throw up.

"Is that so," Mosaic said snidely. He kicked the little goblin as hard as he could in the stomach. Mucous doubled over in pain, crying as silently as he could.

"Take the queen's little brat to the cell down the hall. We can't have these two getting to know each other. Mucous here has been privy to way too much in his time with me, and I don't need him spilling the beans to the Prince of Nobodies."

Kwagar kicked and bit at the huge goblins that were trying to pick him up and take him away. He knew that without Mucous he wouldn't be able to get out of the prison alive, but he had no choice. The mole goblins overpowered him and took him out of the cell. He could see the hallway and tried to make a mental note of which way they were taking him. The mole goblins threw him in a cell only two cells down from the one that Kwagar had been in originally, and they took his chains off his feet. Kwagar was allowed to walk around for the first time in months. The lizard and mole goblins left him in the cell alone, slamming the door behind them as they went. He smiled to himself and then looked around the room. It had a bed with a straw mattress and that was all. But to Kwagar it was like being in the royal suite. He would no longer have to lie on the hard, cold floor. He gingerly sat down on the mattress, feeling the softness go through his whole body.

Suddenly the door flew open and in walked Mosaic.

"Comfy?" he asked.

Kwagar said nothing.

"Don't get too comfortable, my prince. I have to leave for a few days. However, when I return, I want my answers, and you're going to give them to me. Understand!" Mosaic threatened.

Kwagar shook his head in a nervous nod, anything to make Mosaic leave him alone in the peace of his new cell.

"Good," Mosaic said sweetly. "I will come and see you when I get back and we will have a little heart-to-heart talk, okay? You will like my torture chair. It's a lot more comfortable than that bed."

Mosaic's laughter filled the cell as he turned to leave. Kwagar stared at the door as it swung shut for the second time. His insides shook like jelly. He knew without a shadow of a doubt, he needed to be long gone from this prison before Mosaic came back. Bile rose in his throat at the thought of being tortured. He looked at the bed. His comfort would have to be put off until he was home, back in Filligrim Castle where he grew up. As he thought of his home and his bed, a new hope sprang into his heart, a desire filling his very soul, a desire for freedom.

He reached out his mind, stretched out his hand and thought of the largest crack he had ever seen. A second later, the floor began to groan. Slowly at first, then with lightning speed. An ever-widening crack started at Kwagar's feet, and then spread to the opposite wall. It started deepening into the ground, as an unseen force pushed the rock and dirt out of its wake, like a mole digging a tunnel. In

Kwagar's mind the tunnel wound toward Mucous' cell and then upward. He didn't need the goblin to do anything; he would get them out of the prison and into the safety of his kingdom.

Kwagar felt the power flowing from his mind, down his arm and out his hand. Is this what Mystic felt when she used her power? Excitement thrilled him when he realized how big the crack was getting. He could actually see the hole moving toward Mucous' cell, opening and enlarging with enough room for the two of them to crawl in. His arm fell to his side when the tunnel was complete. A loud laughter escaped his lips and he leaped in the air. He had done it!

"I'll bet that old grandmother of mine would die of a heart attack if she were to see this tunnel," Kwagar said out loud.

He got down on his hands and knees and poked his head down the hole. He could see a dim light shining at the far end of the tunnel where the hole opened up into Mucous' cell. Kwagar lowered himself into the hole and began crawling. When he got to the end he could hear Mucous whimpering. Kwagar crawled out of the hole and saw Mucous lying on the ground with fresh bruises on his face, and blood coming out of his mouth.

"Mucous, are you okay?" Kwagar knelt at Mucous' side and helped the little goblin sit up.

"It will take a lot more than this to break me," Mucous said, trying to smile. Some of his teeth were broken. "Hey, how did…" Mucous looked from Kwagar to the hole in the floor. "You did it Kwagar! You really did it!"

"Yes I did," Kwagar said, smiling. "Now, how are we going to get these chains off the wall and off of you?"

Kwagar stretched out his hand and cracked the wall around the pin that held the end of the chains. He pulled the pin with all his might, freeing the manacles.

Mucous looked at the chains that were still attached to his hands and feet, and his face fell. It seemed he had been in some kind of chain his whole life. "I don't see any possible way to get out of them in here," he said, with his lip quivering.

"Well, maybe when we reach the outside of the prison, we'll find something that we can use to take them off."

"I won't be of any use to you with these on. I'll just slow you down." Mucous looked Kwagar with defeat in his eyes. "You should just leave me here."

"No. You're coming with me, even if I have to carry you." Kwagar stood and hoisted the little goblin over his shoulder. He swayed a bit from lack of food and exercise, but the thought of freedom kept him on his feet. Kwagar lowered the goblin into the hole and then jumped in. He put his hand on the side of the crack and thought, *make a hole large enough to take us clean out of these mountains*.

It was tedious work and took a lot of energy from Kwagar's already depleted body, making the fissures in front of him and sealing up the crevices behind him, so that they wouldn't be followed. When the goblins finally figured out that they were gone, they wouldn't have a clue as to how Kwagar and Mucous managed to escape.

Kwagar felt faint and very thirsty and had to stop every ten minutes or so to catch his breath.

"If only I knew how to make water come up from the ground," he told Mucous.

Mucous felt it would go faster if he helped. He worked as hard as Kwagar did, by spitting and smoothing out the rock.

"We'll be out soon and then we'll find some water. At least the rock is thinning. We must be out of the heavier rocks and into more of a rocky soil," Mucous said, spitting dirt out of his mouth. "Why don't you rest for a few moments while I work on the area ahead of us. Then you can try to make a large crack going up; maybe it will come out in the open away from the prison. After all, we've been tunneling for what seems like hours. Down here in the dark, it's hard to tell."

"You're right. I need to rest. If only we had some food and water to get our strength back. I'll just close my eyes for a few minutes and then I'll do as you suggested."

Kwagar leaned back, closed his eyes and let the coolness of the rock seep into his sweaty skin. Concentrating on making the cracks bigger and longer had taken its toll on him. He wondered if Mystic got this tired when she controlled nature.

He thought of the castle in Filligrim and of the times he had spent in the little room in the south tower. The room had a small window in it that you could see for miles across the kingdom. Warm breezes wafted through it, bringing the fragrant scents of flowers from the gardens, the hint of freshly baked bread from the bakery in town, and the leafy smells of the tobacco shop. Kwagar would observe the people milling around, going about in their daily lives. They all seemed so happy and looked as if they didn't have a care in the world.

After he tired of watching out the window, he would lie on an overstuffed feather mattress and read books about his favorite knights and how they always saved the damsel in distress. The servants would bring him his favorite food and drinks and he wouldn't have to leave the tower for days. Eventually, Theodius would insist that he come down and socialize at a ball, which Kwagar hated, or sit in on a council meeting.

Kwagar awoke, startled. He had drifted off to sleep while thinking about Filligrim. But what had driven him from his sleep? He looked around and was surprised to see a light a little ways off from where he was sitting. He could see Mucous staring up at the luminosity with a terrified expression on his face. That's when he heard the goblins. It was a little muffled in the tunnel, but Kwagar understood what they were saying. He also heard the panic in their voices.

"We need to split up," growled one of the goblins. "If we look in different directions, maybe we'll find them. I sent the gargoyles flying in different directions. They won't get far from those nasty beasts."

"The master is going to be very upset when he finds out that the human prince and the traitorous Mucous have escaped," giggled another. "The guards that were on duty probably don't have very long to live."

"He won't find out if we keep up the search. They couldn't have gotten very far," grumbled the first goblin. "Now move out, or I'll take care of you for the master."

"All right! I'll go east and you go west, and I'll meet you back at the prison," said the second goblin. "What if we haven't found them by sunset?"

"Then I guess we can say goodbye to our heads!" the first goblin shouted.

Kwagar and Mucous stared at each other. This was bad. The goblins had checked the cells and found them missing. They wouldn't be able to get out of the tunnel for a while yet, especially with the gargoyles flying around. Kwagar was hoping that he and Mucous would be able to get food and water, but now they would have to stay put until the search for them was over.

"We'll wait here until after dark. Then we'll tunnel the rest of the way out and make our way down the mountain. I'm sure we can make it to River Birch Forest, where the elves will shelter us."

"I don't know how well the elves will accept me, after what my people did to their race," Mucous said, ashamedly.

"They will accept the goblin that helped a Prince of Filligrim escape from Hamamelis Prison. After all, they are my kinsmen," Kwagar said proudly.

WARNING

Grandmother Muckernut's bird shape soared over the tops of huge trees in the direction that she thought the Misfits would take, in order to save Andy from the Dark Lands. At first, flying had been awkward. She had never turned into a bird before. However, she liked the shape more and more all the time. Her body felt light and wonderful. But most of all it was such a freeing experience. Her eyesight was perfect, as well as her hearing. She had been able to hear the Misfits talking for a good three minutes and knew it wouldn't be much farther. She found them in a clearing, eighty miles away from the castle. They were hiking in a straight line toward the Mulberry Forest, with a unicorn leading the way.

Grandmother Muckernut landed in a small tree, a short way ahead of the group and waited till they came closer to her, before speaking.

"Greetings," she called to them in bird song.

"Greetings," Windsor whinnied. "I don't

believe I know you, little bird."

"That's because she's not a bird," Elsfur said, stepping forward. "It's Grandmother Muckernut."

Grandmother Muckernut flew off the branch that she was perched on, and onto the ground. She changed her appearance right before their eyes into the beautiful, rainbow-colored dryad.

"How did you know that it was me?" she asked, smiling breathlessly.

"The rainbow colors on your neck," Elsfur said, smiling back. "Where is Gladdy?"

"That's why I'm here," she said, her face filling with anger. "Gladdy has been taken prisoner at the castle."

"What!" Elsfur yelled, outraged. "Who has done this?"

"I bet I can guess," Shimmer said, stepping forward. "It was Theodius, wasn't it." It was more of a statement than a question.

"Yes," said Grandmother Muckernut, quietly. "Theodius came back to the castle today. He informed us that his name is not Theodius. It's Saber. He also told us that the real Theodius is dead. That's not all. He has an arrest warrant with Queen Noor's signature on it. He's sending Portumus with a huge army to capture all of you and bring you back so that he can imprison you as well."

"Just why would he do that?" Snollygob slobbered, with spittle flying from both ears.

"He said that we are all enemies of the Kingdom of Filligrim, because we are hindering his plan for total domination of all the kingdoms."

"Total domination!" Timmynog bellowed.

"He boasted that the Crown of the Races would look good on his brow. He said that he was going to take Gladdy to the Dark Lands to persuade Andy to tell Saber where the jewel was, or she would watch Saber torture Andy."

"Saber is a cat *and* the Shadow Man?" Elsfur asked, looking perplexed. "How can we solve mysteries, save people and destroy the crown and jewel, if we are locked away?"

A warm morning breeze wafted across all of their faces. But rather than feel comforted by the air, chill bumps rose on their skin, and dawning comprehension on all of their faces. If they didn't get to Andy soon, what they feared most would happen. They would all bow before the same horrible king, forever.

Their hearts began racing, as figures appeared out of the forest, bows drawn and all pointing at the Misfits.

"Shimmer," was all Elsfur had to say. Shimmer turned into the blue mist and drifted into some bushes right beside Elsfur, while Grandmother Muckernut turned into a mole, scurrying down a nearby hole.

"What should I do?" she droned, so quietly that only Elsfur could hear.

"Save Andy. I will find out what is going on in the castle." He sighed and turned slowly toward the bush. Shimmer saw in horror the tears that shone in his eyes. "Be safe. I love you," he whispered. He reached out with his hand and touched the blue mist and Shimmer shivered.

Elsfur turned back around. He nodded to all his friends, and they stepped forward to meet another traitor of Filligrim…Portumus. Elsfur would somehow make him pay for the treachery that Portumus had involved himself in. As Captain of the Guard of Filligrim, Portumus had sworn to protect the people of Filligrim. But now he was helping to imprison the very creatures that could save the Princes of Filligrim.

Elsfur walked up to Portumus, stared at him for a moment with cold eyes and then continued on as quickly as possible, to keep the guard from finding Shimmer.

Shimmer's heart was breaking. All she could see were the tears and the heartbreak in Elsfur's eyes. He had said the words that she had longed to hear since she was a child and first fell in love with him. Why did he have to declare his love now, of all times. Why did it have to be this way? Why couldn't he hate her, so that she would be free to love Andy?

Shimmer sat there for a long time, confused by what she had seen, heard and understood. Saber was the Shadow Man and there was no mistake about that. Would he find the crown and jewel before she could save Andy? Would she be able to rescue the others from the Filligrim Castle? She let another thought pass through her brain. Did Elsfur realize that Andy had started taking her heart and that was why he declared his love for her? Was he going to fight for her? She couldn't believe she was thinking of a life with love in it, when the threat of tyranny loomed so close in the future.

QUEEN NOOR

Still weakened by the goblins' faruva worm gel, Queen Noor sat in the stillness of the morning, staring out the window into the gardens that surrounded most of the Filligrim Castle. She had not been told much by anyone about Andy or Kwagar. Theodius was always insistent that she stay in her room and rest. The apothecary visited every day and said that she was improving. He drugged her with medicine that kept her very groggy and she would sleep at least sixteen hours or more.

Today was going to be different. She had hidden the medicine under her tongue, and when the apothecary wasn't watching, she took the medicine out and put it under her pillow. She was almost fully awake now. If she didn't start running her kingdom again soon, she would lose it to Theodius. Theodius was gaining more and more power every day, as she was losing hers.

She had known all along that Theodius was the traitor in this castle. But she had never had proof. Except for when she had found the traces of black powder on top of the delicate gold box that held the royal seal. Shadow dust. She knew in her heart that he was after something very powerful. "The Crown of the Races," she whispered, as if answering her heart.

A knock at the door startled the queen from her thoughts.

"Your majesty," said two servant girls in unison. Amanda and Taylor were Noor's personal handmaidens. They were beautiful twin girls who were inseparable and always spoke as if they were one person. Amanda had short, blonde, curly hair that surrounded her beautiful face and green eyes. Taylor had lovely, long darker locks with heart-stopping blue eyes. "There is someone here to see you."

"Who is it?"

"It is I," said a deep voice. Someone that Noor had not seen in a very long time. It took her breath away. King Renauldee stood in the doorway. His deep-set, black eyes took in her face.

"Renauldee." It was almost a question. Noor didn't know if she should trust her brain. It had been in such a fog that she didn't know what was real and what wasn't anymore.

She watched as he strode through the door with a look of concern for his daughter-in-law showing in his eyes. Instantly, she wondered what Theodius had told him.

"Noor, are you all right?" he asked, pulling a

chair up next to hers.

"I'm fine," she whispered, feeling ashamed by her appearance. She hadn't combed her hair in days and the dark circles under her eyes made her look gaunt and sickly. "I suppose you talked with Theodius?"

"I saw no one as I came in. Only your handmaidens were there to greet me. They came out into the courtyard as soon as I arrived, and whisked me up here before I could speak to anyone." He looked at them suspiciously as he spoke.

"Why are you here?"

"I thought that would be obvious. I'm here to get answers concerning my grandson and also to see if the rumors about another grandson are true," he said, more hotly than he had intended.

"What you have heard is true," Noor spoke slowly. "My thoughts are a little fuzzy, but I will try to explain. Please forgive me if I don't remember like I should. The apothecary keeps me drugged all the time."

"Why are you being drugged?" King Renauldee asked.

"I will get to that," Queen Noor said with a weak smile. She looked back out the window trying to collect her thoughts. She knew that being honest with King Renauldee would help her out of this situation. She looked back at the king, tears forming in the corners of her eyes. "I did have twins, to answer your question. My father started acting very strange about the time the babies were born. He said that it wasn't necessary to have two babies and he ordered the midwife to kill the older one. She said she would take care of it. I begged him to just let me hold the baby, and say goodbye to him, and then I would give the baby to the midwife as promised. My father said that I could, and after he left with Kwagar, something strange happened. The midwife turned into a beautiful dryad. It was Grandmother Muckernut, Gladdy's good friend. She reassured me that she would never harm the future King of Filligrim. She also said that she had a present for the baby. She put a little necklace around his neck and then Gladdy brought in a baby dragon to bond with the baby. After the ceremony, I asked Gladdy to take the baby far away and raise my son...my beautiful little Andrew, as her own child. I asked her to never tell anyone about him.

"Gladdy told me that there was a land far away, and the only way to get there was with magic. She also said no one would ever find her unless they knew where to look. She left a map with me, just in case I ever needed her to come back. I hid it in a gold box that held the royal seal. One day, not too long ago, I accidentally knocked the box onto the floor and when I picked it up, I found the map gone. I also found shadow dust on the lid and instantly knew that there was a traitor in the castle."

"Why would you think there was a traitor in the castle just because a map was missing and there was shadow dust on the box?" Renauldee asked, absorbed in her story.

"For the most obvious reason, of course. No

one should ever touch the royal seal box, but me. There is a penalty of death for touching that box. Also, someone close to me said that he had heard a story about a certain crown and jewel resurfacing."

"The 'Crown of the Races' is just a myth, Noor. It doesn't exist."

"I think you of all people know it's true, Renauldee. I saw the crown one time, long ago. Becken was taking me through your castle. He had revealed secrets to me about his true mother and about himself that morning. He told me there was something he needed to show me." Noor stood and walked toward the window. "He took me into an underwater passage that led out to the island just off the coast by your castle. The passage was unusual. It twisted and turned in weird directions, as if it had been built to discourage anyone from wanting to find the end. It also had different little traps that would kill you if you didn't know where they were. Lucky for me, my husband knew where every one of them was. When we reached the end of the passage, he opened a door to a treasure room. There in the middle of the room stood a short pillar holding the most amazing crown I have ever seen. It was encased in a beautiful crystal box with an interesting keyhole in the shape of a bird. The crown was so delicate, so intricate. I remember gazing at it with a desire to place the crown on my head. Becken had to nearly carry me out of the room, I wanted it so badly."

"Becken shouldn't have shown you that room," Renauldee said, painfully. It hurt him to say Becken's name. His son had been dead for many years. Noor saw his eyes flash and momentarily morph into sea serpent eyes and then they changed back again.

"Isn't that funny," Noor said, ignoring his anger and then laughing. "I told him the same thing when he told me what it was. However, Becken told me something else that I needed to hear."

She stopped talking and just stared out the window. The silence in the room made King Renauldee uncomfortable.

"What else did he say?"

"Did you know that Becken could see the future?" Noor said, turning to her father-in-law.

"Y—yes. I knew that he could. But I would never let him tell it to me."

"Well, he told it to me. He told me I would have two children. Twins. He also said he would be killed in a battle. Becken also said that someone would claim the crown and become the leader of the races, and that blackness would surround us all."

"That won't happen!" King Renauldee said defiantly, shaking his head. "I have already hidden the crown again in a new place. I had the old tunnel flooded so that no one would ever go there again. Becken told me what he had done, a few days after he showed you the crown. I was furious with him. He knew that it was my kin that had to keep the secret of the crown and he betrayed my family by showing you."

Noor looked at the king with hurt showing in her eyes. "As I recall, Renauldee, I'm part of your family too."

Renauldee sighed hard and rubbed his forehead.

"I know, Daughter," he whispered, ashamed for what he had said. "Please forgive me."

Noor smiled and all was forgiven.

"How is Arianna?" Noor asked, changing the subject.

"She is fine. Feisty as ever," he said smiling, as he remembered Arianna's temper flaring, right before he had left. He lowered his gaze, not wanting to seem so anxious. But he had to find out what happened to Kwagar.

"I know you want to know what has become of your grandson," Noor said, knowingly. "Kwagar is in Hamamelis Prison—" She raised her hand to silence him as he began to protest. "Let me explain what led up to him being captured. When I found that the map was gone and there was shadow dust on the box, I got scared. I formed a plan and told Kwagar most of what was happening. But I asked him to act as if he didn't know anything. Then I went to the goblins that were living as servants in the castle and I asked them to take me to see the goblin king, thinking he would help me. The traitor found out what I was planning and attacked me. I just barely made it out of the castle with my life. When the goblins and I arrived in the Black Mountains, the goblins began to argue about me. They were scared that Prince Mosaic would find out what they had done. That's when Mystic found us. I told her everything. About Prince Andrew and Gladdy, about the shadow dust, and the prophecy that Becken had made."

"You shouldn't have involved Becken's mother. You don't know how volatile that Mystic can be."

"I know it pains you that Becken is not your blood. But he loved you both like you were his blood," Noor said softly, reaching out to touch her father-in-law on the arm.

"I—I miss him very much."

"I know you do. As much as I miss him." Noor looked back at the gardens and swallowed back her tears. "Andrew has a very important part in all of this."

"What is that?"

"Andrew is the only one who can hand over the crown to this traitor, because he holds the key. The necklace that Grandmother Muckernut placed around his neck unlocks the crystal box and releases the enchantments that guard the crown."

"What is Andrew like?"

Noor let out a sob. "I haven't been able to see him. He has been taken prisoner in the Dark Lands. Oh, Renauldee, everything is going so wrong. Theodius won't let me out of this room. The only information I'm allowed is what my girls here can find out for me." Noor held out her hand, indicating the twins. "Please help me, Renauldee. Take me out of this castle."

"Why would Theodius be holding you here against your will? You're the Queen of Filligrim. Take charge of your castle."

"Theodius is the traitor."

She said it so low that Renauldee almost didn't hear her.

"Theodius…he is a traitor?" Renauldee couldn't believe what he was hearing.

Noor nodded. "I believe that something happened to him in the Dark Lands. He went there as a diplomat for my father to speak with Queen Estonia about the war on the other side of the Land of the Fitful. When he returned he came back as a cat. He said that he had some sort of wand malfunction and that it turned him into a feline." She paused as if remembering. "I felt there was something else. That was the first time that I saw the shadow dust. He had been speaking quietly to my father in his chambers, shortly after I had given birth to the twins. When I came into the room, Theodius acted startled, like he had just been caught doing something that he shouldn't be doing. My father was very different and distant up to that point, but after that day my father became worse, a totally different person. He was not the man I knew as a child."

"And you think that Theodius was the cause?"

"Yes. Something was different about my father's eyes. Like he wasn't there anymore. When Theodius left the room, I saw the shadow dust on the floor where he had been sitting. And I knew that something bad was about to happen…."

Voices interrupted Noor. The twins ran to the door and bolted it.

"Hurry, my lady," they said in unison. "Take the secret entrance with King Renauldee and get away now, or you'll never be able to leave and help your sons. We'll hold them off here and then find you."

Noor was grabbing clothes, and throwing them into a bag, when someone started pounding on the door. She closed the bag, grabbed the king's hand, and ran into her bathroom with him, shutting the door behind them.

"Will you please hold my bag? I don't think I will have the strength to hold it and hold on at the same time."

"Yes, I will. Hold on to what?" Renauldee looked around in urgency. "How are we going to get out of here?"

Something yellow in the sink interrupted the two. It was Spongy, a magical sponge that Gladdy had brought to life.

"Your majesty," he said, urgently. "You are in danger."

"I know, Spongy. King Renauldee and I are trying to escape."

"Could you take me with you? I don't think that cat likes me very much. I've been hiding from him here in your bathroom."

"Yes, Spongy. You can come with us."

Queen Noor wrung the little sponge out and placed him in her bag. Then Noor looked at King Renauldee, stepped into the tub and sat down. She pulled him into the tub behind her, then turned on the water faucet, except no water came out. Instead, the wall behind them opened up and the tub slid backward. The king nearly fell on top of Noor. As he took a seat in the tub, he looked back and could see that another tub was rising out of the floor, taking the place of the one they were in. The tub they were in was on some sort of cable system that pulled them down a long hallway, and then it began descending. It felt like a wild ride in a carriage, with demented horses leading the way. It moved faster and faster, twisting and turning in bizarre angles. The tub hit something that King Renauldee thought was a long switch and a bell began ringing somewhere in the distance. Just when King Renauldee thought they were going to crash, the tub slowed down and then stopped abruptly.

He looked around in the darkness, his eyes settling on a light that was filtering around something that looked like a door. Noor got out of the tub and headed toward it. She pushed another knob. King Renauldee could hear ropes and pulleys moving and then a door slid open, revealing a short staircase leading upward. They climbed the stairs out of the darkness and into daylight, which blinded them both for a moment. King Renauldee gasped at the sight before them as he stepped onto the top step. They were standing in the barn. Horses were munching on hay, and griffins were lounging on straw nests, staring at the odd people who had just appeared.

"Queen Noor, I will have you ready in a moment. I heard the ringing of the bell and knew that it was serious." A stable boy was already saddling a horse.

"Caleb," Noor said in hushed tones. "I need you to go to the front of the castle and tell King Renauldee's men to meet us in the forest. This is most urgent. Not a word to anyone where I've gone. Is that clear? After you have told them, go to the hiding place. Your sisters will meet you there.

Then you will come back to me. I'll be with King Renauldee. If you should see Gladdy, tell her what is happening."

"Yes, my lady. You can count on me." He hesitated for a moment as if he had something on his mind.

"Don't worry about your sisters. They are safe."

"Thank you!" he said, with a huge smile.

They led the horse out of the barn and down a narrow path before getting up on it and riding away. Noor was very nervous and kept glancing over her shoulder every two seconds. Things were going smoothly so far. They hid the horse and themselves in a clump of trees and waited for King Renauldee's men. It was a long fifteen minutes. While they waited Noor went on to explain about Prince Mosaic, Kwagar and Andy.

"Somehow Prince Mosaic found out about the whole ordeal, and he prepared for war. He managed to capture me right out of Mystic's cavern and hold me captive. When Filligrim found out what had happened, they had to go to war to save the kingdom and me. I was devastated that both of the boys had fought in the battle." She paused for a moment and then went on. "Apparently, the two of them managed to free me, but they both got captured. Kwagar was captured by the goblins and some Shadow Man, who I believe is Theodius, captured Andrew in the Dark Lands."

"What made Gladdy come back here after all this time?" Renauldee's eyes were dark.

"Theodius the traitor apparently used the map

and went to the other world to retrieve Gladdy. I think the reason he went after Gladdy is because he thinks that she is the key to reuniting the crown and jewel. At least we have that much in our favor. She is only the legend keeper." Noor was quiet for a moment and then she said, "Gladdy calls Prince Andrew, Andy. I want to see him so badly."

King Renauldee turned and smiled weakly at Noor.

"If it is within my power, daughter, I will help you get both of your sons back."

"Thank you, Renauldee," she whispered.

They sat on the horse in silence. They could see the guard approaching in the distance.

"Noor, what I don't understand is what Prince Mosaic has to do with this. Why would he risk war?"

"My handmaidens have managed to get hold of some information. They told me he is in league with Theodius. I'm sure Theodius has promised him something wonderful. Some of the dryads are helping them as well."

"You know the outcome to all of this, don't you? The only way to get my grandsons back?"

"Yes, Renauldee. I do," she spoke softly, feeling the weight of each word. "War, once again. I just hope that all of our allies will be willing to go to war again. It has only been three months since the last conflict. There were a lot of deaths as a result of that battle. Many of the races lost so much. I don't know if they will take a chance on losing the rest."

King Renauldee looked at Queen Noor and

knew what she said was true. Fathers lost sons. Brothers lost brothers. Friends lost friends. War was not a respecter of person or foes.

When the guard approached, King Renauldee mounted his horse and then nodded to all his men. They rode in silence the rest of the day and into the night, not daring to stop until they were back in King Renauldee's kingdom. Queen Noor knew that Theodius wouldn't dare come there. It was the one place she would be safe. She just wished that her sons were there with her as well.

# MOVING UP

Andy lay on his bed staring up at the ceiling. He was bored, and that always brought the familiar feelings about Shimmer to his mind. He had thought a lot about her since he had been in Charlock Castle. However, he kept coming back to the same contemplation. Where was she now? A little voice in his head was always there to torment him. *She's with Elsfur,* it would say.

He scowled and rolled over to his side, his eyes coming to rest on Theodius.

"There's that scowl again," Theodius teased. "Thinking of the girl that turns into a blue mist."

It seemed that Theodius always knew what Andy was thinking, and it was a little unnerving. "I was thinking," Andy said, trying to change the subject, "that we should try and get out of here. I'm about to go bonkers."

"No you weren't, and don't try to change the subject," Theodius said, with mocking eyes. "I like hearing about that blue girl and what she can do. Do you think I will get to meet her someday?"

"I'm sure," Andy sighed hard, a little annoyed.

"Are you going to marry that gal?" Theodius asked, sheepishly.

"You know I can't marry her, Theodius. I'm human, remember," Andy said, more forcefully than he meant to.

"I'll bet that aunt of yours would let you marry her, if you stayed in the Dark Lands."

"Well, that just isn't going to happen. I'm going to get out of the Dark Lands and go back to Filligrim where I belong."

"From what I understand that isn't going to take place very soon," Theodius reminded Andy.

"I'll figure something out. I can be quite a problem solver when I want to be. You'll see. You and I will be eating all our favorite dishes back in Filligrim Castle and laughing and talking with friends."

"When you say friends, do you mean the beautiful blue girl who can turn into a blue mist right before your very eyes?"

"I'm not having this conversation again, Theodius. Shimmer loves someone else. Not me." Andy looked hard at the old man. "*Someone else*," he said again. "Not me!"

"You're kinda touchy on the subject, wouldn't you say?"

"That's because, Captain Bug Eater, you're driving me crazy!" Andy scowled. "I need out of this place!"

Right on cue, someone answered Andy's plea. There was a knock at the door, and it opened. A small gray man with a long, beak-shaped nose entered the room. He was more shadow than he was man and he flickered as he stepped into the cell. His shadowy eyes took in the room and then the two prisoners, coming to rest on Andy.

"The queen requests your presence for supper this evening. I am to get you ready and then show you to the dining hall," he said in a tremulous voice.

"That will be just fine with me," Andy said, jumping up off the bed. "I need to get out of here, before I go mad."

"Please take off that shirt and put on this robe. The queen doesn't want you in the castle with a blood-stained shirt." He threw Andy a gray robe and waited while Andy took off his shirt and then put on the fresh robe. "Follow me." The little man bowed to Andy and then turned on his heel and flickered out of the room.

He led Andy down a dark, narrow hallway with dim lights hanging from the ceiling. Andy could see doors every few feet, which he assumed were other prison cells. The floor was covered in the same dust that Queen Estonia had shed on Andy's bed. The hallway stopped in front of a steep set of stairs which the little gray man began climbing two at a time. Andy followed. A short time later, Andy stood blinking in the brighter light of the great hall of Charlock Castle.

It wasn't bright and cheery like Filligrim

Castle. There were no pictures on the walls; no rugs on the floor, no wood paneling to make it feel homey and no stained glass in the windows. Just gray walls and a stone floor, with shadow dust on the floors.

Andy frowned. He had hoped this would cheer him up. He longed to be out of the confines of the little cell, but it seemed no different in this room. He still felt as if he were in the cell.

Hearing footsteps, Andy was drawn from his disappointment, and he looked to see who was coming into the room. His aunt floated gracefully into the great hall. She seemed more like a ghost than an actual person. The gown she wore was pale pink, which enhanced her gray complexion. She smiled brightly when she saw Andy.

"Andy," she said, coming up to him and kissing his cheek.

"Hello, Aunt Estonia," Andy said, flinching at the touch of her ice-cold lips.

"Claude will take you to one of the palace rooms, where you can take a bath and get into a fresh set of clothes."

"Thank you, Aunt Estonia. That would be very nice."

"I am going to see how dinner is coming along. I hope you enjoy your bath. I have someone I want you to meet. It's my adopted daughter, Jennifer."

"Oh," Andy said, looking at his aunt. "Can't wait."

"Good," Estonia said. "See you in a while."

Andy watched her float from the room, and it chilled him. Claude led Andy up some more stairs to a room on the third floor. The room wasn't as nice as his room had been at Filligrim Castle, but it was still very pleasant. It had a large bed, with a feather top mattress, a small wooden dresser, and a braided rug on the floor. The bathroom just off the bedroom was small, but it had all the amenities.

Claude ran the bath water for him and then left the room. Andy slid into the hot water and drank in its warmth. He couldn't remember feeling so good. He thought of Spongy and it made his heart ache with longing for Filligrim Castle. He pushed the thought away.

He decided that he would play up to his aunt. Try to find out as much information as he could about Charlock Castle and the surrounding lands. Andy had been brought to the castle unconscious and didn't even know which way he would have to go to get out of the Dark Lands.

Reluctantly, Andy stepped from the bath, dressed in an outfit that Claude had left for him and then went out into the hall. Claude sat in a chair a little ways down from Andy's room, waiting patiently. Andy assumed Claude was there to watch his every move.

As he descended the stairs, Andy could smell a wonderful aroma. His stomach growled and Claude looked sideways at him. Andy's face burned bright red for a moment.

"What do you expect?" Andy said a little sour. "I haven't exactly eaten like a prince while I've been here."

Claude just shrugged and went on, ignoring Andy.

When they entered the dining room, Andy could see that his aunt was not alone. A thin girl, with beautiful tan skin, deep brown eyes and long brown hair sat talking and smiling with his Aunt Estonia. They turned toward him when they noticed him staring at them.

"Andy, come in and meet my adopted daughter." Estonia waved him forward. "This is Jennifer."

Andy walked forward and reached out his hand to shake Jennifer's. He was amazed that she didn't have that same gray coloring as everyone else in the castle. She was warm, and her cheeks had a lovely, rosy color to them.

"Nice to meet you," Andy said, blushing a little.

"Thank you. Your Aunt Estonia has told me a lot about you," Jennifer said, very casually.

"Really. I was under the impression that Aunt Estonia didn't know that much about me," he said smiling. His eyes shifted to his aunt's face to get some kind of reaction, but there was none.

"Andy, you've been here a long time and I have been able to hear a lot of your thoughts." Estonia smiled, but it didn't reach her eyes.

"You—read—thoughts now?" Andy asked, bewildered.

"No, no," she laughed. "You talk in your sleep. While I had you up here in the palace, I was able to observe you in your sleep." She looked at him sheepishly. "I hope you don't mind."

"Well, Aunt Estonia, I do mind a little." Andy thought of what his body had looked like when he woke up from the drugs, and he shivered.

"Now, Andy, let's let bygones be bygones. I apologize for my friend. He was a little rough with you."

Andy eyed his Aunt Estonia and then spoke a more bravely than he felt, "I think you have used the wrong word. 'Rough' is not the word that I would have used. However, for now, Aunt Estonia, I will let the subject rest. Nevertheless, I will be bringing up the subject again."

"I don't..." Estonia started to say.

Servants entered the room carrying silver dishes, interrupting Estonia. For that Andy was grateful. He had already had a disagreement with Theodius and he didn't want to have an argument with his aunt right in front of Jennifer.

After they were served, the three of them sat in uncomfortable silence. Andy sat there wishing he knew what to say to the girl. He didn't have any problems talking to Shimmer, and couldn't understand why he was so tongue-tied.

"Andy," Jennifer said. "Queen Estonia said that you might spend some time up here in the palace. It will be nice to have another young person around."

Andy gulped. He had not thought anymore about moving up from the dungeons and leaving Theodius.

"I haven't really decided to move up here yet."

"Come, come now, Andy. I bring my beautiful adopted daughter here to keep you company and you hesitate," Estonia said teasingly.

Andy's eyes flew open in surprise. Jennifer had been brought here for him?

"I—I don't really know what to say," Andy mumbled, feeling the heat rise to his face again.

"Say that you will move up to the palace and join our guest here. She is looking forward to staying here and it would help her out if she had someone more her age to talk to." Estonia smiled at Jennifer. "I could make you, but then you wouldn't be much fun. Making you move would only make you rebel even more against me, so I'm letting you decide."

Andy became very suspicious. Why would his Aunt Estonia go to all this trouble? He looked at Jennifer. And why would this beautiful girl even bother. He had to admit, his curiosity was up, all the way. The two women sat staring at him while he made up his mind.

"I will move up to the palace," Andy said, smiling at the two women.

"Wonderful!" Estonia clapped her hands together.

"On one condition," Andy said cunningly.

"Condition?" Estonia looked at him with hard eyes. "What condition?"

"That you allow Theodius to come with me. We're a package deal."

"What is your fascination with that old man?"

"He is my friend, and I won't leave him down in that dungeon any longer than necessary."

They stared at each other. Andy held his ground. He was not going to let Estonia get the upper hand. Her eyes softened and Andy smelled a victory.

"Fine. Bring that batty old man with you, if

you must. But I don't want him to be roaming around my palace getting everything dirty. Is that clear?"

"Crystal," Andy said, smiling at Jennifer. She smiled back, and his heart did back flips. *Shimmer*, he thought to himself. *Think of Shimmer.*

Why? said another voice in his head. *She is with Elsfur, far away from here.*

"Are you all right, Andy?" Jennifer asked.

"Yes," Andy said, ignoring the voices in his head. "I'm perfectly fine. Pass the potatoes, please."

"I will have Claude fix the room next to yours, right away. Theodius can have the smaller of the two."

"That's okay, Aunt Estonia. I'll have the smaller one."

She glared hard at Andy. He knew that he was pushing his luck.

"Well, maybe the larger one might be nicer after all," he said, trying to please his aunt. "Does the room's window face the gardens?"

"No," Estonia said stiffly. "I have no gardens here. They remind me too much of Filligrim."

Andy flinched and felt bad about what he had said.

"I didn't mean to hurt your feelings, Aunt Estonia." He reached out and touched his aunt's cold hand. "I'm sorry."

She smiled and moved her hand back. Andy noticed that it was trembling.

"You shouldn't touch me without my approval. You never know what might happen," she said quietly.

Andy swallowed hard, as he remembered what had happened to Estonia's father. "It's all right, Andy. I shouldn't be so sensitive." She changed the topic. "Andy, while you were up here in the castle asleep, you mentioned something about magic. Have you have questioned whether or not you have magical abilities?"

"I have questioned different friends about there being magic in our family," he stuttered. "Why do you ask?"

"I feel that it is my duty to warn you about magic, after what happened to me. I am your aunt after all. You need to forget about magic. It's bad in every way. Always remember the story that I told you about my family. It will only lead to heartbreak." She stopped speaking when her voice cracked. After she composed herself she said, "Promise me."

"I promise, Aunt Estonia," Andy said, looking at her stricken face.

As time wore on, Andy found that he was fascinated by everything that Jennifer said. Her laugh made jelly of his insides. Her chocolate-colored eyes seemed to bore a hole right through to his soul. He felt all giddy inside, especially when she was speaking directly to him. When she spoke it was as though he forgot he was a prisoner in a castle in the Dark Lands. Instead he felt as though he was enjoying dinner with a date.

He shook his head. He couldn't imagine why he was feeling this way. Their meal ended on a very high note. He had learned quite a lot from his

Aunt Estonia about the Dark Lands. How far the nearest farms were. How many people lived in the Dark Lands, which to Andy's astonishment was over five thousand. The most useful piece of news was that the border was only a day's ride from the castle.

Claude walked into the dining hall as they were finishing their meal. "Theodius is in the palace room as you requested, your ladyship," he said, addressing Queen Estonia. He then handed her a piece of paper. "Will that be all until supper?"

"Thank you, Claude. We were just finishing with lunch, so you can show my nephew to his room and that will be all for the afternoon." Estonia read the paper and a look of panic crossed her face.

"Is something wrong, your ladyship?" Claude asked.

"There is a sickness in the village. It's apparently very bad. This note is from the apothecary. He warns not to go out of the castle until he can find a cure. Make sure all of the castle doors are locked and post some guards at each door, that way no one will be able to get in or out of the castle. This evening you can serve Andy, Theodius and Jennifer in their rooms." She waved her hand at him. "I will see you when you bring me my supper this evening."

"Yes, your ladyship."

Andy stood. "Thank you for the lunch, Aunt Estonia. Also, thank you for bringing Theodius up from the dungeon. It was very nice of you," Andy said as sincerely as he could and then he turned his attention on Jennifer. "It was nice to meet you. I look forward to seeing you tomorrow. Maybe we can play a game or something."

"I look forward to it as well. Especially since we won't be able to go outside. Have a good night's sleep, Andy." Her voice tickled Andy's ear and his breath caught in his throat. Andy looked one more time at her face; and then he departed with Claude.

He analyzed the afternoon as he climbed the stairs. What was wrong with him? He had acted like a total idiot. Andy decided to talk it over with Theodius later.

Claude left Andy standing in his room. Andy stared at the bed. It had been a long time since he had felt the softness of a real bed. Looking out the window at the afternoon sun, thinking about the lunch, his thoughts kept returning to Jennifer. But his heart argued with him, trying to put some common sense into his head.

What about Shimmer? it said.

FREE ADVICE

Shimmer had collapsed into a ball, lying on the ground. Her tears wet the earth below her head. She lay there for a long time. A few feet away, Grandmother Muckernut sat waiting for Shimmer to cry until there were no more tears. She could feel the agony coming from Shimmer and she felt very sorry for the girl.

"Shimmer," Grandmother Muckernut finally spoke, very tenderly. "We need to leave before they realize you're not with the others and they come looking for you."

Shimmer raised her head and looked at the beautiful dryad.

"My heart is broken," she whispered.

"You have loved Elsfur a long time." It wasn't a question.

"All my life."

"What is the problem then? I heard what he

said to you when he left."

"I'm torn between Andy and Elsfur," Shimmer answered truthfully.

"Andy?" Grandmother Muckernut looked puzzled. "I guess I missed something."

"I had to let Elsfur go," Shimmer started speaking. "He's promised to Wisteria. So I started looking in other directions. Andy is so warm and kind. My heart liked the direction it was taking...."

"But Elsfur has decided that you're the direction that he wants to take?"

"I don't know," Shimmer said, shaking her head. "I really don't know."

"Does he know that you like Andy?"

"I'm assuming that he has guessed."

Shimmer looked past Grandmother Muckernut. The sun was going down in the sky. She had been on the ground longer then she should have been.

"Let's get a move on. If you want to talk some more, we can talk on the trail. But we need to get to Mulberry Forest as soon as possible." Grandmother Muckernut looked around, worried.

Shimmer rose and dusted the dirt off her clothes. She wiped the tears from her face with the back of her hand and then smiled at Grandmother Muckernut.

"I need to put this matter out of my head for a while," Shimmer said, picking up her things and walking over to where Mistletoe was hidden in the brush. She got on the horse and helped Grandmother Muckernut get on behind her. Daisy landed on the horse's head. She had been very quiet while Shimmer and Grandmother Muckernut had been talking.

"I wish they hadn't taken Windsor. Mistletoe will get tired faster carrying the two of us," Grandmother Muckernut said.

"We're light enough. She'll be fine. I just hope all the prisoners are all right. Gladdy is too old to be in a prison cell." Shimmer looked back toward the way they had come.

"Gladdy is in a very nice cell as far as prisons go. She at least has a comfortable bed." Grandmother Muckernut patted Shimmer on the back and then nudged Mistletoe forward.

All three rode in silence for most of their journey, only commenting occasionally about which way they should go. Hours later, they came to an arch covering the path.

Looking through the arch, they could see the forest darken the farther it went in. The arch was covered in vines with nasty looking thorns and blood red flowers that smelled sickly sweet.

"This is where Gladdy comes from?" Daisy said, staring into the arch.

"This is the beginning of Mulberry Forest," Grandmother Muckernut said. "Gladdy actually comes from the Land of Chaldeon."

"Where are the guards?" Shimmer asked.

"We are here."

Two very impressive elves appeared out of thin air, making Mistletoe jump and nearly lose her passengers. The elves' muscular frames were very sleek and they were dressed in dark green tunics and thigh-high boots. But that was not what caught Shimmer's eye. It was their faces that made her gasp. They were pale silver, with cat yellow eyes and circular carvings all over their skin.

"I'm Paowyn and this is Thornthistle," said the shorter of the two elves. "We are the guardians of the Arch of Mutador, the pathway into Mulberry Forest."

"I am Shimmer Misfit, an Asrai warrior. This is Grandmother Muckernut, Leader of the Dryads," Shimmer said, indicating with her hand. "And this is Daisy, a pixie from Toadstool Village. We seek passage to the Dark Lands through the Mulberry Forest."

Paowyn looked at Shimmer with interest.

"I have only heard about the Asrai people in legend. What is your power?"

"If I may dismount, I will show you."

Thornthistle drew his sword and stepped into attack mode. All three of the riders on the horse sucked in air. Paowyn held up his hand and looked at his friend. Thornthistle relaxed, but his sword stayed out of its scabbard.

Very alert, the two elves watched Shimmer as she dismounted the horse and then walked cautiously before them. She bowed to them. Then as she stood, she ran her hand the length of her body, and disappeared into a blue mist in front of them.

"I turn into a blue mist," she droned.

They watched in awe as she turned back into the blue girl again.

"Most impressive," said Paowyn. "I have heard tales of an old Asrai woman in the Black Mountains who can control everything around her.

Do you know her?"

"Mystic," Shimmer said. "Yes, I know her. She is a marvel. No one has power like hers."

Paowyn eyed her. "What is it that you seek in the Dark Lands?"

Shimmer stood there debating on how much information this elf needed. She would rather tell the king of Mulberry Forest.

"We seek someone very close to Princess Gladiola. We are her emissaries," Grandmother Muckernut spoke before Shimmer could. What she said about Gladdy caught Shimmer off guard. Her face didn't show any question, but her eyes held Grandmother Muckernut's for the briefest of moments. Questions would need to wait for now.

"His majesty hasn't seen his niece for a very long time, but she still holds favor with her uncle. You may pass," said Paowyn. "However, I would advise you to stay on the path. Others of my kind may not be as receptive."

"You are most kind, Paowyn, Guardian of the Arch of Mutador. I will remember to speak highly of you to his majesty."

This pleased Paowyn and he bowed very deeply. The two stunning elves stepped aside and let the horse and riders pass through the arch. Daisy peeked over Grandmother Muckernut's shoulder, looking back to where the two elves had stood. They were no longer visible.

The atmosphere changed the instant they rode through the arch. The air was the perfect temperature. The smell in the air was sweet and very pleasant. Music played from somewhere that was most inviting. A feeling of calm and happiness wrapped around them like a warm blanket. Everything in the forest was brilliant and alive with color.

"Why on earth would Gladdy ever leave this place?" Shimmer asked.

"The elves are very good at making a forest feel like it's the only place to be. They treat their trees as though they were children. Almost spoiling them."

Daisy looked at Grandmother Muckernut. "What do you mean, spoiling them?"

"Well, look at this place. There is music playing for the trees. Flowers are planted in strategic places so that the forest has the right fragrance. Magic enhances the colors so that birds and beautiful insects and animals will visit this forest, and the trees will not be alone."

"They do all that just for trees?"

"Yes. The trees are what these particular elves live for. If the trees are unhappy, then the elves are unhappy."

"That's going overboard," Shimmer said, appalled. "Just for a tree?"

"Don't let anyone hear you say that..." Grandmother Muckernut stopped talking. Harsh whispers came from all around them. "Well, that was just rude!"

"What was?" Daisy asked.

"The trees are talking about the two fat, old women on the mule," Grandmother Muckernut said angrily.

"Well, at least they aren't talking about me,"

said Daisy, smugly.

"I wouldn't speak so fast. I won't tell you what they said about you," Grandmother Muckernut giggled.

"Well!" Daisy said, stamping the air with her foot.

As they went deeper into the forest, Shimmer began to notice more elves along the path. They all had the same markings on their faces and arms as Paowyn and Thornthistle, and all of them wore long robes in different shades of green. Some of the elves carried baskets and tended to the plants along the path. Others carried large hand fans and walked among the trees, fanning the trees' bark. Magical harps and flutes floated around, weaving in and out of the trees, playing strange but soothing music.

"Grandmother Muckernut," said Shimmer, turning in the saddle. "Why do these elves have carvings on their skin, when Gladdy does not?"

"Gladdy has them on her skin. She just doesn't allow them to be revealed. It's a safety precaution. She is a princess after all."

"Are her markings the same as all the others?"

"No, hers are different. They show royalty."

Shimmer didn't understand what Grandmother Muckernut was talking about, but she didn't ask any more questions. Something had caught her eye and it took her breath away. Their horse had stopped at the rim of a narrow, round valley, in the shape of a bowl. Massive trees with sleek, white bark ran in a spiral pattern all the way around and down to the middle of the basin. Looking down on the valley, it resembled a city with high-rise buildings. Topped in the trees were the houses of the elves. Lush vegetation and beautiful, exotic flowers grew densely all around the trees and the various paths that encompassed the homes. Waterfalls from three different rivers flowed over the edge of the valley rim and ran down to the center where the water circled a small island and then flowed off into dark tunnels at the base of the valley. Mist rose up from the waterfalls and created beautiful, shimmering rainbows giving the valley a magical appearance. White fluff from different plants floated on scented breezes from the orange and magnolia blossoms. Four ornately carved bridges, with four large silver lampposts standing beside each bridge, connected the valley to the island, where a huge red mulberry tree stood in the very center of the island. Luscious fruit hung in large clusters all over the tree.

Shimmer, Grandmother Muckernut and Daisy all looked at each other and smiled in wonderment. Shimmer nudged Mistletoe forward. They followed a path in the same spiral shape as the trees all the way to the bottom of the valley, passing curious elves with the same designs etched into their skin. Also, to the three women's astonishment, satyrs and a few centaurs could be seen along the way.

At the bottom of the valley they rode alongside the river where water nymphs surfaced to watch the travelers pass by. Grandmother Muckernut looked at them curiously. Their bodies looked almost human, except their skin was blue-green and scales covered the front of their torso. They also had webbed hands and feet and short, golden hair curled around their pointy faces.

"Welcome," one of them said. Her eyes flashed bright purple and then she dove beneath the water.

Grandmother Muckernut leaned forward and whispered in Shimmer's ear, "Why are all of these different creatures in the realm of the elves?"

"I have no idea."

"Because," came a booming voice, "I have given them refuge from the Shadow People, who have chased them here."

The three women turned around to see who was talking to them. Appearing next to the enormous mulberry tree, the elf king's form glittered like thousands of tiny, sparkling stars, before coming into focus. His face bore the same markings as the other elves, except his were red like someone had taken a marker and drawn them on his face. He wore a dark brown robe and a belt made from the bark of the white trees. He was most impressive, standing at least two feet above any of the other elves in the forest. But that was not what got their attention. It was his crown. It grew out of his head and resembled a stump of a tree and was embedded with gold leaves.

Shimmer, Daisy, and Grandmother Muckernut rode across the bridge to the island and then dismounted, never taking their eyes off the king. They stood by their horse and bowed their heads.

"I am King Silverthorne, second king to my brother King Foxglove. I am King of the Mulberry Forest and the Land of Chaldeon. Why have you entered the Mulberry Forest?"

Grandmother Muckernut stepped forward and

bowed. "Your majesty, I am Vinca, also known as Grandmother Muckernut to my people and close friends, leader of the...."

"I know who the three of you are," the king said, cutting her off. "What do you want?"

"We travel to the Dark Lands seeking...."

"The Dark Lands have become a problem for our people and for others that live near my realm," King Silverthorne boomed, sweeping his hand in the direction of the centaurs and satyrs.

"We seek the Prince of Filligrim," Grandmother Muckernut said, feeling a little frustrated being cut off by the king. "He was taken by a Shadow Man three months ago...."

"I know that Prince Kwagar was taken, but your information as to where he was taken is wrong. He was taken to Hamamelis Prison, home of the goblins," he said, cutting her off again. "However, my sight cannot see that far."

Grandmother Muckernut turned and looked at Shimmer. She didn't know how much information they should give away about Andy.

Shimmer stepped forward and whispered to Grandmother Muckernut, "I think you should tell him, he obviously can...."

"Read your mind," King Silverthorne said. "It's more like hearing your thoughts. Some people are louder than others. You, Shimmer, are very loud. Who is this Andy person? He seems familiar."

"Andy is Kwagar's twin brother, your majesty. He was hidden in a faraway land until his mother thought it was safe to bring him back. I think you know how King Anasee was becoming…."

"I know about King Anasee and his eccentricities, Vinca. What you don't know is that King Anasee was being used like a puppet by a dark figure that I cannot see."

"The Shadow Man," Grandmother Muckernut whispered to herself.

"That would be my guess, since all I see are shadows concerning that area," King Silverthorne said, smiling for the first time.

King Silverthorne sat down on a throne that had not been there a few minutes before and took a long look at Shimmer, Grandmother Muckernut and Daisy.

"Queen Noor is very cunning, hiding one of her children for so long. I take it that my niece Gladiola had something to do with this."

"Yes, your majesty. She took the child to help out Queen Noor," Daisy said.

"I was wondering why I couldn't hear her. She was out of my hearing distance. I hear my family louder than anyone else. She must have passed through the labyrinth."

"Yes, your majesty. She raised Andy as though he were her own child."

"What is his true name?" the king asked, looking at Grandmother Muckernut.

"Prince Andrew Misfit, your majesty," she answered.

"There is something that you are blocking from my hearing. Why is the Shadow Man so interested in Prince Andrew?"

"He is holding him ransom for something very

precious."

"Hmm…come and sit with me. I want to speak with you further on this matter, and also I want to talk with you about the Dark Lands." King Silverthorne gestured toward two chairs that had appeared with the sweeping of his arm. "I can't hear the Shadow People and as a result it is causing great distress in my realm. I have been able to keep them out, however, though I don't know for how long."

"I don't understand your majesty," Shimmer said. "Do you mean that the Shadow People are trying to leave the Dark Lands?"

"I'm saying, my dear, that the Shadow People are infected with something and they have decided to try and take over my realm."

"Do you know what has infected them?" Daisy asked, fearfully. "Andy is in the Dark Lands. What if he becomes infected?"

"I have my suspicions. I have warned my elves not to kill the Shadow People if they can keep from it. The Shadow People are…or were our friends. They come by the hundreds and strike where they think my defenses are the weakest. I have enchantments that keep them out, but for how long, I cannot guess. Some of my elves have come in contact with the Shadow People and it doesn't look good for them. They have gone into a very deep sleep. Also, they are turning black as if they were rotting. If you go to the Dark Lands it is possible you will not live long. The Shadow People will destroy you."

"We have to try. I cannot sit here and let Andy

stay in that place," Shimmer said most insistently.

"I will not open the gate in the Land of Chaldeon that leads into the Dark Lands. It is too risky. Shadow People might get in, killing my people and everything else in this realm," King Silverthorne said. "So I will not let you go through that way. However," the king held up his hand when Shimmer started to protest. "However, if Grandmother Muckernut, leader of the dryads, can turn into a dragon and fly to the Dark Lands by way of the Land of Chaldeon, then maybe there is a chance that you might find Prince Andrew and see how you can assist him."

"I don't have that capability," Grandmother Muckernut said sadly. "There has to be another way."

"Couldn't you try?" Shimmer asked, desperately.

Grandmother Muckernut sighed really hard. Frustration was building more and more in her heart.

Finally she said, "I will try for you. However, I will need time for the transformation." Grandmother Muckernut had never tried something so monumental before. She didn't want to tell Shimmer that it might take as long as three weeks. Instead she turned to the king and asked, "Are you sure there is no other way?"

"None that I can think of. You may go to the Land of Chaldeon and by then maybe a solution will present itself. I will send elves to assist you in getting to the Land of Chaldeon. After that only you, Grandmother Muckernut, may leave. The other two will have to stay in my realm."

"Could you tell us your suspicions about what is happening to the Shadow People?" Daisy asked King Silverthorne.

King Silverthorne sighed really hard and looked at the mulberry tree. He stood, walked over to the tree and seized a cluster of the red fruit. As he ate, he contemplated on what he would say. Slowly he began, "What I'm about to tell you must be held in the strictest of confidences."

"You have our word, your majesty," Grandmother Muckernut said.

"The famous stone that you once held in your trunk when you were a tree, Grandmother Muckernut, has far greater power than you could have foreseen. I could hear the jewel's thoughts so I knew the evil that empowered it. The stone was one of the reasons the races couldn't mix with humans. I don't know exactly why it affects the mixed humans in such a bad way. My speculation is because it was made from magical beings, with one exception: humans. That is also why I'm guessing that if the stone were to come in contact with a human that is of mixed race, then the consequences would be drastic."

"You think the Shadow Man already has the stone?" Grandmother Muckernut, Shimmer and Daisy all said in unison.

"I don't know if he has it. However, it would be one reason why the Shadow People are infected. I will guess one more time by saying that I don't think the Shadow Man has the jewel yet. But it must be in the Dark Lands. Whether it has been found by someone accidentally or maybe traded for, one can only assume."

"Y-you mean they're infected with evil?" Daisy gasped.

"Yes."

Silence filled the little island.

"Your majesty," Grandmother Muckernut finally said quietly. "There are two things you should know. The imposter posing as Theodius, the great wizard of Filligrim is the Shadow Man. He killed the real Theodius and assumed his identity. He came back from the Dark Lands disguised as a cat. Everyone believed his story that he had a wand malfunction, resulting in his becoming a feline. He now calls himself Saber. We have solid proof that he is the Shadow Man. The other detail I must tell you is that he has taken Gladdy prisoner...."

"What!" King Silverthorne shouted. "My niece, Gladiola, Princess of the Land of Chaldeon, a prisoner!"

"Yes, your majesty. We both were taken by surprise by Saber this morning. He has also captured Elsfur and Windsor, the unicorn."

"Queen Noor needs to handle her kingdom better. Taking my niece prisoner is an act of treason by Filligrim and I will be sending warriors to take back what is mine."

"I'm afraid that would not be a wise thing to do," Grandmother Muckernut said, ignoring the rude comments about Queen Noor and Filligrim. "You see Saber has put...."

"Enchantments around the palace," King Silverthorne finished her sentence for her.

"Yes."

"I will see what can be done about that," King Silverthorne said stiffly. "Stay here for a while and rest. I will have food brought to you and then you may begin your journey toward the Land of Chaldeon. Grandmother Muckernut," King Silverthorne looked hard at her. "I will give you some free advice. Don't get your hopes up about Prince Andrew. He may have already met with his doom, just being in that atrocious land."

"I know your majesty. However, I refuse to think that way. Life could not possibly be that cruel."

"Instead of finding Prince Andrew, you should try and find the stone. I have two relics that were made by my father's father. One that will allow you to walk anywhere in the Dark Lands, and the other will assist you in finding the Jewel of the Races. Once the stone is found, you must destroy it."

"Is there a certain way to destroy the jewel?" Shimmer asked.

"The Shadow Queen must use her magic to destroy it, and I doubt that she will ever do that."

"Why not?"

"Because, just like the fairy that gave her own life to make the jewel magical, so must Queen Estonia end her own life." King Silverthorne said this so quietly, all three of the women had to strain their ears to hear him.

After a few moments of letting the news sink in, Shimmer said, "Well, I don't believe that Andy is dead. I think I would feel it in my heart. I say that we go as planned to the Land of Chaldeon and let Grandmother Muckernut fly toward the Dark Lands to find Andy."

"As you wish. I will summon my guard to take you there." King Silverthorne faded before their eyes, leaving them all astonished.

"Are you sure about this, Shimmer?" Daisy asked.

"You're his pixie, what is your heart telling you?"

Daisy closed her dainty eyes. She didn't know if she really felt him or if it was sheer desperation of wanting him not to be dead, but she finally said, "I think he's alive."

A GOTHIC DRAGON

"I'm going with you," Shimmer whispered to Grandmother Muckernut, as they traveled with a group of elves to the Land of Chaldeon. It had been several hours since they had left King Silverthorne and they were almost to their destination.

"I don't know, Shimmer," Grandmother Muckernut said, looking around at their company. "It's very risky to disobey the king."

"I know it is, but I have to try," Shimmer whispered back.

"I can't believe that he has something that will help us find the Jewel of the Races. Lucky that we came this way instead of through the Black Mountains. Also, I want what he has to give us that will ensure our safety. Both of them must be very powerful talismans. I'm surprised he would part with them, knowing what is going on outside his gate."

"You two had better hush," Daisy said quietly, while eyeing several of the elves. "The elves are trying to listen in on your conversation."

An elf with long dark, raven-colored hair and sparkling blue eyes, sitting on a black horse, kept eyeing Shimmer. Shimmer kept looking at him as well. After a while, he nudged his horse closer to Mistletoe and spoke to her. His voice was smooth and deep.

"I am Thane. Do you know me?" he asked.

Shimmer thought that the question was strange. He had just told her who he was. "I guess that your name is Thane."

"No," he laughed, a baritone sound from deep within his chest.

Shimmer smiled back at him.

"I am Gladiola's brother. She has spoken of me, hasn't she?"

Grandmother Muckernut and Shimmer looked at one another and then back at Thane. Both shook their heads no.

"I know of you," Daisy piped up. "She spoke often of you when she and I were in the other world. She missed you very much. She said that when you were born, she was already a lot older, and that you were more like her child than her brother."

"Yes. She raised me until I was thirteen. Then she went to Filligrim to work at the castle for Queen Noor and to help Theodius. She wrote

172

letters telling me how Queen Noor had become her best friend. She also told me that Theodius had asked her to be his wife."

"Wife!" All three women said, in astonished unison.

"Yes." Thane's eyes misted. "The last letter I received from her said that her marriage to Theodius had been postponed because he had received orders from King Anasee to go to the Dark Lands. She also said she was having to go away on a secret mission for Queen Noor."

"I bet she will be glad to see you again," Grandmother Muckernut said. "It may be a while before you can see her."

"I—I don't understand," Thane said, a little bewildered. "What do you mean?"

While Daisy, Grandmother Muckernut and Thane listened, Shimmer explained their whole situation to Thane. Starting at the very beginning about the fake kidnapping of Queen Noor, retrieving Gladdy and Andy from the other world, the war with the Goblin Prince, the imprisonment of Gladdy and Grandmother Muckernut, plus their talk with King Silverthorne—Grandmother Muckernut and Daisy interjected every once in a while. They left out the part that King Silverthorne asked them not to mention to anyone. Thane listened intently to every word Shimmer said.

"So this Andy, he is like a son to my sister?" Thane asked, after Shimmer had stopped speaking.

"Yes, and if we don't get to him soon, I'm afraid that he may either become a Shadow Person himself, or die from the epidemic."

"And my uncle, King Silverthorne, won't let you go through the gate in the Land of Chaldeon?"

"That's right. He said that he couldn't take the chance that a Shadow Person might enter into his realm."

"I will think about what to do while we ride the rest of the way to the city," Thane said. "You will probably lodge in the Bastion Tree. It is my uncle's home. I will find you there later on." He rode on ahead and left the three women looking puzzled.

"What does he mean, 'He'll think about what to do'?" Daisy asked.

"I don't know. But I hope he will help us," Grandmother Muckernut said.

Shimmer remembered that the Land of Chaldeon was the main region of the Mulberry Forest. Most of the forest elves lived there. Except for a sign that said they were entering the Land of Chaldeon, and a lot more elves and homes, everything was exactly the same. The elves were plainer than the elves the three women had first encountered as they entered the forest. Only a few had the carvings on their faces.

The air was thick with tension. Elves, men and women, were dressed in battle gear, and no children were to be found.

"Wow, they look as if they are ready for battle," Daisy said.

"Yes," replied one of the elves in their party. "The Shadow People are coming by the thousands to our gate and we don't know how much longer it will hold. King Silverthorne has reinforced the gate with enchantments. However, the enchantments are diminishing; we think it's as a result of the sickness that is infecting the Shadow People. The king feels it is the sickness of the Shadow People that is causing it to fail. We have already lost so many of our kinsmen."

"I thought you were safe inside the gate," said Grandmother Muckernut. "How could you have lost so many?"

"Quite a few elves were on their way back from trade days in the Dark Lands forest. We have a trading post there where we trade different food, tools and provisions for our people, with the people of the Dark Lands."

"Did someone close to you come in contact with the Shadow People?" Shimmer spoke softly, feeling her own pain.

"My younger brother is a blacksmith. He loved the Shadow People of the Dark Lands. He looked forward to traveling there to make tools for them."

"I'm sorry for your brother and you as well," said Grandmother Muckernut. "I will soon be traveling to the Dark Lands. Maybe I can find out what is going on."

"Be careful. My people were permitted to go to the trading post, but no farther. The land is infected with the dark queen's magic. The land will destroy you if you set foot past the trading post."

They stopped at the base of three colossal trees. Each tree was as wide as the portcullis at the castle in Filligrim. They joined into one large tree halfway up where a most impressive structure was built. It looked as though someone had taken three large, round wooden balls and placed them precariously, one on top of the other, in the middle of a tree. The limbs of the tree grew straight out of the top of the topmost ball and then cascaded down, much like a weeping willow tree, with gold leaves and bright fuchsia blooms. The sight of the Bastion Tree was breathtaking.

The three women were led up steps that wrapped around all three trees to a spacious room with carved wooden furnishings. A large table sat in the center of the room, with bowls of steaming hot food in the middle of the table and enough plates and glasses for the king and guests. At the head of the table sat King Silverthorne, with a twinkle in his eye.

"How do you like my home?" he said merrily.

"It is very impressive," said Shimmer.

"Please have a seat at my table. You must be hungry from such a long journey."

"Thank you, King Silverthorne. That is most gracious of you," said Grandmother Muckernut.

"My nephew tells me that you had a talk with him on the way here. He has offered to help you in any way that he can," said King Silverthorne, getting right down to business. "I, however, feel his place is here with his people, and not on some wild goose chase after a prince that wasn't even heard of until three months ago."

"We are not asking for your nephew's help, your majesty," said Shimmer sharply. "We just want to get to our destination and help our friend. Thane feels he owes something to his sister and wants to help retrieve her son."

"He is not my niece's son! He is Queen Noor's

son. You would be wise to remember that!"

"She raised him from the time he was just a day old. I think that qualifies her to be his mother. I also think that Queen Noor would agree with me."

"Shimmer, daughter of Ellisdale...."

"How—" Shimmer said, cutting off the king.

"How did I know your father's name? I knew your father from long ago, and he would not have approved your tone of voice toward a king."

"I—I'm sorry your majesty. I was forgetting myself. I should not have spoken that way to you. Please forgive me."

King Silverthorne sighed and sat silent for a moment. He looked around the room, not wanting to look at his visitors.

Then he finally said, "I am sorry for my sharp tongue, Shimmer. Gladdy is a kind and caring elf and I know her heart. If you say that she is the mother of this Prince Andrew, then she is his mother. Thane loves his sister very much. She was like a mother to him as well. I will let him help you. However, for me to let him help you I would still have to disarm my enchantments, and that is something I'm not willing to do. In order for you to fly over the enchantments that surround the Land of Chaldeon, you would have to fly pretty high. The only animal or being that can do that would be a dragon."

They ate in silence for half-an-hour while Shimmer's mind raced for solutions to their problem. Then, a loud roaring outside interrupted them. Grandmother Muckernut ran to a nearby window. Shrieking from delight, she turned and looked at Shimmer and Daisy.

"Our problems are solved," she said confidently. "Now, I won't have to change into a dragon, and you can go to the Dark Lands with me."

"What are you talking about?" Shimmer asked.

"Come and have a look for yourself."

Daisy, Shimmer and King Silverthorne came to the window. Standing among a crowd of onlookers stood an enormous dragon with a red and blue iridescent hide, five metal horns sticking out of his head and gold-rimmed glasses perched on his nose. Flopsy, the twin brother to Flipsy, stood roaring at his onlookers. Everyone covered their ears.

Flopsy roared, his English accent even more pronounced as he said, "Where is Shimmer Misfit, daughter of Ellisdale! If you have harmed her, elves, I will tear this forest apart!"

Shimmer ran from the room, down the stairs and with open arms right up to the dragon. "I have never seen a more beautiful dragon in my whole life, Flopsy," yelled Shimmer over the roar.

Flopsy stopped roaring and looked down at Shimmer.

"I thought these elves had captured you. So, I came to your rescue," he announced proudly. Then he looked around bewildered and slowly said, "You aren't in danger?"

"No, silly. King Silverthorne is helping us."

"But, Elsfur said you were in danger."

"Elsfur was wrong," Shimmer said, with anger boiling in her stomach. "Where did you see Elsfur? I thought he had been captured."

"He has. I have Denny, Andy's mirror friend." He pointed to a small hand-held mirror tied around his neck. The mirror was part of the Mirror Friends Network, a network of magical mirrors, which were given only to the royals at the Filligrim Castle. A young man in the mirror, with blond hair, grinned and waved at Shimmer. "They put Elsfur in a cell with a mirror. The idiots!" Flopsy growled. "I sent Denny around the castle through other mirrors, to find out what was going on. He came back saying that he had found Elsfur and all the others, including Gladdy. Denny said that Elsfur wanted me to come and save you."

"That elf...."

Shimmer's retort about Elsfur was cut short by a loud vicious roar above her head. Everyone began running for cover. Shimmer looked up to see an awesome sight. A dragon, a little smaller than Flopsy, was flying above them. It landed with a shuddering thud right beside Flopsy. Thane sat astride the dragon, looking most impressive in battle gear. The dragon was deep purple in color and had sparkling diamonds embedded in the hide of her underbelly. She had reddish-brown tufts of hair sticking out of her head with a few hot pink streaks in it. She wore a huge gray and black-striped hoodie, with a skull and crossbones on it, and little red hearts floating above the skull. Her talons were tipped with black nail polish and her back feet were adorned with enormous, black high-topped tennis shoes.

"Don't come into my forest and threaten to tear it down, beast," the dragon roared at Flopsy. She, too, talked with an English accent. "Or I will make shish kebabs of your flesh!"

"I—I, um…" Flopsy said, voice wavering.

"Who is this?" Shimmer asked Thane, most impressed by the dragon.

"This is Hannah," Thane said, beaming.

"Wow! I don't think I have ever seen a gothic dragon before. You are very impressive. I love the hair," Shimmer said with a grin on her face.

"Thank you, I try to keep up my appearance," Hannah said, eyeing Flopsy with obvious dislike. "Unlike some dragons, I try to represent a fine quality, so that my rider will look even more impressive. Thane looks impressive, don't you think?"

"Oh, indeed he does," Shimmer said, trying hard not to laugh. "Where do you come from, Hannah?"

"I am from Eldfjall, the same kingdom as Flipsy and Flopsy. I served their father King Granite as a dragon-o-gram for years, until I was old enough to finally serve a prince."

"You did?" Flopsy said, bewildered. "I don't remember you, and I have been to my father's palace many times."

"Your ego is so large, you can only see your head. That is why you have never noticed me." She turned her attention back to Shimmer. "Some dragons think they are superior to others, because they are bonded at birth to a human prince."

"I don't think I'm better than you. I—I was always on business when I went to see my father and that is probably why I never noticed you. I will apologize for my behavior if that will make you feel better."

"I'll think about it," Hannah said, dismissively.

Flopsy opened his mouth to say something and then clamped it shut again.

"Well," Thane said awkwardly. He jumped down from Hannah's back. "Flopsy, can you tell me how Gladdy is doing? I hope they haven't hurt her."

"She is well. I wish there was some way to get her out of that castle. I'm so large that my wings won't let me get close enough for her to get on me through the tower window. We could really use Gladdy to retrieve Andy."

"I know. However, there is no time for that. We must go ahead and try to rescue my sister's son. I have a plan..." said Thane.

Thane was cut off by a noisy crash coming from a small clump of trees to his left. Huge blue eyes peered out at them.

"I don't believe this!" Hannah said, exasperated. "Haylee, come here!"

A young dragon, a lot smaller than Hannah, bounded into the clearing and edged right up next to Flopsy. She looked at him, starry-eyed. Her skin was a midnight blue with soft, shimmering light blue wings. Her bright, sapphire-colored eyes accented the small mark on her cheek, identical to the Mulberry Forest elves.

"You're King Granite's son, aren't you," Haylee blurted out quickly.

"Haylee, you need to go back to your nest, immediately. You cannot come with us. We're going on a dangerous mission and you might get hurt," Hannah said, with authority.

"I can go where I please. You're not the boss of me, Hannah."

"While you are visiting in this forest, I am. Now go!"

"What if I were to go and try to rescue Thane's sister and bring her back here, then would you let me go?" she asked, almost pleadingly.

"Absolutely not. You are not to go anywhere. Now go back to your nest!"

Haylee hung her head and walked a few feet away, only to be stopped by Shimmer.

"Haylee, wait. Why don't you stay here with us while we discuss our plans and then you can go back to your nest? I'm sure Hannah wouldn't object to that."

Hannah looked at Haylee and then grudgingly said, "I guess she can stay. But, when talks are over, you go back to the nest."

"Yes, Hannah."

She perked up and sidled back over to where Flopsy was, looking very moony.

"Once again," Thane said eyeing the two dragons. "The plan...."

"I'm guessing that plan involves Hannah," King Silverthorne said, interrupting Thane for a second time as he, Daisy and Grandmother Muckernut, and a young elf carrying weapons, approached.

"Yes it does, Uncle," Thane said, exasperated.

"Hannah is a Land of Chaldeon dragon. I don't want her involved. What if she were to become infected?"

"Uncle, she is a dragon...."

"And since she is a dragon," Shimmer said, cutting Thane off, "she will have a better resistance to most infections. Tell us your plan, Thane."

"I think we should scout out the land right after dark. Maybe even get as close to the castle as possible. If Shimmer can sneak into the castle without being seen, and find Andy, we could get him out of there and no one would be the wiser."

"That sounds good to me," Shimmer said.

"I don't know about that, Shimmer," Grandmother Muckernut said. "What if you're caught? Queen Estonia won't like you coming into her castle uninvited. It could mean your imprisonment, or death."

"Stay here if you want to, Vinca. But I will do whatever it takes to rescue Andy." Shimmer folded her arms across her chest and her lip protruded out in a very serious pout.

"Don't ever use my birth name again, Shimmer," Grandmother Muckernut said, slow and warningly. "I will accompany you and Thane to the Dark Lands. I just don't want to rush in and ruin any chance we might have in saving Andy."

"I'm—I'm very sorry, Grandmother Muckernut. I shouldn't have been harsh with that. You're right. We need to think things through more."

"And I don't like being cut off by you, Shimmer," King Silverthorne said sternly.

"I apologize, your majesty," Shimmer said, bowing. Her tongue seemed to be getting her into trouble every time she opened her mouth. "It won't happen again."

"See that it doesn't!" King Silverthorne shot Thane a look of disapproval. "Here." He held out his hand to Shimmer and dropped a small pouch into her hand. Shimmer opened the pouch and looked inside it. She pulled out one of the artifacts and looked it over. It was a small, smooth black river stone with three pale white rings around it. "The rings will glow when it gets close to the stone of power. The other relic will only allow the wearer to touch Queen Estonia's land. If all of you are to step on her land, then all of you must be linked together by holding hands," King Silverthorne informed her. "I have also brought you some extra swords. I'm sure that when you find Andy, he will not be armed." The young elf stepped forward and handed Shimmer several swords, bowed and then backed away. "I will give you permission to leave, but I don't like it."

King Silverthorne looked at Shimmer, Grandmother Muckernut, Daisy and Thane, nodded, and then turned to go back to the Bastion Tree.

"I guess I'll have guard duty for the next fifty years for helping you," Thane said jokingly, while watching the king's retreating back. "Boy, I don't look forward to that."

"I'm sorry to you as well, Thane," Shimmer said. "I know this is putting you in a hard position." She turned to Grandmother Muckernut, "What is your plan?"

"I think we should go just before sunset. Circle

low so that we can get a good view of the castle grounds and then fly out to the plains to discuss our plans."

"That sounds good to me. There's just one problem. If the Shadow People are on the plains, what do we do then?"

"We'll go to the Dwarf City or Mystic's cavern. I doubt the Shadow People have made it that far."

"Well, I for one am ready to fly," Hannah said, proudly stretching out her impressive black, leathery wings and making them flutter.

A faint humming sound filled the air. Shimmer looked around for its source and her eyes came to rest on Flopsy. The humming sound was coming from his chest. He was staring at Hannah intently with sparkly eyes.

"Oh brother," Shimmer mumbled. "That's all we need. A love-struck dragon."

Elves approached the group and brought a saddle for Flopsy and strapped it to him. Then Shimmer stowed away the swords in one of the pouches on the saddle and mounted Flopsy, followed by Grandmother Muckernut. Daisy had been placed into one of Shimmer's pockets for the ride. Thane crawled back on Hannah and nodded to Shimmer.

"Well, let's go. I haven't flown on Hannah in a long time," Thane said, a little excited. "I'm looking forward to an adventure."

Shimmer smiled at him. Her heart leaped a little at the prospect of perhaps seeing Andy very soon.

"Let's go, Flopsy," she said, grinning with excitement herself.

Haylee watched with pride as the two powerful dragons leaped into the air. The back draft from their wings bent the grass and trees in the clearing. Haylee inhaled the sweet air through her nostrils and contemplated the idea that was forming in her head.

"I may not be able to go with you, but I can do something about Gladdy," she said, giggling to herself.

Waving and yelling her goodbyes, she waited until the others had completely left the clearing and then pretended she was going back to her nest. As she passed a fairy in flight, she began humming to herself. She exulted in how she could be so sneaky about things she was determined to do. When she was well away from the clearing and prying eyes, she changed direction and flew off toward Filligrim Castle.

AN OLD MAN REMEMBERS

Andy woke feeling like a million dollars. Excitement filled his chest and he jumped out of bed. He couldn't wait until he saw Jennifer. He dressed quickly and was putting on his shoes when someone knocked on his door. His smile widened into a huge grin that he had no control over. He nearly ran to the door, but stopped and tried to calm himself. He couldn't let Jennifer see him acting so goofy. He slowly opened the door. His heart fell somewhat as he looked into the black toothy grin of Theodius.

"Oh," was all he said.

"Well, hello to you too. What's the matter? Am I not pretty enough for you?" Theodius teased.

"I was just…."

Andy stopped as he looked at Theodius' mischievous face. He wouldn't give Theodius any fuel for his teasing fire.

"I know whom you were expecting." Theodius walked over and sat down next to Andy on the bed. "I think you should start concentrating again on the little blue girl and leave the other one alone. I don't know what it is about that Jennifer girl, but there is something suspicious about her."

"There is nothing wrong with Jennifer! And as for Shimmer, she has made her choice. She chose Elsfur," Andy said, sharply.

"You don't know that," Theodius said, his face becoming so somber, it shocked Andy a little.

"I—I do know that," Andy stammered.

"No, you don't. For that matter, she could be on her way here right now to rescue you."

"I highly doubt that. I won't let you ruin my good mood, Theodius."

Andy began humming as he walked into the bathroom. Theodius listened to the running water, then walked to the window. He stared at the sky. His heart willed Andy's friends to hurry to the Dark Lands. He just knew his little friend was in danger. He just couldn't think of why.

‌ಶ•ೀ

Andy looked down from the landing at the top of the stairs to see Jennifer seated in a chair in the foyer. Excitement stung every nerve in his body as he descended the stairs two at a time. Just being with her made him feel so alive.

"Well, don't you look lovely today," he said as he approached her. She was wearing a green dress made from a silky fabric and she had swept her hair up into a ponytail.

"Why thank you," she said, beaming up at him. "What are we going to do today?"

"I thought we would eat brunch, since I slept so late, and go and explore the castle. I don't think Aunt Estonia will mind."

"I think that would be a great idea. I'm starving!"

They found the buffet table loaded with fruit and breakfast items, and feasted leisurely. They talked about Andy's world and he listened as Jennifer spoke about where she was from.

"So," said Andy. "When did Aunt Estonia adopt you?"

"Well," Jennifer laughed. "She didn't really adopt me. I have known your Aunt Estonia since I was a child. My parents passed away when I was very young. A friend of the family introduced me to Estonia and she took a liking to me. I stay with her every now and then and when I do, she always introduces me as her daughter. It's just a little inside joke between her and me."

"Oh well, it's nice that you have someone you can call family," he said, smiling at her.

"So, where do you want to go first?"

"I think I would like to go to the library," Andy said as he finished eating his food. "I want something to read at night when I'm not in your wonderful company."

Jennifer blushed. "I think that's a magnificent idea as well," Jennifer said, giggling. "Shall we go?"

Andy proffered his arm and she gladly accepted it. As they entered the library, the scent of leather and old paper accosted them like an old friend. Andy smiled in astonishment as he looked at the thousands of books his Aunt Estonia had acquired. He would have never thought that she would like reading so much. They meandered separately, browsing the many volumes of history books, genealogy, and castle records. Towards the back of the library Andy found a little sitting area with well-worn chairs, a table and a candelabra. Large amounts of wax lay hard on the table as if someone had spent many nights reading by candlelight. Andy swallowed a lump in his throat, as he thought of his Aunt Estonia sitting here night after night, lonely, with nothing else to do with her life. She was a prisoner in her own land.

Andy chose one of the more comfortable chairs and picked up the nearest book. It was a love story written mostly in songs and poems. His stomach lurched as he flipped through the pages of the sickening love story. *How can someone be so sappy?* he wondered in disgust.

Andy laid that book down and picked up another book about how to build bows and arrows, and how to make flint arrowheads. He began to read. It was so interesting that he lost all track of time. He could have stayed there all day, but decided he was being rude leaving Jennifer alone for so long. As Andy put down the book, his eyes traveled over the nearest shelf. They came to rest on a tiny familiar symbol etched in the wood. It was a bottle with a wilted flower. Andy stood and walked over to the shelf and traced the bottle with his finger. This gave him an idea. He took a few steps back and looked around at the other shelves that were close by, and sure enough there were the other symbols etched in the wood. The moon and stars, the lightning bolt, the book with the strange writing, the balancing scales, the three legs, the burst of flames, and the tree with the falling fruit. They were the symbols from the doors that he, Daisy and Gladdy had found in the Filligrim Castle, when they had been following the Shadow Man. Andy got excited. Was this the way back to Filligrim Castle? Could this be how the Shadow Man traveled back and forth between lands? His heart leaped with joy. Maybe he could get back to the castle.

"Jen—" Andy began to shout out, but something made him shut his mouth. The voice of Theodius and his cautioning words to him in his room. Should he trust Jennifer? What if Shimmer was coming to rescue him?

He turned when he heard footsteps behind him. Jennifer was smiling at him.

"You called?"

"What—oh, I was just wondering if you had found anything to read. I've got my book." He bent over and picked up the mushy love story by accident.

"*My Wandering Heart Hears A Song,*" Jennifer read out loud. "I didn't think you went for love stories."

"Uh—well, you know," Andy stammered over his words, wishing he had grabbed the right book. "I've got to learn how to be dashing somehow. Sorry I left you alone for so long. I—I just couldn't put the book down." He pulled Jennifer towards the door. "I'll go and put my book in my room so I don't have to carry it around with me. It might get in the way. While I'm upstairs, I'll check on Theodius."

"Is there something wrong with Theodius?" she asked, a little suspiciously.

"No," Andy shook his head trying to come up with something without lying. "I just like to keep tabs on him. You know how Aunt Estonia is about him." Andy wrinkled up his nose and did his best impression of his Aunt Estonia, "If he gets any dirt on my furniture, it's back to the dungeon he goes."

She laughed, "You're right about that."

Andy found himself staring into her eyes. She was drawing him in, making him feel lightheaded. He felt as if he were in a trance. She stood on tiptoes and leaned in, so close that Andy could smell her wonderful perfume. Seeing her perfect mouth, he leaned his head down, and just as he was about to kiss her, he saw Shimmer's beautiful face swim before his eyes. He shook his head and breathed deeply. He backed away from her and noticed that one of her eyes was turning orange. He was about to ask her about it, and then it turned back brown.

"Um…I—I better go and put this book away," he laughed nervously. He looked at her eyes again.

Maybe it was just my imagination, he thought. He smiled at her and then began running up the stairs.

❧

Jennifer watched Andy's retreating back as he ran up the stairs to his bedroom. Her eyes began glowing orange and rage twisted her beautiful face. The bangs on her forehead turned the color of orange sherbet. Deciding to see what Andy was up to, she put her foot on the bottom step of the staircase. She jumped as a cold hand stopped her, clamped down on her arm, and then spun her around. Standing before her was a huge dark man, more shadow than human. She stepped back a little, nearly falling on the second step. She didn't like being so close to the Shadow Man.

"You need to watch yourself," he said pointing to her hair. "You're going to give yourself away."

"I can handle it," she said. He watched as her eyes and hair turned back to a more human color.

"How is our prisoner today?" His deep voice reverberated around the foyer and made the hair on the back of her neck stand on end.

"He's fine. He will be back down shortly," she said a little anxiously. "He just went to put his book away and then we're going to explore the castle."

"Watch him," he hissed at her, spittle hitting her in the face. "He is not to be trusted. I want you to find out where he put his birdcage necklace and what he knows about the crown. Is that clear?"

"Yes, Saber," she said, cowering a little. "I just don't understand why you couldn't have done it when you had him drugged. In a drugged state he should have given you every piece of information you asked for."

"Because he's strong," Saber said, agitated. "I've never seen anything like it before. It must be the dragon blood he has running in his veins. Do you always have to question me, Apricot? Just do as I ask!"

His hand flew up as though he wanted to strike her, and she covered her face. More than once over the past three months she had felt the anger of the Shadow Man, and she couldn't wait until she was rid of him. He had promised her that if she retrieved the information that he wanted, she would be able to leave the Dark Lands for good.

"I will get the information," she said through her tears. Then she begged, "Just don't hit me anymore, please."

He glowered at her a moment longer, and then pushed her away. She sat down hard on the stairs and watched as he turned and left through a secret passage just a few feet away.

"I can't believe I left my beautiful forest for this," she lamented to the empty foyer.

~∘~

Andy barged into Theodius' room without knocking. He couldn't wait to tell him his news. Theodius was staring out the window and didn't turn around when Andy walked in.

"Theodius, I have to talk to you," Andy said breathlessly. "I have found something that might help you and me escape from this castle."

Theodius turned and looked at Andy, but didn't speak.

"When I was in the Filligrim castle," Andy began. He spoke quietly so no one would overhear him. "Gladdy, Daisy, and I found a room that had doors leading to nowhere in it. On the doors were symbols. One had a moon and stars on it, another had a bottle with a wilted flower, another had a tree with falling fruit, another had a book—"

"With strange writing on it!" Theodius practically yelled, interrupting Andy.

"Yes, how did you know that?" Andy asked.

"Because, I have seen that room before."

"What do you mean, you've seen that room before. You said you didn't know where Filligrim Castle was."

"The reason I know is because that room was one of the ways to my laboratory," Theodius said grinning widely. Andy backed away a little and felt his stomach lurch. There, sticking out between two of Theodius' black teeth, were the remains of a bug.

"Theodius," Andy said, thoroughly grossed out, "Aunt Estonia provides more than enough food for us. Why are you still eating bugs?"

"Old habits are hard to break." Theodius began sucking at his teeth trying to remove the rest of the bug. "Is that better?"

"Yeah," Andy said slowly, rolling his eyes. "Back to what you just said. What do you mean 'your laboratory'?"

"My mind has been clearer since I've been in

this room. I am remembering who I used to be. You might want to have a seat," Theodius said, gesturing toward the bed. Andy ignored him and Theodius went on. "I am Theodius the Wizard."

"What. No way!" Andy said, practically shouting.

"It's true. King Anasee told me that Filligrim was having problems with Queen Estonia. The king asked me to go to the Dark Lands and make Queen Estonia more agreeable. However, when I got to the Dark Lands, I was arrested, drugged and put in the dungeon. They tortured me for long periods of time. I tried to fight back with magic, but my magic wouldn't work here. I started forgetting who I was, until you came. There must be something in that dungeon, or maybe the food, that was keeping me from remembering. Ever since I have been in this part of the castle, my memories have been coming back."

"I don't understand. If you are here, then who is in Filligrim Castle acting like he's you?" Andy asked, bewildered by what Theodius had just told him.

"I would assume an imposter."

"I think it's the Shadow Man. That Saber person." Andy grinned at Theodius. "But, how on earth is he able to turn into a cat? Queen Estonia said that she was the only one with great powers in the Dark Lands."

"Sounds like someone has fooled your aunt."

"I guess so," Andy said. He smiled at Theodius. "And you built that room with all of the doors?"

"Yes, I had a lot of secret experiments and I didn't want anyone to stumble upon them. So I made a secret laboratory. Somehow Saber found out about it. Probably when he tortured me. He loved to take me there and make me suffer."

"That must have been what I heard," Andy said, excited over solving a piece of the puzzle. "When Gladdy, Daisy and I found the room, I heard the most horrible screams. It must have been you."

"It probably was," said Theodius, matter-of-factly. "I can't imagine Saber taking anyone else there."

Andy sat staring at Theodius in awe. To be talking so nonchalantly about being tortured. He shivered and changed the subject.

"So you're the real Theodius, huh? Gladdy will be so glad that you're okay."

"How—how is Gladdy?"

"She was great the last time I saw her. I bet she's worried sick about me though."

"I sure miss her. She had the most beautiful eyes," Theodius said, remembering. "We were going to be married when I returned to Filligrim."

"Married?" Andy laughed. "I didn't know you two were serious."

"Yes, we were very serious. I loved her very much." Theodius turned and walked back to the window and asked, "So, how are we going to get back to her?"

"Tonight when everyone is in bed, you and I are going to sneak back down to the library. Since you know so much about those symbols it should

197

be easy for us to open some sort of secret passageway."

Theodius turned back to Andy.

"I want out of this castle and back to the one I love, Andy. I will do whatever it takes to get us there."

Andy heard the conviction in Theodius' voice. Something he had not heard before. He felt sorry for the old man. Sixteen years of his life had been spent in prison and Andy was determined to set Theodius free.

"I will have to spend more time with Jennifer today. I have to keep her happy. However, I'm starting to think like you, Theodius. She's not who she says she is and she is definitely working for Aunt Estonia, or maybe even the Shadow Man."

"You be careful, Andy. We're dealing with evil here," Theodius said, turning to face Andy. "Evil that is growing. I can feel it."

"I will," Andy said, reassuringly. "You stay up here until I come to get you. Tell Clyde that you want to eat supper in your room. Tell him that you're not feeling well."

"That would be the truth. I haven't been feeling well for a few days."

"It's probably because you're eating so many bugs. You need to cut that out and eat some normal food."

"You eat bugs for sixteen years and see how hard it would be to kick the habit."

"Oh, believe me," Andy said, grinning, "I could quit. I'm just glad I never took up the habit."

They both laughed and then Theodius hugged

Andy. Andy swallowed the lump that stuck in his throat. Theodius had become like a father to him while he had been in the Dark Lands. He hoped he would be able to see Theodius marry Gladdy. Then Andy really could think of him as his father.

KING FOXGLOVE
HELPS A GOBLIN

King Foxglove sat on a branch high up in a tree. He watched the plains with his bird-like eyes. Green creatures were flooding out of the Dark Lands and into the plains. Some of them were coming towards River Birch Forest. He jumped when Shade called quietly to him.

"My lord, what are those creatures?"

"I'm not sure," King Foxglove said. "They resemble Shadow People, yet—"

Elves didn't know fear, but those creatures were creating feelings that King Foxglove had never felt before.

"Shade, you and Meadow go to the edge of the woods and place a barrier wall in front of the forest. I don't want any of those things getting into my realm."

"As you wish, my lord," said Meadow.

He watched his two faithful servants jump from tree to tree like trapeze artists and make their way toward the plains.

King Foxglove was deep in thought, when he heard rumblings coming from the ground. He jumped down out of the huge oak and stood very still. Someone or something was digging just below his feet. Just as he knelt down to put his ear to the ground, the ground began to push upwards, then collapsed back into a hole. King Foxglove jumped back and drew his sword. He watched amazed, as a head began protruding up through the hole. Familiar eyes on the head came to rest on him.

"Kwagar!" King Foxglove shouted with joy. "Is that you?"

Kwagar blew dirt out of his mouth and cried, "Oh, thank goodness! King Foxglove! I have never been so glad to see someone in my whole life. I need your help. My friend is seriously hurt."

"What friend?" King Foxglove asked, bewildered by what he was seeing.

"Hold on a moment, I'll show you."

Kwagar put his head back into the hole. King Foxglove began to worry when he didn't return. Then the ground began to tremble so violently under King Foxglove's feet that he thought it was an earthquake. The ground burst open, knocking King Foxglove to the ground and flinging dirt, roots and debris everywhere. King Foxglove eased over to the edge of the now enormous hole and found Kwagar standing there holding a small, unconscious goblin.

"How did you...?" King Foxglove's voice trailed off as he looked at Kwagar. The boy was skin and bones. His face was covered in a thick beard and his hair hung past his shoulders. But it was not how Kwagar's body looked; it was his eyes. They were sunk into his head and looked hollow and lifeless.

"Here," King Foxglove said, sticking out his hand. "Let me help you out of that hole and then we can talk."

Kwagar handed up the small goblin to King Foxglove and then crawled out of the hole as King Foxglove carefully laid Mucous on the ground. King Foxglove's ears twitched as he heard the running approach of Shade and Meadow. He turned and watched their swift return.

"My lord," Meadow said, barely winded. "Are you all right? We heard a loud noise and came straight away."

"I'm fine. It's Prince Kwagar that could use our help, or rather his goblin friend."

King Foxglove pointed to the small goblin lying on the ground.

"Isn't that Mucous?" Shade said, a little confused.

"Yes it is," interjected Kwagar. "And if we don't get him some medical attention, he will surely die."

Shade bent down and gently picked up the little goblin.

"If you don't mind, my lord, I will carry him," Shade said, with concern in his voice.

"Yes, that will be good. Meadow, you help

Kwagar. I will lead the way."

They made their way down a dirt path through very dense forest. King Foxglove had to use his sword many times to hack through the underbrush. They walked for quite some time. Kwagar didn't think he would make it much farther. He was starved for both food and water and his legs felt like rubber. Just when he was about to tell the king that he couldn't go on, they came to a bridge with a fast rushing river flowing beneath it. Kwagar could see elves camped just on the other side.

As they entered the camp, merriment and music could be heard. Some elves were dancing around a huge fire, while others stood in groups boastfully discussing their different skills as archers, three-quarter staffing, and wrestling. All of them stopped to watch the party of elves and Kwagar enter the camp. What intrigued them most though was the goblin that Shade was carrying.

With Shade carrying Mucous, the three elves and Kwagar headed toward a large tree just on the other side of the camp. King Foxglove touched a knot in the tree and a door opened. Stairs inside the tree descended deep underground and ended in a large room. A wooden table and chairs holding bread, a strange green plant and a pitcher sat in the very center of the room. Clay jars with weird substances dripping from them lined one of the walls opposite of the door. A bizarre fire with green and red flames crackled merrily in a pit beside the jars. Hooks with drying flowers and roots hung from the low dirt ceiling, filling the air with their aroma.

Shade laid the little goblin on a rudimentary bed in the corner and began tending to him. King Foxglove motioned for Kwagar to take a seat at the table. Meadow poured him some water from the pitcher. Kwagar drank deeply, quenching his great thirst. It had been so long since he had swallowed clean water. This water immediately gave him back his strength and most of the tiredness left his body.

"Wow, I feel better already," Kwagar said, smiling. "Where does this water come from?"

"It passes through the Dark Lands and then onto our land by way of the Golden River," King Foxglove said.

"Thank you, it was delicious."

"You are very welcome, Kwagar. Tell me, son of Queen Noor, when did you learn how to use your Asrai powers, since you didn't have Mystic to teach you, as was planned."

Kwagar looked at King Foxglove. "I had to get out of that prison. Prince Mosaic has appointed himself king now. He was going to torture me. He said that he wanted information about the Crown and Jewel of the Races. I acted like I didn't know what he was talking about. I didn't want to be tortured so I used my powers to get us out of there."

"I'm glad you made it out alive," King Foxglove said, patting Kwagar on the shoulder. "You rest and enjoy something to eat. I will tend to Mucous and then I have to speak to my brother, King Silverthorne. There is something bad going on in the Dark Lands and I must find out what that is." King Foxglove gestured toward another makeshift cot in the other corner. "You can rest on that cot if you like. My home is not as grand as my brother's. I prefer to live simply as our people have always lived, without all the grandeur."

"Thank you, your majesty. Your home is like heaven to me, after where I've been."

"You're too kind, Kwagar."

King Foxglove gathered some herbs from one of the nearby clay jars. The herbs were mustard yellow and gave off a repugnant odor. Kwagar found himself holding his breath as he watched King Foxglove squeeze out juices from the herbs into a cup. Discarding the herbs, he took the cup over to where Mucous lay. He began bathing the goblin in the substance, washing all of his exposed limbs and face. Instantly, Kwagar could see the little goblin's wounds disappear. Shade managed to take the manacles off the goblin's small wrists and King Foxglove rubbed the herbal solution on the bruises, healing them almost instantly. A moment later, Mucous opened his eyes and looked at the king and smiled.

"King Foxglove," he said weakly. "I must be dead. How can this be possible?"

"Don't you remember?" King Foxglove asked. "Kwagar saved you from the prison. You're safe now, Mucous. You may stay in my kingdom as long as you like. Mosaic will never harm you again."

Mucous began crying. "Thank you, your majesty," he whispered.

"You rest. Shade will take care of you and be your protector."

"It will be my honor," Shade said, with a huge smile.

"Thank you, Shade," Mucous said, as he closed his eyes once more to sleep.

Kwagar felt relief that his little friend would be okay and that the elves would take care of him when Kwagar had to leave. The elves were kind folk and had a way with making you feel wonderful when you were around them.

Kwagar watched as King Foxglove went over to the wall at the far end of the room. A mirror in a thick, wooden frame was the only fixture that hung on the wall. King Foxglove knocked on the very center of the mirror and then stood back, waiting patiently. Then King Foxglove's reflection disappeared and was replaced by a scene of a little island with a beautiful throne sitting in the center, next to an odd tree. Stunned, Kwagar watched as a very majestic-looking elf appeared and then sat on the throne.

"What is it, Brother? I'm a little busy," King Silverthorne growled.

"I need to talk with you about what is happening with the Shadow People. They don't look like themselves these days," King Foxglove said.

"That's why I'm so busy. They have attacked my lands and people."

"What do you mean, they have attacked you?" King Foxglove asked. "Queen Estonia wouldn't dare attack the elves. She must be out of her mind."

"I don't think it's her, my brother. The Shadow People are infected with some sort of disease. They have turned green and have pustules all over their bodies."

"A disease? What would cause a disease in the Dark Lands?"

"Can't you think of something so evil that would cause the darkness in the Dark Lands to become darker?" King Silverthorne asked, teasing with his brother.

King Foxglove stood there staring at his brother for a moment, thinking of all the possibilities.

"The Jewel of the Races...."

"That would be my guess," King Silverthorne said.

"But how could that be?" King Foxglove asked, confused.

"I can't see what has transpired. My vision is growing dim," King Silverthorne said weakly. "Whatever is happening to the Shadow People is affecting me as well."

"What can be done to stop this?"

"I don't know. Some of the Shadow People have infected some of my elves. Apparently all they have to do is touch you and you go into a deep sleep. Also, the elves that have been touched are turning black, as if they are rotting."

King Foxglove sighed hard.

"Is there anything I can do for you and your people, my brother?"

"No. Stay away and behind a barrier. I don't doubt that they will be coming your way soon."

"I saw them just a while ago, coming this way. I had Shade and Meadow set up barriers at the forest front."

"You will be in my thoughts, Brother. I only hope we withstand this bombardment."

Kwagar stood up from the table and started walking toward the little cot that King Foxglove told him he could lie on. King Silverthorne leaned to one side in the mirror to get a better look at Kwagar.

"Who is that bedraggled person in your chambers, Brother?"

"That would be Prince Kwagar from Filligrim Kingdom."

"How did that little whelp escape from Hamamelis Prison?" King Silverthorne shouted in shocked surprise. "No one has ever escaped from there!"

"It seems our little Prince here is half Asrai Warrior."

"Prince Becken?" King Silverthorne said, as if he was seeing something in his mind. "Ah, Mystic. I see it now."

"I saw it a while ago," King Foxglove said, smiling. "You should have seen it, Brother. He was tunneling underground and—"

"His head popped out of the ground like a daisy," King Silverthorne laughed.

"See. Your sight hasn't left you, Brother. You just needed a good visual and it came back."

"No, I don't think it's come back. I think it's just from the prompting. Speaking of Asrai Warriors, I had visitors today."

"Who would be brave enough to visit you?" King Foxglove laughed.

209

"Shimmer the Asrai, Daisy the pixie, and Grandmother Muckernut of Hemlock Forest."

Kwagar ran forward toward the mirror.

"What were they doing in your kingdom, your majesty?" he asked, eagerly.

"They were on their way to the Dark Lands. Seems your newfound brother is being held captive by Queen Estonia. My nephew and two dragons accompanied them."

"But how can they go to the Dark Lands if the people are infected?"

"I warned them not to go. However, Shimmer wouldn't take no for an answer. She was determined to go. Matters of the heart and all."

"So, she has let Elsfur go at last. Well that's good. Maybe he will do the right thing and finally marry my daughter—"

"I must go and help Shimmer," Kwagar said, cutting off King Foxglove.

"You're not going anywhere in the shape you're in. You will rest. It will take them some time to get to the Dark Lands, even flying on dragons."

"I have to go now. If my brother is in danger, then I need to help him."

"You rest at least two hours. I have to figure out how we can even get out of River Birch Forest without letting in those creatures."

"I have my barrier so high that only a dragon can fly over it," King Silverthorne interjected.

"That's a bit extreme isn't it, Brother?" King Foxglove teased.

"You haven't seen one of those creatures up

close, have you?" King Silverthorne muttered.

"No, I haven't. But I'm going back to the forest's edge to see for myself," King Foxglove said, laughing at his brother's expression. "Thank you for all the information, Brother. I will talk with you later if I learn anything new."

"One more thing, Brother," King Silverthorne said hastily. "If the jewel is in the Dark Lands, it will need to be destroyed."

"Yes, I realize this. But Queen Estonia won't give up her life willingly."

"She will if you make it happen," King Silverthorne replied, coldly. "But she has to be holding the jewel when her life goes out, or it won't be destroyed."

"Yes, Brother, I understand," King Foxglove said solemnly.

King Foxglove and Kwagar watched as the reflection of the island went blank and King Foxglove's came back.

Turning to Kwagar, King Foxglove said in a deflated voice, "Go and rest, Kwagar. I will wake you in two hours. In the meantime, I will find a solution to our problem." He looked directly into Kwagar's eyes. "Your brother will be saved, and the Jewel of the Races will be destroyed."

Kwagar nodded. He knew that it was not in an elf's nature to just kill someone. But, that was what would have to be done if the jewel were to be destroyed. Then he thought of something.

"Your majesty, I have a plan already," Kwagar said, brightening. "I am Asrai. I can move the earth. I will dig us a tunnel. All you have to do is bring along a little food, and some of that wonderful water that renewed my energy, and point me in the right direction. I will take care of the rest."

King Foxglove stood there looking at Kwagar, trying to picture him tunneling under the earth like a mole. He grinned as a plan formed in his mind. Making it to the Dark Lands might just be a stroll in the park after all.

LITTLE DRAGON TO THE RESCUE

Haylee was feeling pretty good about herself as she flew toward Filligrim Castle. She was confident that her plan would work. First she would fly up to the towers, where they were keeping the prisoners, and find Gladdy. Haylee hoped that she would be able to get close enough so that Gladdy could get on Haylee's tail. Then she would take Gladdy and set her a safe distance from the castle. After that, when the coast was clear and no one had discovered what she was doing, she would then do the same for all of the other Misfits that had been taken prisoner.

As the Filligrim Castle came into view, Haylee got a little nervous. What if her plan failed and she was captured? What if she wasn't able to get everyone out? She inhaled a large gulp of air and let it out. A small burst of fire came with it.

"Oops," she said to herself, smiling.

As a small dragon she still hadn't quite got the hang of controlling her fire. It would come out at the strangest times, but mostly when she was anxious. Once she had caught King Granite's tail on fire at a banquet. She had just graduated from dragon school and was the head of her class. Every year the graduating class dined with the king and the head of the class would give a speech. Haylee had just started speaking when she hiccupped, and fire spurted all over the king's tail. It took her a while to get over the embarrassment of that incident. She hoped with all her heart as she flew toward Filligrim Castle, that she wouldn't set the castle on fire and burn up everyone that she intended to rescue.

She circled way above the highest tower trying to see if there were a lot of people in market that day. Luckily, it was late afternoon, so most of the people would be at home preparing for the evening meal. Also, she looked for the guards that would be posted on the walls surrounding the Keep, but found hardly any.

"Theodius must think that his spell is impenetrable," Haylee said, giggling. "Or he would have more guards posted."

Haylee swooped down toward the highest tower and circled it until she found a window. She couldn't believe her luck. She could see Gladdy lying on a bed, asleep.

"Gladdy," she said quietly. "Wake up. I've come to rescue you."

Gladdy opened her eyes and looked at the enormous sapphire eyeball that was peering at her through the window.

"My, my, what do we have here?" Gladdy asked, smiling.

"I'm Haylee, a dragon from—" Haylee began to say, but Gladdy finished her sentence.

"The Land of Chaldeon," Gladdy beamed. "I know the dragons from my land."

"How did you know where I was from?" Haylee asked, astonished.

"Because, you have the mark," Gladdy said proudly. Subconsciously Haylee's paw covered the circular mark just below her eye, and she blushed. "Did my uncle send you to me?"

"Aaaactually," Haylee said, a little drawn out, "I came on my own. No one knows that I'm here. I'm sure King Silverthorne will have my head when he finds out."

"Not if you rescue me and the others. Then my grumpy old uncle won't have anything to say but praise," Gladdy said. "I'm assuming that is why you are here."

"Yes, that is why I have come. My sister Hannah thinks I'm a baby and that I have no business doing anything other than staying in the nest all day. So I'm proving to her that I'm big enough to do just as much as she."

"I can see how big you are," Gladdy said, very amused. "Now, how are you going to rescue the others and myself? I presume you have a plan."

"Oh sure," Haylee said confidently. "You will need to climb up here on the windowsill. I will turn around so that you can get on my tail and then while you hold on very tight, I will fly you down to the forest where you will be safe. Next, I will find all of the others and do the same with them. After that, if Flipsy can fly, we will take a few of you to the Dark Lands and meet up with Shimmer, Thane and Grandmother Muckernut."

"Wow, that sounds like quite a plan."

"I know. Right!" Haylee said, with much enthusiasm.

Deciding that she liked the plan, Gladdy made up her mind to go for it. *I just hope I have the strength to get off the bed*, Gladdy thought.

Still in a weakened state, Gladdy's old frame sat up and willed her body off the bed. It took every ounce of strength she had to stand up. She had been getting weaker and weaker ever since Grandmother Muckernut had left. As she stood there all the blood went to her head, causing her to get dizzy. She shook her head and moved toward the table where her mirror lay. She could see the reflection of a very concerned Hattie Mae, staring up at her from the reflective glass.

"Are you sure about this?" Hattie Mae asked. "You look like you couldn't shoo off a fly if he landed on your nose. What if you fall? You're so frail, you might break every bone in your body."

"Oh, she won't fall," said Haylee. "Besides I would catch her if she did."

"Put me in your pocket," Hattie Mae said. "I'm coming with you. I might be a huge help when we get to Charlock Castle in the Dark Lands."

Gladdy nodded and then smiled weakly at her.

She picked up the mirror and slid it into her pocket. She couldn't talk. She needed all her strength for what she was about to do. She began climbing onto the table. *You can do this*, she thought as her foot slipped off the edge. She steadied herself, then climbed up again. Gladdy had just stood up on the table when a noise pricked her ears. Someone was coming up the steps. From the sound of it, several people were approaching the tower's uppermost floor.

Gladdy forced herself to move faster. She began pulling her body up towards the windowsill. Her lack of muscle made the climb that much harder. Haylee could hear the guard approaching as well. She moved a little higher so that her mouth was in line with the window. As Gladdy stretched her arm over the window ledge, Haylee stuck her tongue out and wrapped it around Gladdy's arm and started flying backward, pulling Gladdy as she went. When Gladdy was firmly on the windowsill, Haylee turned herself around so that her tail was right in front of Gladdy.

Wind blew Gladdy's hair and it felt so refreshing. Gladdy breathed in the fresh air and felt her strength begin to return, since she was now above the spell that Theodius had put on the castle. Her body began transforming until she looked youthful again.

"Jump!" Haylee hissed softly. A rattling of keys clanked against the door. "Jump!" she said again, only this time it was a low roar.

Gladdy looked back at the door. She could see Portumus standing on the other side of it. He looked at her and she smiled at him. He couldn't see Haylee because Gladdy was taking up the whole window. A look of concern crossed his face. He thought she was going to jump to her death. He thrust the keys into the keyhole trying to unlock it faster, but it was too late. Portumus looked up just in time to see Gladdy push herself off the windowsill and onto Haylee's tail.

"Take me out of here," Gladdy said, laughing.

"You got it," Haylee said, joining her in the mirth.

Gladdy turned around and waved at Portumus who had just climbed onto the table and was staring out of the window in shock.

"What about the others?" Gladdy shouted.

"I'll set you down near the dragon paddock and then go back for whoever else I can get. Hold on."

Haylee flew toward the backside of the castle and then began to descend. Just as she soared close to the dragon paddock, a huge dragon shot up right in front of Haylee. Haylee started back peddling her wings to keep from flying into Flipsy. Gladdy almost fell off of Haylee's tail. Flipsy, so colossal in size compared to Haylee, hovered right in front of her.

"Who are you?" he roared. "And what are you doing with Gladdy?"

Before Haylee could answer, Gladdy shouted, "Get out of the way, Flipsy! Haylee is trying to rescue me. I can't hold on much longer. I'm slipping."

Flipsy moved to one side and Haylee continued towards the ground. She gently set her tail down on the ground and Gladdy got off. Flipsy landed beside them.

"I've got to go back and get as many as I can before they have time to sound the alarm," Haylee said hurriedly. "Flipsy, stay here and protect Gladdy. Do not let anyone near her. If you have to, take her away from here."

She leaped powerfully into the air and flew off toward the castle, leaving Flipsy with his mouth hanging open.

"What is going on here?" Flipsy asked Gladdy.

Gladdy told him all of the events that led up to that moment. They watched as Haylee made quick trip after quick trip to rescue as many Misfits as possible. She managed to set free Elsfur, Snollygob and Timmynog. Gladdy couldn't imagine how Haylee was able to get Timmynog out of such a small window. All of the Misfits rubbed their arms and touched their faces, for they too had suffered the affliction of old age from the enchantment that was placed on the castle.

"What about Mystic?" Gladdy asked, as Haylee set Snollygob on the ground.

"There was a guard at the window as I passed by. He shot arrows at me but missed," Haylee said proudly.

"What's the plan?" Elsfur asked. "I don't think Haylee can carry more than one of us to the Dark Lands."

"I can carry Snollygob and Gladdy. Flipsy can carry Timmynog and you."

"There is no way Flipsy can carry Timmynog and me. He's just recovering from serious injuries."

"I can," said Flipsy, not wanting to be left out. "I'm much stronger now. If I get tired, I'll just set you down and rest for a while."

"I don't know," Elsfur said slowly.

A trumpet sounded a warning up at the castle.

"Elsfur, we need to make a decision fast," said Gladdy. "Besides, Flipsy has had three months to regain his strength. Just look at him. He seems good as new."

"Okay, we'll try it. But if you get tired, Flipsy, you have to promise me you will set us down and rest."

Flipsy crossed his heart and held up two talons. "Upon my honour as King Granite's son, I promise." He smiled, spreading his mustache and beard wide. Everyone smiled back at him.

Just then a griffin came hurtling toward them. Astride it was Caleb the stable boy.

"Gladdy," he shouted, very rushed and out of breath. "I saw you escape and knew I had to reach you before anyone else. Queen Noor has escaped the castle with King Renauldee. They are making their way for the Crystal Sea Palace. I thought you must know. My sisters and I are leaving as soon as they saddle their mounts. I have brought you some weapons that I had stashed in the stable. I hope they will be of good use to you."

"Thank you, Caleb. This is the best news ever," Gladdy said, breathing a sigh of relief and accepting one of the swords. "Now, go before you are caught. Tell the queen that we are going to rescue Andy and bring him to her."

Caleb smiled. "That is great news. I know she

will honor you forever for saving her son."

The words bit deeply into Gladdy's heart, but she didn't let it show. She only shook her head and stood back as the griffin took off and soared toward the barn. They watched as two more griffins joined it in the air, flying off toward the horizon.

The rest of the Misfits put on their weapons, mounted up and the dragons jumped skyward, just as soldiers began running across the bridge towards the dragon paddock. They shot arrows into the sky, missing both of the dragons. They flew for quite a long time.

"Do you think it would be possible to get something to eat? I'm very hungry," Gladdy shouted at Haylee, as her stomach began to rumble.

"I'm hungry as well," Snollygob chimed in.

Haylee looked at Flipsy and signaled for him to begin descending toward a lake that she had spotted. It looked like it was about a mile away. After they had landed, Elsfur and Timmynog hunted for berries or whatever else they could find to feed everyone, while the rest drank from the lake and rested. Everyone was pleased when Timmynog brought back a huge bunch of groodle berries.

Looking at the sky, Haylee could see that most of the day had slipped by. The clouds had turned a glowing orange and purple, and the sun was sinking into the horizon. She grinned as she thought about what Hannah would say to her for rescuing all of the Misfits. All she could hear in her head was praise. If she had been realistic, she would have heard how she was going to get it for disobeying Hannah.

Their stomachs had just begun to feel full when Flipsy jumped to his feet and began growling. Elsfur went into attack mode as well, drawing his sword from its sheath.

"What is it?" Timmynog asked, pulling out his sword.

"All of the Misfits need to get on a dragon now!" Haylee said, with flaring nostrils. "There is something bad in those woods."

As the Misfits started scrambling onto the dragons, a low, rumbling, chanting sound rolled through the woods and began to grow louder and louder.

"Dryads," Gladdy whispered. Then she yelled, "Get us out of here."

Creatures began emerging from the woods in various shapes and sizes. Then they changed into different colored dryads. They stared at the Misfits with malice in their eyes. The dragons unfolded their wings, preparing to jump into the sky when the dryads began screaming and running towards the dragons. Some of them leaped onto the dragons with great agility. The Misfits fought the dryads, hitting and kicking at them. Elsfur slashed with his sword, striking at the ones that were attacking him. Haylee managed to get off the ground, but Flipsy was having a harder time. The dryads were swarming him. Haylee hovered close to Flipsy. She concentrated with all of her might and breathed in a large gulp of air. As she felt the nerves in her stomach and imagined poor King Granite's tail on fire, she could feel the heat in her belly boiling like a volcano. She smiled and let out a huge spurt of fire, scorching a lot of the dryads, forcing them to retreat. This gave Flipsy the space he needed to get off the ground. Soon both of the dragons were flying again. Gladdy leaned over Haylee's shoulder so she could see what was happening below. Many of the dryads were running after the dragons. As they ran around the lake, they turned into various animals such as horses, deer and large cats so they could run faster. Gladdy watched them until they finally disappeared from view.

"How on earth did they know where we were?" Gladdy said, sitting up and breathing a sigh of relief.

"Who knows," said Elsfur, yelling over the wind. "They could have been tipped off by Theodius the minute we escaped, or they could have been residing in that forest, then recognized who we were and attacked us. Either way, they know where we are going. It's just a matter of who gets there first. I think we will have the advantage though, because dragons are the fastest creatures in this world."

"Flipsy and I will beat them to the Dark Lands," Haylee beamed. "I just know we will."

Flipsy looked at Haylee and just shook his head. His scabbed-over wounds were hurting him and he was feeling very tired, but he was determined not to let the others know.

As they flew, Haylee filled the others in about the plague, what was happening with the elves in the Land of Chaldeon and about the two different devices that King Silverthorne gave to Shimmer to help find the jewel of the races and to keep them safe when they traveled through the Dark Lands. She also told them about Thane and Hannah helping to retrieve Andy.

The epidemic was what concerned Gladdy the most and how fast that it had spread. What if Andy had contracted the plague? Her heart went out to him. She had always been there for him when he had been sick. She only hoped that Queen Estonia had kept all that was in her castle safe. She willed the dragons to fly faster. She knew that she shouldn't think bad thoughts. She must keep a more positive attitude for Andy's sake. So she willed her spirit to brighten and her heart soared right along with the dragons as she thought about seeing Andy again. If he were sick she would make him better. *Soon*, she told herself. *I will see him soon.*

MARCELLA THE SHEELY

Shimmer clung to Flopsy and shivered from the cold air. Her stomach had major butterflies from the rising and falling of the dragon. She ached from being on Flopsy for so long, and her stomach felt like her throat had been cut as it growled in protest from hunger. It had taken a lot longer than Shimmer had thought it would to reach the Dark Lands. Hours upon hours of flying on the dragon's back, over some pretty rough terrain.

The Shadow People had been a gruesome sight. Shimmer grimaced as she recalled the thousands of Shadow People practically crawling over one another to get through the barrier that separated them from the elves. She hoped the elves would be safe and that she and the others would be able to find the jewel and stop this terrible plague that was infecting the Shadow People.

"We're almost to the Dark Lands," Grandmother Muckernut yelled. "I can see the castle in the distance."

Shimmer looked to where Grandmother Muckernut pointed. The castle of the Dark Lands loomed ominously before them. The small town that surrounded the castle stood empty and looked so forlorn. Shimmer stiffened at the thought of Andy having to stay in such a horrible place for so long. Had he given up the hope of being rescued?

The evening sky darkened and little light was left for them to see by. Flopsy and Hannah descended to just over the tops of the trees. Shimmer could see the Golden River below them, slithering like a black snake in the dimness of the night. She could see that the roof of the castle was unguarded. She signaled for Thane to land Hannah on the roof of the castle and told Flopsy to do the same.

"Marcella the Sheely," Shimmer said to everyone after they had landed. "I think I should go and talk to her. Maybe she has seen something new."

"I don't know about that, Shimmer," Grandmother Muckernut said slowly. "She can be pretty tricky. Especially if she's still stirred up about the goblins."

"Marcella the Sheely is in the Dark Lands?" Thane asked.

"Yes. Elsfur said he had talked to a farmer who was friends with Marcella the Sheely. She is the one that said the Shadow Man had Andy on the horse with him."

They gazed down at the river shining in the pale moonlight.

"How come there aren't any guards on the roof?" Thane asked nervously. "You would think there would be at least one guard."

"Maybe every one of them has the epidemic by now," Daisy said, coming out from Shimmer's pocket. "That might mean that Andy is infected by now as well."

"We mustn't think that way, Daisy," said Grandmother Muckernut. "We can't start panicking. It will only get us captured or dead, and I for one don't want either one."

"Well, what are we going to do? We can't stay up here all night," Shimmer said impatiently.

"I'll go," Daisy said to the group. "I'll just fly down and have a conversation with her."

Before anyone could protest, Daisy took off flying toward the Golden River. Even flowing in the Dark Lands, the Golden River was a sight to see. It originated in the Dalley Mines, where the dwarves quarried for their gold. The dwarves would throw away bucketfuls of the precious metal when it was found to have impurities, thus causing the river to turn gold.

Daisy flitted quickly along to the river's edge, slowing as she neared one of the bridges. She could see the drainpipe shining in the moonlight. Heaps of little animal bones littered the water's edge underneath the pipe. Seeing the bones made Daisy think twice before approaching. Then she got an idea. If she used some of the invisibility dust that she kept in her pocket for emergencies, maybe Marcella wouldn't be able to catch her. She had started keeping invisibility dust with her at all times, ever since she had accompanied Gladdy and Grandmother Muckernut to Hemlock Forest. Gladdy had said that it was just for a precaution and that you never knew when the stuff would come in handy. Daisy smiled as she remembered Gladdy giving her the little pouch, and wished she were here now.

She took the little pouch out of the pocket of her purple flower petal dress and opened the drawstrings. She took a pinch and sprinkled it over the top of her head. She giggled a little when she thought of Andy. He had used the invisibility dust while they had been together in Filligrim Castle. She laughed as she remembered him being just a pair of floating eyeballs. But just as fast as that memory came, another one took its place. She remembered why she was here. She had to find out what had happened to her beloved master and prince.

Cautiously she flew toward the opening of the pipe. It was pitch black inside. She stopped when she heard raspy breathing.

"Who approaches my home?" An old ragged voice asked. "I can smell you, but I can't see you. Why?"

"My n—name is Daisy Misfit. I am from Filligrim C—Castle," Daisy shivered, nervously. "I—I have to speak to you a—about my f—friend that is being held captive in this c—castle."

"Why are you speaking so funny? I'm not going to hurt you. Where are you?"

"I'm a little cold," Daisy fibbed. She was embarrassed that her voice was shaking so badly. She also avoided answering where she was. She didn't want to risk being caught by the Sheely.

"I don't think that is the reason," cackled Marcella. "You're afraid of me, aren't you?"

"Yes, I am a little," Daisy admitted, a little more bravely than she felt. "Who wouldn't be, when there's a pile of bones under my feet? Can you help me? Your friend, the farmer, told a friend of mine that you saw the Shadow Man ride across the bridge one night with a boy across his saddle. Do you remember?"

"I remember, fairy. I'm not dumb!" Marcella hissed. "And as for those bones, I have to eat. However, I don't eat pixies. Do you think I want to be cursed? Even I know that eating a pixie or a fairy will bring repercussions on my life.

Daisy agreed with the Sheely in her mind. Killing a pixie or a fairy was a very dangerous business. The Fairy Godmother always knew when a pixie or fairy died, and usually how it died. If a pixie or fairy were murdered, the person who committed the murder would suffer a terrible death at the hand of the Fairy Godmother.

"Tell me again why you are here," Marcella said, her breath rattling. As she spoke, Marcella moved closer to the end of the drainpipe. Daisy could see her cold eyes and slimy, long seaweed-textured hair that outlined Marcella's glistening features. "And this time, try to control your speech."

"A friend of mine," Daisy said, exhaling slowly, "is being held captive by Queen Estonia, up at Charlock Castle. Have you heard anything about him? His name is Prince Andrew."

"Ahhh," Marcella said. Her voice bubbled as if she were speaking underwater. "You are speaking about the young man that Saber brought back to the castle. He is alive. He shares a cell with a wizard."

"Wizard? What wizard?" Daisy asked.

"Theodius, the wizard from Filligrim Castle."

"Theodius is alive?" Daisy said, not believing what she was hearing. "We were told that he was dead."

"Sounds to me as if someone lied to you," said Marcella, as she inched her way forward.

Daisy floated there, stunned. Her head was filled with questions, and she didn't know what to ask next.

"Do you know what started the sickness that is infecting all of the Shadow People?" Daisy asked, finally deciding on her next question.

"Nasty, nasty," Marcella cackled.

"What is?"

"The epidemic that the farmer started. His farm is by the river, close to River Birch Forest. He is a friend of mine named Morgan. I saw him the day he came into town. He had green streaks and pustules covering his skin." She began laughing. "He could have been my twin brother."

"That's nice," Daisy said, getting impatient. "What happened to Morgan?"

"Morgan collapsed into the butcher's arms, and

that is how the epidemic started. It was like an avalanche of rocks tumbling down a hillside. First the butcher, then one after another of the town's people fell to the ground. When they got up, they would be covered with the same nasty stuff that covered Morgan. After he saw what was happening to all of the Shadow People, he ran back toward the way he had come. I assume he ran home."

Her voice fell as she finished her sentence and Daisy couldn't tell if Marcella was sad about this fact or not.

"That sounds bad."

"Yes, I guess. There was one thing different about him than all of the other Shadow People. He was still himself. The others weren't."

"What do you mean?" Daisy asked.

"He just acted like he was a sick Shadow Person covered in icky green stuff. As if he just had the flu. But the others acted crazy, like they weren't human anymore."

When Marcella finished saying this, Daisy could see the leer on Marcella's face, as if she enjoyed what had happened to the Shadow People.

"You say he ran back home."

"He ran in that direction." Marcella was in full view now and Daisy could see her pointing west.

"Do you know if anyone in the castle has been infected by the epidemic?" Daisy asked.

"I haven't seen anyone from the castle. I believe they have locked themselves away from anyone in the Dark Lands, so they would be safe from the outbreak."

"I just hope you're right," Daisy said, with

hope filling her heart. "Thank you for your time, Marcella the Sheely. If there is any way I can return the favor, just ask."

Daisy was about to turn and fly away when Marcella stopped her.

"There is one thing you can do for me," she said.

"What would that be?" Daisy replied, her heart skipping a few beats as she turned back to the Sheely.

"I want to return to the Crystal Sea, the home of my birth."

"The Crystal Sea! Do you know how long it would take us to get to the Crystal Sea from here!" Daisy shouted.

"It's what I request," growled Marcella. "If you didn't really mean to help me, then you shouldn't have said you would."

"You're right," Daisy said. "I apologize. I can't help you right at this moment, but I will help you when my friends and I rescue Prince Andrew and rid this land of the plague."

"How long will that take?" Marcella moaned.

"However long it takes," Daisy said. She was growing tired of the conversation.

"Promise me that you will come back for me." There was harshness in her words that didn't tread too lightly on Daisy's heart.

"I promise," Daisy said, through gritted teeth.

"Fine. I will be expecting you and your friends as soon as this mess is over. Don't forget, pixie, or tragedy will befall you and there is nothing your precious Fairy Godmother can do. So I suggest that you don't break your promise."

Daisy swallowed hard. She knew if she went back on her promise that Marcella would be justified in Daisy's death.

As she flew out of the river toward the castle, she chided herself for opening her big mouth and promising something that she shouldn't have to Marcella the Sheely. Daisy didn't know how or when she would be able to fulfill the promise.

LADY APRICOT REVEALED

D aisy found all of her friends still on the roof of Charlock Castle, looking expectant and anxious. She smiled and they all relaxed.

"Well," Thane said. "What did you find out?" Out of all of them, he was the most tense. He didn't like being up on the roof for so long and he wished he could hurry the others to make a decision on what they were going to do.

Daisy explained everything that Marcella had told her. The group was elated to find out that Theodius was still alive, especially Grandmother Muckernut. "Oh, thank goodness," she said, breathing a sigh of relief. "Gladdy will be so happy and relieved to hear that."

"I know she will," Daisy said.

"I can't believe that it was my friend Morgan who started this whole plague mess," said Thane. "I wonder what happened to him. I wonder if he is okay."

"Marcella didn't know, only that he ran off back toward his home," Daisy said. She could see that Thane was very worried about his shadow friend. She tried to change the subject. "Now, what is our plan?"

The plan that Shimmer, Grandmother Muckernut, and Thane came up with while Daisy had been talking to Marcella the Sheely, was to circle the castle and see if there was a point in which they could let Shimmer off. Grandmother Muckernut and Daisy would be in Shimmer's pocket. Shimmer would enter the castle, find Andy and hopefully not get caught.

Lights from the castle began to creep on, as someone went from room to room lighting lanterns. The group circled once and then found a room with a balcony. The door was open and from her vantage point, Shimmer could see that it was empty.

"Let me down here, Flopsy. I'll go through that door. If I'm not back in one hour or less, you'll know that I have been captured."

Flopsy agreed and dropped Shimmer onto the balcony. Then he, Hannah and Thane flew off to find a tree in which they could perch and watch the castle.

Shimmer took Daisy and Grandmother Muckernut out of her pocket and watched as

Grandmother Muckernut transformed into her dryad form and Daisy flew up into the air. All three looked around at the deserted room. It was decorated plainly with only a small bed, a table and chair.

"We must be in the servants' quarters of the castle," Shimmer whispered. "Let's find the stairs. Then we can go down to the dungeon."

"Lead on," said Grandmother Muckernut. "But I had better change into something small so I won't be noticed.

As Grandmother Muckernut changed into a mouse, Shimmer tiptoed over to the door and opened it a crack so that she and the others could get out. Then she bent over and ran her hand the length of her body, changing into a blue mist as she went.

"Let's go," she droned.

The three of them slipped through the cracked door and down a long, dimly lit hallway. Not a sound could be heard in the castle and this worried Shimmer. What if Andy and everyone else in the castle had come in contact with the plague? After walking for a few minutes and exploring some of the rooms, they found a staircase behind a wooden door and decided to investigate. The stairs led down to two other doors. One of the doors opened into a long dark hallway that looked as if it hadn't been used in years, and the other opened to another set of stairs. Above the door was a sign that read: THE DUNGEON. It was in fancy handwriting, like a woman had written it.

"That was easy," Daisy snickered.

"Yeah, I hope everything else goes this fast," said Shimmer, materializing into her solid self. She stood in front of the door with her hand on the doorknob, as though she was debating about something. "Okay," she finally said. "We don't know if there will be guards, or other ways to get out of the dungeon, so we will need to be extra cautious while we are down there. I think I will turn into my misty self, instead of going in as a solid form. Daisy, I want you to hover as close to the ceiling as possible. Grandmother Muckernut," Shimmer looked down at the mouse, "maybe you should turn into a small fly. That way you can stay with Daisy."

"That sounds good to me," Grandmother Muckernut squeaked.

They descended the stone stairs cautiously. The corridor was dimly lit with flame torches. Steel doors lined the stone hallway that attached to the bottom of the stairs. Each door had a very small opening about the size of Shimmer's fist. She tried peeking into each opening as they passed door after door. In several of the poorly lit prison cells were Shadow People. They were a little unnerving to look at. Most of them were so dark you couldn't even tell that they were human. *Maybe they weren't human anymore*, Shimmer thought. The last cell they came to, before the hallway turned a corner, scared all three of them very badly. Inside the cell was a gargoyle. It was lying on its side and drool was dripping out of its mouth. Even in its unconscious condition it made Shimmer shiver just looking at the ugly creature. The smell from the creature burned her eyes and nose.

"Why on earth would they have a gargoyle locked up in this castle?" Daisy whispered. "And what's wrong with it?"

"It looks as though they have it drugged, which is a good thing for us," Shimmer droned. "If he weren't drugged, he would have already come through that door and killed us. Let's keep moving. He makes me nervous."

They turned the corner and looked in every cell until they came to the end of the hallway. Andy was nowhere to be found. The last cell door in the hall was open slightly and Daisy flew in. There were two beds and an old wooden table with a lamp on it. On one of the beds was a bloodstained shirt lying on some dirty bed sheets. Daisy's heart started beating faster.

"Shimmer, come in here," Daisy called out. Shimmer floated into the room and stopped beside the bed. Daisy pointed at the shirt. "That's Andy's shirt!"

"Are you sure? Oh my gosh, it *is* his shirt!" Shimmer exclaimed in surprise, turning back into her solid body. She leaned over and picked up the bloody shirt and then stuffed it into the pocket of her robes. "We'll take this with us. Maybe they have taken Andy to the main part of the castle for some reason. Let's head up that way and see what we can find."

"We need to keep an eye on the time," said Daisy. "I don't want Thane and the dragons to think we've been captured. They might storm the castle and then we really would be in trouble."

"Yes," Shimmer said, sighing and staring at the bed. She ran her fingers over the blanket and then turned toward the door. "We better hurry."

Down a short hall from what they assumed to be Andy's cell was a small flight of stairs. Shimmer opened the door and found that they were on the main floor of the castle not far from the steps that led to the upper floors. Shimmer hesitated when she heard voices. Someone was coming down the stairs. She peeked her head out a little farther to see who it was. Her insides turned to jelly. There was Andy only a few feet from her! He was standing with some girl. As the girl spoke Shimmer realized that she had heard the girl's voice before, but where?

"I had a really good time today," Shimmer heard Andy saying. "Dinner was awesome. Queen Estonia has a wonderful cook. I've got great plans for tomorrow."

She had to get his attention. She eased the door shut and turned back to Grandmother Muckernut and Daisy.

"Andy is right outside the door," Shimmer whispered excitedly. "But he is with some girl. We need to get his attention and get him away from her. Grandmother Muckernut, can you fly out and buzz in his ear? Tell him that we are here."

"You bet I can," Grandmother Muckernut buzzed in her little bug voice. Shimmer opened the door just a crack and Grandmother Muckernut zoomed out, flying towards Andy. She was almost to Andy when she heard a familiar voice. She searched for the source and then realized it was coming from the girl that was standing in front of Andy. Grandmother Muckernut flew past Andy and landed on the banister of the stairs. She stared at the girl. Grandmother Muckernut couldn't move because she was in shock.

"See you in the morning, Andy," Jennifer said, leaning forward. She tried to kiss Andy on the lips, but at the last moment Andy turned his head and the kiss landed on his cheek.

"See you in the morning, Jennifer," Andy replied as he turned and trotted up the stairs.

Grandmother Muckernut watched as the girl called Jennifer whirled around and walked off. As she walked away, the tips of her hair turned a bright orange color.

Lady Apricot!" Grandmother Muckernut buzzed. "I knew it was her! I have to warn Andy."

She flew up the stairs and followed Andy down a hallway and into a bedroom, lighting on a wall next to the bed.

"Theodius," she heard Andy say. Her heart filled with a mixture of joy and sadness as she observed the old man to whom Andy was speaking. Theodius had aged so much as a result of being a prisoner, that if Andy hadn't spoken his name, Grandmother Muckernut would not have known who he was. Even Andy didn't look the same. Not only had his face features matured, he was darker, as though there was a shadow covering his skin.

"We'll wait for a few hours and then go down to the library. We have to make sure everyone is asleep, so we won't be caught escaping."

Grandmother Muckernut's antennae perked up

at this information. She knew she needed to reveal herself now and tell them about the rescue party. She transformed. Andy jumped when he turned around and found Grandmother Muckernut standing there.

"Awww…" he yelled, before he could stop himself. "Grandmother Muckernut, you're here!"

"Shh…" she shushed, holding up a finger to her lips. "Be quiet or someone will hear you."

He ran to her and embraced her as he would if it had been Gladdy standing there. Tears filled his eyes as he admired her beautiful face. Her brightness and color stood out in the drab, colorless room.

"Have you come to rescue us?" he asked breathlessly.

"Yes, Andy, I have," she said, embracing him again. "We have been so worried about you." She looked at Theodius. "Theodius," she said as she went over to hug him as well.

"Did you bring anyone with you?" Andy asked, as hope filled his heart. What he really meant was, *Did you bring Shimmer with you?*

"Yes. Also Thane, King Silverthorne's nephew, along with Daisy and Shimmer."

"Thane?" Theodius said. "You mean Gladdy's brother is here with you?"

"Yes, he is," said Grandmother Muckernut. "I have to tell you something before I go and get Daisy and Shimmer. The girl that you were with just a while ago…" she started to say to Andy.

"You mean Jennifer?"

"Yes. That is really Lady Apricot in disguise."

"Lady Apricot? You mean the dryad that was in the forest when I first met you?"

"Yes. I'm guessing that Saber brought her here right after the battle."

"Saber? You know his name? But how?" Andy asked, bewildered.

"Saber is the Shadow Man, but he is also the person who has been posing as Theodius."

"I was right, Theodius!" Andy said, grinning. "If Lady Apricot is here and we know where the Shadow Man is, where is Prince Mosaic?"

"At last reports he had taken Kwagar to Hamamelis Prison in the Dingy Mountains."

"Is anyone trying to rescue Kwagar?" Theodius asked.

"No," said Grandmother Muckernut sadly. "They have posted gargoyles around the prison."

"Ah," Theodius said.

"What do you mean, 'Ah'?" Andy said, his voice rising. "He is just as important as I am. You should have gone there first."

"Andy, you need to calm down. Gargoyles are horrible creatures with poison-tipped fangs and talons. They can smell a creature a mile away. There is no way to get close to the prison without dying. We'll figure out how to rescue Kwagar. It's just going to take a bit of planning."

Andy thought about this for a moment. Kwagar must have been captured by the goblins when Flipsy took off and left Kwagar on the cart, on Phantom Road, during the battle. His heart hurt for his brother.

"There are a few more things we need to

discuss. But first we need to get you and Theodius out of this castle," said Grandmother Muckernut soothingly. "I will go and retrieve Shimmer and Daisy."

They watched as Grandmother Muckernut turned back into a fly. Andy opened the door just a crack for her and she flew out to find Shimmer and Daisy.

RUNNING OUT OF TIME

As Lady Apricot sat down on the bed, her dryad form reappeared. It was very draining to remain human-like for so long. She lay back on her pillows and felt a weird sensation go through her, a prickling of the hairs on the back of her neck. Something was going on, but she just couldn't put her finger on it. Rolling over, she opened her bedside table drawer, and got out her handheld mirror. She looked at the image peering back at her. A bright red fairy with dim, glowing wings cowered at the sight of Lady Apricot. The fairy's stunning face wore an expression of sadness. She was wearing manacles on her wrists.

"Slave, find out where Blueberry is. I want to speak with her."

"Yes, your ladyship." The fairy curtsied and then flew away.

The mirror went blank for a moment and then a dryad with cobalt blue hair and eyes to match, filled the frame.

"Lady Apricot, how are you this evening?" Blueberry said, with a sneer that, more often than not, accompanied her features.

Apricot rubbed her temples. "What news do you have for me?"

"Wonderful news actually," Blueberry said, smiling. "The Misfits at Filligrim Castle have escaped. We ambushed them as they landed at a nearby lake. We would have recaptured them; however, they have two dragons with them. The smaller dragon blew fire over some of the dryads, wounding some and killing others. The Misfits are now flying toward the Dark Lands. Most of my dryad army is in heavy pursuit."

Apricot sat up abruptly. "Really," she said, enthusiastically. "That is splendid news. I will be held in high esteem by Saber for recapturing them here in the Dark Lands. I will have Pinecone ready the troops. Thank you for making my day."

"You're most welcome, Lady Apricot," Blueberry said, her sneer becoming even more pronounced.

The mirror went blank. Apricot blew on it and another dryad appeared.

"Lady Apricot," said Pinecone, bowing her head slightly. She had short, choppy, dark green hair that stuck out all over her head, as if she had pine needles for hair. Her almond-shaped eyes were a murky jade green.

"We will be having company, Pinecone. Make sure everyone is ready," Apricot's voice was slick as oil. "I don't want any Misfits getting away. I want the Shadow Man to be pleased with me, is that clear?"

"Yes, your ladyship."

"The Misfits are coming here riding two dragons. That shouldn't be too hard for you to miss. It will be fairly easy to recapture them. You haven't seen any dragons yet, have you?"

"As a matter of fact I saw two dragons just a while ago. They lighted on top of the castle and then flew away to another part of the forest. I couldn't tell if they had anyone with them. It was too far off."

"What!" shouted Apricot, as she jumped off the bed. "How long were they on the castle?"

"About fifteen minutes, I would say."

"Why didn't you contact me?" Apricot hissed. "They could be in the castle trying to steal Prince Andrew away as we speak. Get up here and bring a few dryads with you!"

Apricot hurled the mirror onto the bed and ran for the door. Throwing it open wide, she ran wildly down the hallway toward the stairs. She had to stop them from taking Andy out of the castle.

৯৽৽৻

Shimmer flew into Andy's arms and bear-hugged him, then reluctantly let him go. Andy smiled at her and then at Daisy. It was so good to see them again. Shimmer was just as beautiful as ever and she truly acted like she had missed him as much as he had missed her.

"We were worried that you might have been infected by the epidemic," said Daisy. "Apparently everyone in the Dark Lands has been contaminated."

"Queen Estonia sealed the castle the moment she found out about the epidemic, and allowed no one in or out."

"We have to get out of here, meet up with the dragons and Thane, and find the jewel. King Silverthorne said that the jewel might be the source of the epidemic."

"The jewel?" Andy said. He stood there for a moment. He hadn't thought about the jewel in such a long time. His memory was becoming clearer. He had buried the jewel along with his birdcage necklace, just before Saber had taken him. Relief filled him. He hadn't told Saber where the necklaces were. He had resisted the torture and kept the secret to himself.

"Yes, the Jewel of the Races," Daisy replied.

"I know where the jewel is," Andy said, smiling.

"You do!" everyone said in unison.

Andy told them of how he had fought with the goblin *Lock* and how just before the goblin fell from Flipsy's back, Andy had snatched the pouch with the jewel in it from its neck. He described how he wandered the Dark Lands and found the river, and how he buried the two necklaces to keep them safe, by a large tree near the river, just before the

Shadow Man seized him. "But you can't walk on the Dark Lands without it harming you, if you have come with bad intentions. The Dark Lands are infected with Queen Estonia's magic."

"We know all about that," Shimmer said. "King Silverthorne gave us an artifact that will help us travel in the Dark Lands safely."

"Great," said Andy. "How do we get out of here?"

"I'll fly to the dragons and bring them back," said Daisy. She flew up to Andy and placed her little hands on his face and looked his face over, as if trying to memorize it. She had been so worried about him. But now, everything was going to be just fine. She beamed with satisfaction as she pecked him on the cheek with her tiny lips. "I'll be right back. Don't you move."

"I'll be here," Andy said.

They all watched her fly out of the window and into the darkness.

ຈ໌ຈ

Lady Apricot felt as though a dragon had just given her a horde of treasure as she listened to the conversation behind a door in a secret passageway that led to Andy's room. Saber had chosen the room so that Apricot would be able to keep tabs on him. Apricot's insides were jumping for joy. She would be able to give the jewel to Saber and recapture all of the Misfits, all in one night. Then Saber would release her and she would be free to take her place as leader of all dryads in Hemlock

Forest. However, she needed to get to that jewel first. Everything would depend on how well she played her cards. She turned and tiptoed away from the door down to the entryway to wait on Pinecone and the other dryads. As she waited she heard footsteps on the landing and peeked to see who was there. Queen Estonia was walking toward Andy's room. This was going to ruin everything. She had to do something about Queen Estonia. Then a plan began to form in her mind.

Just then the door to the hidden passageway opened up and Pinecone and several other dryads stepped through.

"Follow me," Apricot mouthed quietly. She motioned with her hand toward the top of the stairs.

⮞⮜

"King Silverthorne said there was a way to rid the Dark Lands of the epidemic," Shimmer said.

"How are we supposed to do that?" Theodius said. He had been very quiet up to this point, taking in every word the Misfits had been saying.

"We will have to find the Jewel of the Races and destroy it."

"How can you destroy a jewel with such an immense power?" Andy asked.

"By killing me," Queen Estonia said, coming through the door. "That is what you had planned, isn't it? Did that fool of a king Silverthorne send you to my castle to destroy me?"

Grandmother Muckernut stepped toward Queen Estonia. Her tall, sinewy frame looked impressive next to the queen. She knew the answer would infuriate the queen, but she would be ready for anything Queen Estonia threw her way. "Yes, King Silverthorne said it was the only way to cure your people from the affliction they are suffering from. No one wants to end their life, but if it helps others to live...."

"Has anyone ever helped me?" Queen Estonia said with bitterness. She stepped forward and stood face to face with Grandmother Muckernut. "My life has been cut short already. I have no life other than the prison we stand in right now. I have never felt the delight of marrying someone; never felt the happiness of having my own children. *Forever* stuck in a shadowy world of darkness and sorrow. Do you know how that feels?"

Everyone stared at Queen Estonia. She walked over to Andy and looked into his eyes. "For the first time in a long time, life was starting to bloom with color within my very soul. Andy is the reason for that." Her voice quivered and black tears ran down her face. She faded for a moment, but became lighter as she spoke again. "A light kindled within my black heart, making it warm as sunshine. I could see a future with Andy as my son, standing by my side as we ruled together in this kingdom." She turned and looked at Grandmother Muckernut and Shimmer. "Now, you have come and messed everything up for me. You were going to take away any happiness I might have enjoyed. However, I can't allow—"

"Aunt Estonia," Andy said, cutting her off. "Please don't hurt anyone here. Let them go and I will stay with you and rule the kingdom just as you planned. Just please don't hurt anyone. Remember your father and the soldiers and how you felt when you hurt them. Try to control your emotions."

"There is not a day in my life that I don't think about my father or those soldiers that I murdered. Each thought rips my heart right out of my chest, to the point of suffocation...." Her words softened as she looked at Andy again. "You listened to me, Andy, without judging me. Being able to confide in someone for the first time in my life about those tragic events has been very freeing."

"Then let them go," Andy pleaded. "Don't add to your memories. Not that way. Please!"

"Andy, I can't—" Queen Estonia walked briskly to the door. Andy thought she was going to run away so he stopped her by grabbing onto her arm. At the same moment Daisy, followed by Thane, crawled through the window, distracting everyone from what was going on in the room. No one noticed that Lady Apricot had stepped through the open door, grabbing Queen Estonia and sticking a knife to her throat, until they heard a little cry escape the queen's lips. Andy was forced to let go of his aunt. What he wouldn't give to have a sword at that moment.

"Well, well, well. What have we here, a family reunion? I was expecting different Misfits, but you will do," Apricot said, nastily. Pinecone and the other dryads burst through the door with their swords drawn. "So much information I have accumulated this evening. Thank you, Andy, for telling the whereabouts of the Jewel of the Races and the birdcage necklace. My master will be thrilled to have both in his possession. When he has the crown, he will become the ruler of all of Filligrim and I will have Hemlock Forest as he promised."

"You will have nothing," Andy said acrimoniously.

"Oh now, my little Lamby Toes. Is that any way to speak to me?"

Andy laughed, "Yes, I think you need to be brought down a little. You are starting to think too highly of yourself, Jennifer. Oh, I forgot. That is not who you really are, is it? You are second to Grandmother Muckernut, and that is all you will ever be. Never a first! Do you really think that Saber will let you rule your own kingdom? You are fooling yourself. Once the jewel is set in the crown, everyone will bow down to him, including you. Everyone will become his slave, and I mean *everyone*!"

Andy's last word hung heavily in the air.

"Not me," Lady Apricot said, shaking her head, but Andy's words had brought doubt, and it was showing in her eyes. "He told me I am his favorite and that I can have anything I want, if I found out where the jewel and crown were."

"Don't you get it!" Andy practically screamed. "He *won't* give you anything. He wants it all for himself. And I bet he will destroy you once he has it."

"Never!" Lady Apricot pulled the knife from Queen Estonia's throat, shoved it into her back, and then pushed her into Andy's arms. She smiled at them as they all moved for their swords.

"I wouldn't do that if I were you," she said as her dryads stood ready to fight. "Now, I will go and get the jewel, while you stay here and try to keep the good queen from dying. Goodbye, Andy. I once thought that you and I could have had something together. A marriage perhaps?"

"I would die, than have you for my queen," Andy said through clenched teeth.

"That won't be a problem."

Lady Apricot threw a small round ball to the floor. It erupted into a blinding flash of light, giving the dryads and Lady Apricot the perfect opportunity to flee. Once Andy recovered his vision, he struggled under the weight of his aunt to lay her on the floor. Black blood poured from her wound and also from the corner of her mouth. Shimmer ran to the bathroom and retrieved some towels.

"Let's get her to the bed," said Thane. "Then we can examine the wound."

He and Andy hoisted the queen onto the bed. Shimmer cut open the queen's garment. The wound was deep.

"If she dies before we get to the stone, all is lost," Shimmer said, looking at Andy.

"Andy," Queen Estonia said, weakly. "I'm sorry I was so selfish. Please forgive me."

"You don't worry about that right now."

"I didn't know...that was what Saber wanted, honestly," she sobbed. "You have to believe me."

"I do," Andy said, smoothing his aunt's hair and feeling the cold with each stroke. "You couldn't have known that he was after the Crown of the Races."

"Get to the stone before—before Lady Apricot gets there. I—I will do what you want me to do. I want to save my people from the epidemic. They have been so good to me. Just bring me the stone." Queen Estonia winced in pain. "I will try to keep the land from hurting you if I can."

"What about the dryads? Is there something you can do about them?" Andy asked desperately.

"No. I made a pact with Saber. The land won't hurt him or any of his friends. There is nothing I can do about it," the queen said, sadly.

"You just rest," said Shimmer. "King Silverthorne gave us a talisman that is supposed to keep us safe on your land."

Queen Estonia smiled weakly. "King Silverthorne is a fool. There is nothing that can stop the magic, except me. When you are fighting tonight, there mustn't be any magic performed by anyone, not from this land. I won't be able to stop what goes on if magic is used. Do you understand?" Andy nodded. She grabbed Andy's arm and looked desperately into his eyes. "Andy, go—go to my room. Find—find the silver powder in the chest by my bed. Take it down to the dungeon. There is a gargoyle locked in one of the cells. Blow—blow the powder into the gargoyle's face. Tell it that you are its master. Take it with you to help fight the dryads. But be careful what you tell it though…make sure you tell it not to kill—kill any of your friends." She released Andy, going limp.

"Go, and do what has to be done."

They all looked at one another with hope in their eyes. A gargoyle to help them fight was like having a whole army.

"We may need more, even with the gargoyle. Who knows how many other dryads are accompanying Apricot to the river. It could be a whole army," Grandmother Muckernut said.

"I will get Claude to stay with Aunt Estonia," Andy said, jumping to his feet. "You signal to the dragons that we are ready to leave. After I get Claude, I will run down to the dungeon and get us a gargoyle. Then we can be on our way. Surely we can get to the river by dragon a lot faster than they can on foot."

"You don't know how fast a dryad can run, do you?" Grandmother Muckernut mumbled, as Andy ran out the door and down the hall to retrieve Claude.

THE MOVING OF THE JEWELED TREE

King Foxglove leaped back as a Shadow Person with green skin and pustules covering its body ran forward and hit the barrier protecting River Birch Forest. The barrier shocked the Shadow Person, knocking him backward several feet onto the ground. The Shadow Person sat up, shook his head, and then stood up to try again. Hundreds of Shadow People were hitting the barrier that kept King Foxglove's kingdom from harm. They tested the blockade over and over again, trying to find weaknesses.

"Wow," said Shade. "They are persistent. Are you sure you want to leave our people just now? What if they are able to get in?"

"Our people can take care of themselves. Besides, if they do get in, I don't think they will be able to find the elves. Our hidden city is just that, hidden."

King Foxglove and Shade jogged back to where Kwagar was putting water, food and herbs into pouches that would be hung from their backs. Meadow was depositing shovels down the hole that Kwagar and Mucous had tunneled out of.

"Are we ready to go?" King Foxglove asked, as he picked up his bow and quiver and slung it over his shoulder.

"Yes we are," said Kwagar. "Did it look as if the barrier will keep out the Shadow People?"

"I'm sure it will hold just fine. Those creatures are very nasty. My advice to all of you if you see one in the Dark Lands is to get away as fast as you can. Don't try to fight them. They look very strong and I don't want to chance any of you contracting whatever they have. Apparently the elves don't fare very well. They go into a deep sleep and start to rot. So run, is that clear?"

All of them shook their heads in agreement and then Kwagar got down in the hole. He looked at the three elves and smiled. King Foxglove nodded his head for Kwagar to start. Kwagar picked up his water skin, took a long drink and then turned to face the wall of earth. He felt so good when he drank the water. It was like energy coming to life inside his gut, giving him strength. He held out his hand and let the power flow through him and out of his fingers. The earth moved with a tremendous force that nearly knocked the three elves down. Kwagar's power was gaining strength. He smiled just thinking of Mystic. She probably would have jumped for joy watching her grandson becoming a true Asrai.

King Foxglove, Shade and Meadow all looked at each other, shocked by what they were watching. The earth was moving even faster than they had anticipated. From the way the earth was moving, they wouldn't even need the shovels they had brought with them. King Foxglove checked his compass and directed Kwagar as he split the earth into a giant tunnel. He rounded it so perfectly that the elves didn't even have to walk hunched over. There was plenty of room for them all.

Even in a flat run above ground, it would take hours to get to the Dark Lands from where they were. Kwagar hoped that the short cut he was creating with the tunnel would cut off some time. They had to get to the Misfits and help them. He thought about Prince Mosaic and where he might be. Did he go to the Dark Lands to see the Shadow Man? Would he be one of the problems that they encountered when they got to the Dark Lands?

After a while Kwagar picked up a routine for tunneling through the ground. He would tunnel for a while, then drink and eat his herbs, rest and then start the whole process all over again.

"I sure hope Andy is okay," he said to King Foxglove as he was resting.

"Andy is a resourceful and brave kid. I bet he is doing just fine."

"I couldn't believe it when my mother told me I had a brother. I was so excited. I have always felt out of place in the castle and also a bit lonely. Always wishing for someone to play with...talk to."

"Now you have Andy. And when this is all

over, you and he can get to know each other better."

"I suppose so," Kwagar said thoughtfully. "I just hope we reach Andy and the rest of the Misfits in time. Who knows what is going on above ground right now." Kwagar yawned and stretched, then drank deeply from his water skin one last time. He got to his feet and looked at the wall in front of him and wondered how much farther he would have to carve the tunnel in order to come up in the Dark Lands.

As if reading his thoughts, Shade spoke, "Only a few more miles and then we will be in the Dark Lands. You have done very well, Prince of Filligrim."

Kwagar nodded at the elf and then held up his hand and closed his eyes, envisioning a perfect round tunnel. The power flowed through his arm once again, blasting through the earth and separating it into a round hole. When he and Mucous had been tunneling, after they had escaped, Kwagar needed Mucous to form and shape the tunnel. Now, it was as if his ability had taken on the goblin's ability as well. Moisture seeped into the earth, while flat stones rose up to shape and mold the earth into an ideal passageway that could be used for years to come.

About an hour later, Shade came and put his hand on Kwagar's shoulder.

"If you can make a hole large enough in the roof of the tunnel so I can get my head and shoulders through, I will see where we are. I believe we are close to our destination."

This was good news to Kwagar. He smiled as he worked. He even added stairs, so Shade didn't have to strain in reaching the hole to look out into the night.

Shade smiled at Kwagar as they inspected the steps. "Most impressive. Thank you for making it so convenient. I will check to see what is going on. Everyone will need to be very quiet."

Everyone watched as Shade climbed the stairs and poked his head through the small hole. He turned his body in a clock-wise motion, trying to observe the whole area, and then stopped suddenly. Shade stood there for a moment as if trying to make sense of what he was seeing. A sound like a hurt animal could be detected.

He jumped off the stairs and walked over to King Foxglove. Leaning in close he whispered, "There is a Shadow Person up there. He is lying on the ground, crying."

King Foxglove's brow wrinkled in thought.

"I'll go and have a look," he whispered. "You three stay here and be vigilant. I may need your assistance."

"My lord, I must protest!" Meadow said. "It should be me, not you, who goes up there. Who knows what you will encounter."

"I will be fine," King Foxglove said with finality. "Just be on your guard."

They watched as the king mounted the stairs and wiggled his body through the small hole. Kwagar could see stars dotting the night sky after the king disappeared. Shade and Meadow pulled their swords from their scabbards and stood ready.

Kwagar tried to read the elves' faces, but no sign of worry was there. Kwagar, on the other hand, was very nervous. He joined the elves and pulled out the blade that had been loaned to him by King Foxglove. The elf-made sword gleamed in the darkness. Just holding it made Kwagar feel a lot safer. A minute later, King Foxglove poked his head back through the hole and motioned for Kwagar and the elves to join him. Shade went first, followed by Meadow, then Kwagar.

The night air fanned across Kwagar's sweaty face. It felt wonderful to breathe the fresh air. It reminded him of when the Misfits had come out of the troll cave, just a few months before. Kwagar couldn't believe that it had been three months since they had traveled to the distant land to retrieve his brother and Gladdy, and he longed for that time again. Things were only a little out of control then. Now, the whole world seemed to be falling apart.

A sobbing man, curled up in a ball on the ground, brought Kwagar from his reminiscences. The man was a shadow man; only he had green skin with weeping sores covering his arms, hands and face. Kwagar stepped back in revulsion. He watched as King Foxglove leaned over the man, then reached out to touch him.

"Don't touch me!" the shadow man shouted. "Unless you want this curse."

"How did this happen?" King Foxglove asked.

Sitting up, the shadow man said, "I ate from a small tree deeper in the woods, by the river. The fruit looked so good, like beautiful jewels. But when I bit into it, I noticed that the flesh of the fruit was black inside. It sickened me and I threw the fruit away. Not long after, I began feeling bad and I passed out. When I came to, I was like this."

The shadow man fell back, howling with grief. The elves and Kwagar looked at one another uncomfortably.

"What is your name, son?" King Foxglove queried.

"I am Morgan," the man blubbered. "I went to town to see if I could get some help...I didn't know...."

"You didn't know what?"

"I didn't know that—that I would spread—that I was..." Morgan was making no sense to Kwagar. The man was full of such anguish that it brought tears to Kwagar's eyes.

"That you would spread the disease," King Foxglove finished.

"Yes."

"What kind of fruit would cause an epidemic this catastrophic?" Kwagar asked.

King Foxglove stood there staring up at the sky in thought, and then he said, "You are right, Brother." Kwagar looked at the king as though he was out of his mind, and then realized he was talking to King Silverthorne. Since they were brothers, they must be able to talk with one another through their minds. "We will seek out the tree and destroy it." He looked back down at Morgan, "Can you show us where the tree is?"

"I think I can. I tried to get back to it earlier, but I kept passing out. My horse and wagon are still near the tree, so if we find them, we will find the tree. My head is a little fuzzy, so bear with me."

They watched as Morgan got unsteadily to his feet. He swayed for a moment and Shade reached out to catch him. King Foxglove jumped at Shade just in time.

"Don't touch him," King Foxglove said. "Remember, it's deadly to us. We'll just have to let him take his time."

They walked for a long time. To Kwagar, it seemed as if Morgan didn't know where he was going. Several times they walked in a circle. Morgan would realize it was the wrong path and then start off in a new direction. The elves and Kwagar glanced at each other with looks of exasperation.

Once they had to climb a gigantic tree to avoid other infected Shadow People, leaving Morgan on the ground. Finally, after walking a couple of hours, Kwagar could hear the river nearby. As they neared the river, however, the elves' pace began to slow, as if they were walking in very deep mud. Kwagar hadn't noticed that the elves had slowed down. "What is going on?" Kwagar asked as he walked back to where they were standing.

"It's because the Dark Lands are tainted with Queen Estonia's magic," Morgan said. "If you have evil intentions, the Dark Lands will destroy you."

"But why isn't it affecting me? I can walk with no problem."

"Maybe it is because you are an Asrai," King Foxglove said. "The whole 'controlling nature' thing."

King Foxglove struggled, trying to move his

feet. His ears twitched as he heard the approaching sound of many feet walking through the forest. He looked around the forest. Their voices were not far off. They were speaking dryad language. He tried to stay calm. Thankfully they were hidden pretty well behind bushes. He peered through the darkness toward the river. There, glinting in the moonlight, was a small tree with sparkling golden fruit that looked like jewels. King Foxglove's heart began to pump frantically.

"Start digging, ladies," a dryad said, as they came near the spot where the little tree was planted. King Foxglove could understand every word they said, since he had spent time with dryads as a child. "Lady Apricot will be here any moment and I want to be able to hand the jewel over to her.

"Morgan," King Foxglove mouthed to the shadow man. "We have to keep those dryads from getting that stone."

"I can't help you," Morgan said sadly. "Besides, there is no stone, only a diseased tree that will make you wither away and die."

"Morgan, you have to help. The jewel must have been the seed for the tree. It must have grown out of it or something. If we have the stone, we might be able to cure you."

King Foxglove began staring at the sky in a trance-like state once again while everyone watched. "You're right, Brother." He looked at Morgan. "Take my hand, Morgan. If we're holding hands, maybe the land will think I'm part of you. I will be able to move."

"No, your majesty," Shade practically shouted.

"You will be infected."

"I have to get to that jewel before they do," King Foxglove said desperately. "It cannot fall into the hands of the dryads. That would be disastrous. They will hand it over to the Shadow Man and I won't let that happen."

"Let me do it, my lord," Meadow whispered. "I will give my life for you. If there is a cure, than you will find it and make me better. You know how to make potions better than anyone. Please, let Morgan take me."

"There will be no potion-making for this epidemic." King Foxglove sighed. "This disease will only be cured by the destruction of the jewel. If I can't do what it takes to destroy the stone, then you will be forever doomed. I am an elf lord. When I took my father's place, I vowed to never do evil, and killing the Shadow Queen in my book is doing evil."

"Taking Queen Estonia's life is not evil," whispered Kwagar. "If it cures thousands of lives and rids us of that cursed jewel, then that is what must be done."

"That is your opinion, Kwagar," said King Foxglove. "I just can't take a life, unless my life is in danger."

Kwagar looked toward the tree. Moonbeams fell through the trees, illuminating the golden fruit. It was beautiful even in the darkness of night. "I will go. Since I am able to move about, I can go after the jewel. And if you can't do what it takes to kill Queen Estonia, then I will do it for you. I can also inflict damage to the dryads."

"No," said Morgan. "You must do nothing to the dryads. The land will see you as a threat and kill you."

"Fine, I won't hurt anyone. Maybe I could tie them up in the roots of a tree." He stared a moment longer at the tree and then began smiling. "I have an idea. I am Asrai, after all. I will move the tree slowly and steadily, out of the way. They will never miss it. It's obvious that they don't know that the jewel is tied to the tree."

"That just might work, my lord," said Shade.

"Okay, you can try it," King Foxglove said. "But if they see what you are doing, you must lead them away from us. We won't be able to defend ourselves if we are discovered."

"I will do my best, don't you worry."

Kwagar nodded and then left, choosing a path leading to the other side of the jewel tree. He could only hope that if he were to be revealed, he would be able to lead the dryads deeper into the Dark Lands away from the elves and Morgan.

After he was situated behind a wide oak tree, Kwagar began reaching out, pretending that he had just lassoed the tree with a rope. Pulling on the lasso with his mind, the tree slowly began to move. Kwagar would stop about every six inches, waiting for a minute or so, making sure that no one had noticed the little traveling tree and then proceeded moving it. After about fifteen minutes the tree was hidden behind a dense bush. Kwagar made his way back around to where the elves and Morgan were.

"Good job," King Foxglove said. "Now we can wait until they leave and get the jewel."

"What if the sun rises before they leave?" Meadow asked. "They will be able to see us."

"Good thinking," said King Foxglove. "Kwagar, see if you can move us somewhere."

King Foxglove held out his hand and Kwagar took it. Kwagar started walking, but King Foxglove didn't move.

"Well, that didn't work. Is there any way you could carry us?"

"If I drink some of the water, I think I will be able to."

After Kwagar drank the water, he began the task of carrying his friends one at a time to a spot a little farther away, behind a small clump of trees and rocks, but where they could still see the bush where the little tree was hidden.

"If they spot us, I want you to run, Kwagar," said King Foxglove. "You are now a very valuable commodity and I would hate for you to fall into the hands of the enemy."

"They won't know that I'm an Asrai."

"I don't think it will take them long to figure it out. You're supposed to be in Hamamelis Prison. No one has ever escaped that prison."

Kwagar smiled with pride at King Foxglove and then they turned to watch as the dryads dug hole after hole. A while later, they heard the sound of many feet running in the woods. The elves and Kwagar drew their swords. A group of multi-colored dryads walked into the clearing. The dryads spread apart and then bowed their heads as an orange-colored dryad walked to the front of the group and toward the dryads that were digging. The dryads that were digging fell to their knees and bowed their heads as she approached.

"Lady Apricot," the lead dryad spoke. "We have yet to find the jewel, but we're working on it."

"Hurry! Those Misfits can't be far behind me and they have dragons."

The elves and Kwagar looked at one another.

"Dragons," they mouthed in unison.

THE STINKY GARGOYLE

Andy and Daisy approached the gargoyle cell with caution. Andy had been able to smell the gargoyle, even standing at the top of the stairs. Its musky scent reeked throughout the whole dungeon.

"He didn't smell as bad when Shimmer and I were here before. From what I've been told about the creatures, their musky scent is at its height when he is awake and smelling something that he would like to eat," Daisy whispered.

"Thank you for helping my nerves," Andy said, sarcastically. "Maybe I should let you go in there and blow the powder on him and I will stay here just in case."

"No way!"

"If he is awake, I sure hope that cell door holds him."

"I'm sure Queen Estonia has it reinforced by magic," said Daisy reassuringly.

"I hope you're right."

"Why don't you come and find out," growled a voice from behind the door. "You might make a good appetizer, before I break out and devour all of your friends upstairs."

Andy looked at Daisy in surprise. How did the gargoyle know about his friends? "I have something better," Andy said. "How would you like a dryad dinner? They look much tastier than we do. They come in all sorts of colors. You could pretend that you are eating popsicles."

"I like the smell of the pixie that is there with you," laughed the gargoyle. "Perhaps we could make a deal. I kill the dryads and you give me the pixie as a bonus."

"No deal," Andy said, horrified at the thought of the gargoyle eating his friend. "Besides, she is so small, she wouldn't even fill one corner of your belly."

"I love the taste of pixies. They are such a nice delicacy. Long ago, I would go to Toadstool Village and eat until I was full. Of course that was before the Fairy Godmother moved in and passed a law that beasts like myself could no longer go there. "

"Thank goodness. You're horrible!" Daisy shouted.

"I just like what I like. And I like pixies."

"Well, you're not getting pixie today. You're getting dryad." Andy was getting impatient. They had already spent too much time talking to the gargoyle. He nodded to Daisy. The plan had been for Andy to keep the creature busy so that Daisy could get into a position to blow the powder into the gargoyle's face. She made her move and flew above the small opening in the door, waiting for just the right moment.

Andy stepped forward and looked through the small window. There, looking back at him, were a pair of deep, blood-red eyes that made Andy's insides quiver. The monster was salivating as he looked back at Andy. Then the gargoyle grinned, exposing even more of the long tusks that hung from his mouth.

"Uh," Andy said, nervously. "You don't think you could move a little closer to the door, do you?"

The words were barely out of his mouth, when the gargoyle charged insanely at the door. Andy jumped back, trembling and then fell to the ground. Andy stared up in horror as the gargoyle pressed his face against the little window in the door. The gargoyle slid one hand with his razor sharp claws through the window and wrapped it around one of the bars.

"Is this close enough?" he said, as a deep rumbling laugh rose from his chest.

"Yes, it is," Daisy said, zooming directly in front of the gargoyle's face. She blew the silver powder right into the gargoyle's nose.

The gargoyle sneezed and started to roar with anger, pounding on the door and shaking the bars in the window. However, as Daisy and Andy watched, the gargoyle's eyes glazed over and he began to stare blankly. Andy got up and walked over to the door.

"Well, that was easy enough," Andy said.

"You haven't opened the door yet," Daisy said.

"That's true. Now listen to me," Andy said to the gargoyle. He tried to make his voice sound authoritative, but he was shaking so hard it wasn't working. "I need you to help us with a battle that we will be fighting with the dryads. You are only to harm the dryads and no one else. Is that clear?"

The gargoyle nodded.

"Also, when the battle is over, you are to stay with me. I may need you again. Do you understand?" Andy was feeling somewhat like a general.

The gargoyle's eyes slid into focus and looked at Andy. "Yes, that is clear. I wouldn't take the whole bossing me around thing for granted though. One day, I might just take your head off and use it for a sandwich."

Andy blinked.

"Well, let's get going, shall we?" Daisy said nervously, as she handed Andy the key to the cell door. Andy held the shaking key with both hands as he placed it in the lock. He stood there a moment and then gulped. He hoped his aunt was telling him the truth about that silver powder, or he was about to become a gargoyle's evening meal.

The door swung outward and Andy stepped back, giving the creature some room. The gargoyle hunched over his enormous gray frame so that he could fit through the door. One of the gargoyle's massive wings hung for a moment. The monster spread the wing out, pulled it though the door, and then collapsed it again. He looked menacingly at Andy.

"This way," Andy said, pointing a shaking finger toward the steps of the dungeon. Andy eyed Daisy as they followed the massive monster up the stairs.

When they got to the landing the gargoyle's smell increased. Andy covered his nose and mouth with his hand. Daisy did the same. Soon little tooting noises could be heard from the creature's backside.

"Ugh, could you cut that out, please?" Andy said in disgust. "We have to breathe here!"

"I can't help it," the gargoyle growled. "I smell something really appetizing. You have brought me a whole smorgasbord of food."

"Yeah, well, you will be able to sample only the food that's called dryad. Understand?"

"Oh, I understand plenty," the beast said.

When they got back to Theodius' room, Andy moved in front of the gargoyle.

"Okay, foul creature of the night. These folk won't take kindly to all the farting. They have to breathe too. So control your bodily functions. Okay?"

"I will try," the gargoyle grinned. "You wouldn't happen to want to give me your arm to chew on for a snack? I might behave better."

Andy looked at him in shock.

"Uh...no!"

Andy turned around and opened the door. Just as he walked in, the gargoyle pushed him to the floor and pounced on top of Grandmother

Muckernut, roaring triumphantly.

"Oh my gosh!" Andy screamed, jumping to his feet. "What are you doing?"

"I'm going to eat me a dryad," the gargoyle said, whipping his head around to look at Andy, his enormous pupils pulsing with elation.

"*Not her*!" Andy shouted. "*She is a friend*!"

"*What*?" he barked. "You said I could have dryad for dinner."

"I know. But she is my friend and you are not going to eat my friends! Is that clear," Andy said sternly. "Take note of every face in this room. They are *not* on the menu."

"Fine," the gargoyle grumbled, while getting off of Grandmother Muckernut.

Grandmother Muckernut got up with the help of Theodius and Shimmer, all of them looking horror-struck. Andy just shook his head and tried to calm his shaking arms.

"Boy," Andy laughed nervously. "When Aunt Estonia said to be careful about how I instructed this beast, she wasn't kidding. Are you okay, Grandmother Muckernut?"

"Well, I was almost gargoyle fodder," she said, examining her body. "But there is no damage done."

Really loud tooting could be heard coming from the gargoyle. They all looked at the gargoyle and then covered their noses.

"Oh, that's revolting!" said Shimmer as she ran for the door. Out in the hallway, still pinching her nose she said, "We better find the room where Flopsy dropped us off. Geez, we may not have to worry about fighting the dryads. His farting will kill us all before we get there."

࿎࿎

Even though they were in a hurry, the Misfits, elf and dragons took a few minutes to catch up with each other. The little reunion between Theodius and Thane gave everyone in the room high spirits. Thane shook Andy's hand vigorously. He was so excited to be meeting his sister's son. Andy admired Hannah's cool gothic look and thought she would be a big hit with all his friends back home. Saving Flopsy for last, Andy hugged his enormous neck as the huge dragon clung to the railing of the balcony. He could hear a deep, happy rumbling emanating from the dragon's chest. Tears of joy poured from the dragon's eyes, soaking Andy's head and back.

"I'm so glad to see you. I just knew you were alive," Flopsy said, as he perched with his hind legs on the balcony where Shimmer, Grandmother Muckernut and Daisy had first entered into the castle. "Flipsy will be so glad as well."

"I'm glad to see you also, Flopsy," Andy said, drying Flopsy's tears off his hair and face with his shirtsleeve.

"What about me?" Denny said, his reflection showing in the small handheld mirror.

"You as well," Andy said, beaming at Denny. Andy looked at Flopsy. "Did you see which way the dryads were running?"

"Off toward the plains. They can really run!"

"Yeah, we're a little worried about that," Andy said. "Do you think you can out-fly them?"

"I don't know," Flopsy said, doubtfully. "When I said they could run really fast, I mean *they could really run*. Also, they do have a head start."

"Well, let's get going then. We have a whole race to save and a dryad who needs to be done away with." Andy said these last words with venom rolling around each word. Shimmer retrieved swords from Flopsy's saddle and handed them to Theodius and Andy. She watched as they strapped them around their waists. Thane and Grandmother Muckernut got on Hannah, while Andy, Shimmer and Theodius got on Flopsy. Daisy stowed away in Shimmer's pocket. Flopsy was the first dragon to take off.

Sitting astride Flopsy, Andy looked back at the castle and watched as Hannah took off, followed by the gargoyle, which leaped powerfully into the air. As he flew, the gargoyle looked very impressive up in the night sky. His gray skin gleamed in the moonlight and his shadow looked intimidating on the ground below.

Andy smiled and thought, *We might just have a chance after all*. With two dragons, a gargoyle, an elf, a dryad, an Asrai Warrior, and a wizard, Andy was feeling more confident. Not to mention his Aunt Estonia keeping the land from destroying any of them.

Upon closer inspection of the gargoyle, Andy could see a vapor of heat following the creature's backside, much like you would see shimmering heat rising in the desert. Andy shook his head and laughed. *How could one creature have so much gas?* Andy thought.

The gargoyle flew really fast. He rocketed out ahead of them and stopped, hovering until the rest caught up with him. Then he began flying circles around them and loop de loops. All the while he was talking about how he had been a prisoner so long that he almost forgot how to fly. He zoomed so fast around them that in the dark the gargoyle's blood-red eyes reminded Andy of someone taking a burning stick out of a fire and writing in the air with it.

Then the gargoyle began singing. Everyone covered their ears and winced in pain.

"Will you please stop singing," Andy shouted.

The gargoyle stopped and looked at Andy. "Why? Don't you like my singing?"

"No. You sing like a piece of chalk scraping over a chalkboard. It's awful!"

"I will have you know that in my land I am a very good singer. Gargoyles come from miles around, just to hear me sing."

"I can't imagine that. They must be desperate creatures to listen to that caterwauling," retorted Hannah. "And it doesn't look like you have forgotten anything. You don't look very dignified or scary flying like that. All willy nilly."

"You know, the taste of dragon is beneath me. However, I would stoop to get rid of a pest like you."

Flopsy roared so loud that everyone covered his ears. He craned his neck and looked the gargoyle in the eyes. "Touch her and you will die at my claw, gargoyle! I will chew you up and spit you out."

Hannah side-glanced at Flopsy and smiled.

"Bring it on, fat boy," the gargoyle sneered.

Flopsy whirled around so fast that he almost lost his passengers.

"Okay, that's enough!" Andy said, holding on for dear life, while trying to stop a fight before it began. "Let's stop making so much noise, for one thing. And for another, you, Mr. Gargoyle, are only allowed to eat dryad. How many times do I have to say that?"

"As many times as it takes," he snarled.

"Then I'll remind you as much as it takes that I'm master over you now, and you will obey me."

"Or what?" The gargoyle's mouth watered staring at Andy, and drops of saliva dripped out of his mouth.

Andy gulped. He hadn't thought of what he would do to make the monster behave. He knew his Aunt Estonia probably always used magic on the beast.

"Or he'll have his two dragons make mince meat pie out of you," said Hannah, hotly.

"Why don't all of us make the rest of the flight in peace and quiet," said Theodius, bringing the conversation to a sudden close.

Everyone looked at him. Silence fell through the group for the rest of the short trip. Andy looked at Hannah gratefully for what she said. Pictures of the gargoyle trying to eat him came into his head. He was very glad at that moment that he had the dragons with him.

The gargoyle eyed everyone, and then flew a ways ahead of the group. They watched as he suddenly stopped and began hovering. He held his hand up and then pointed down, signaling for the group to land. When they were on the ground, the gargoyle motioned for them to follow him. He began sniffing the air, as if he smelled something really delicious. They had walked for half a mile when the gargoyle turned and looked at them with a triumphant smile on his face. He then pointed to a clump of trees not too far from where they were standing. Several dryads were digging with shovels, while others were watching. Andy could see Apricot.

The gargoyle sniffed again and his face contorted in confusion. Andy could see that something was wrong.

"What's the matter?" Andy whispered, looking up at the massive figure.

"I'm smelling elf and a human, with a touch of Asrai blood."

Andy looked at Thane. "Of course you are. Thane is an elf, I'm a human and Shimmer is right here, who just happens to be Asrai."

"No," the gargoyle grumbled softly. He held up one of his long, razor sharp talons and pointed in another direction, not far from where they were standing. The gargoyle's stomach rumbled with hunger. "It's coming from there."

Andy squinted in the dark. A beam of moonlight fell not far from where they stood, illuminating a small clump of trees and rocks. Andy could see an arm waving at them from behind one of the rocks. He grinned as Kwagar's head popped up just for a moment. They stared at each other and beamed. Kwagar's appearance shocked Andy. His brother was thin and ragged. Relief washed over Andy. His brother was safe!

Thunder rumbled above their heads, then lightning flashed across the sky, signaling the coming storm.

THE INVISIBLE TWINS

Gladdy's legs were feeling bowed from sitting on Haylee for such a long time. She just knew that when she got off, she would be walking like she had been sitting on a barrel for a year. How was she supposed to protect herself or anyone else in this condition? The dragons were no better off. They had been flying for hours without a break, trying to stay ahead of the dryads that were following them.

Gladdy looked back the way they had flown. In the distance she could see tiny dots of different creatures running toward the Dark Lands. If the dragons rested for even twenty minutes, the dryads would be upon them. Flipsy was looking bad. He had just gotten over the stabbings from the battle in the Black Mountains and now he had to fly hundreds of miles just to keep his friends safe from the evil that was following them.

Gladdy turned around and patted Haylee on the neck. She had been so impressed by the little dragon's spirit. The wind picked up and storm clouds threatened rain. Gladdy eyed the clouds uncomfortably. It was one thing to be on the ground when it was about to rain. It was a whole different story when you were thousands of feet off the ground, flying right under and sometimes through the clouds.

Suddenly, lightning cracked and startled Flipsy. He jumped and Timmynog fell, catching the thin membrane of Flipsy's wing.

The dragon roared. "You're pinching my wing. Let go!"

"Are you crazy?" Timmynog shouted. "I'll fall."

"I'll catch you. But you have to let go or all three of us are going to be in serious trouble. I can't flap my wing. Haylee, start descending."

Haylee swerved and flew under Flipsy in case Timmynog fell. They flew down trying to get closer to the ground.

"Haylee," yelled Gladdy over the wind. "You won't be able to hold us all if he falls."

"I have to try," Haylee said. She looked up at Timmynog and moved closer to him. Just then Timmynog lost his grip and hit Haylee in the neck, knocking all of them sideways. Gladdy managed to hold on, but Snollygob lost his seating and fell, followed by Timmynog. Gladdy screamed as she watched her friends plummet toward the earth. Timmynog reached out for Snollygob and pulled him to his chest as the earth rose up to meet them.

He looked back at Flipsy. The huge dragon caught Timmynog and Snollygob in his talons just feet above the ground. He back-peddled his wings and then gently set them on the earth. Gladdy and Elsfur dismounted Haylee and Flipsy, and ran to help their friends to their feet.

"I'm so glad you two are all right," Gladdy said, hugging both of them.

"You aren't the only one," Timmynog boomed. "Thank you, Flipsy."

"I'm just sorry this happened. I don't understand why I startled so. I have flown through clouds with lightning and thunder hundreds of times and never got scared," said Flipsy, shaking his head.

"I think it's because you are so tired," said Gladdy, patting Flipsy on his shoulder. "After all, you just got over the attack from the goblins. Also, you've just flown hundreds of miles without stopping."

"Speaking of hundreds of miles without stopping," Elsfur said, pointing toward the direction they had just come. The dryads were almost on top of them. They were all screaming a loud battle cry.

"That's not the only problem we have," Snollygob said. He was pointing in the opposite direction. Diseased Shadow People were running swiftly toward them as well.

"Oh my goodness," Haylee said. "We've got to get in the air."

"I can't," said Flipsy. He extended his wing and showed them the huge hole that had been burned in it as a result of the lightning. "I was so startled, I didn't realize that I had been hit."

"Haylee," Elsfur said. "Get Gladdy to safety, now!"

"No, I won't go!" Gladdy yelled. "You need what I can do."

She turned and looked in the direction of the Shadow People. She knew that if they got to the Misfits first, the Misfits were dead. The dark sickness would fall on the Misfits and they would never be able to rescue Andy. At least they had a chance fighting the dryads. She raised her hand and pointed at the Shadow People and yelled, "You will not touch us."

Wind began to blow, whipping Gladdy's hair and clothes. Her eyes turned solid black. Elsfur and the others jumped back away from Gladdy as energy began building in the air like static electricity. All around her were sparks of bright light. A green glow began to form at the tips of her fingers, in a round shape like a small ball. Finally, when it was as big as an apple and the Shadow People were close enough, the green light shot out of her extended hand, blasting the first wave of Shadow People. Most of the Shadow People, who were in the lead, fell and moved no more. Others that were behind them stumbled, falling only long enough for Gladdy to do what she had to do next. She looked to the sky. Her eyes changed to a deep purple color. She concentrated hard on the clouds, and then held up her other hand, pointing her index finger. A thin, purple-tinted wall of energy came down from the clouds to the earth, extending for miles in both directions. The wave of Shadow People broke upon the barrier, only to be shocked and knocked backwards. The rest of the Misfits drew their swords, worried that the barrier wouldn't hold for long. Gladdy collapsed to the ground, sparks fading. The energy to make the barrier made her very weak.

"Gladdy," Haylee said, nuzzling the elf. "What is the matter?"

"I'm spent. I haven't used magic in so long, it has taken all of my strength away." She looked at the other Misfits as they looked at the Shadow People. "Don't worry, the barrier will hold."

"That's good," Elsfur said, looking at Gladdy with concern. "Haylee, take Gladdy to safety. That is an order!" Gladdy didn't protest this time.

"Yes, Elsfur. But I will be back to help as soon as I get her to safety."

Elsfur nodded his head in approval, and then watched as Timmynog picked up Gladdy and slung her onto Haylee's back. They both stood back and watched the small dragon leap into the air. Haylee looked back down at the Misfits on the ground, tears running down her snout. She knew she must hurry and get Gladdy to safety and get back to the Misfits. She just hoped they would be alive when she returned.

Rain began to pour down on their heads. Elsfur looked at the Shadow People as they ran forward, hitting the barrier.

"At least she will be safe in the Dark Lands," he said. "If looks as if every Shadow Person from the Dark Lands is on the Bitter Plains."

"I agree," said Timmynog as he wiped water from his eyes. "I hate fighting when it is raining."

"We'll just have to do our best," Elsfur said. "Is everyone ready?"

They all nodded. Elsfur, Timmynog, Snollygob and Flipsy turned to face the dryads. Elsfur counted at least thirty-five dryads that had managed to follow them from the lake. They spread out and then each one took a ready stance. Elsfur looked at his small group of companions. Each one of them had on his warrior face. His chest puffed out with pride. He would be in battle once again with his closest friends. His thoughts turned to Shimmer for a brief moment, wondering if she was safe. Wondering if she had managed to rescue Andy. The thought of her gave him the strength he needed. He readjusted his hands on the hilt of his sword, as rain dripped from his hair onto his face. He was ready.

A dryad in the shape of a black panther was the first to reach the Misfits. When she was several yards away, she shape-shifted back into a dryad, pulled swords from leather sheaths that were attached to her very long legs, and lunged at Timmynog. Her clothing was black and tight-fitting for battle and her long, black-panther-spotted hair flew behind her. She moved with blurring speed, but she was no match for Timmynog. He hit her with his fist in the face and she fell to the ground, unconscious. He looked at his hand like he had never seen it before and then smiled.

"Oh yeah," he beamed at Elsfur. "I'm the man!"

"No, my friend, you're the giant!" Elsfur laughed.

They gave each other a high-five, turning just in time to start battling with quite a few dryads. Snollygob was fighting two dryads at once. One had short choppy hair cut like a Mohawk. The hair ran in a straight line down her back and she was covered in dark spots. Her clothing was made from animal skins and she laughed like a hyena. The other dryad was a dark beauty, with rich black skin and eyes to match. She was much taller than the other dryads, with very lean, sinewy arms and legs. She moved with the grace of a gazelle. Her robe was made from very fine purple silk and she wore gold-colored sandals on her feet.

Snollygob fought the two women with the skills that he had acquired while he was in the Royal Guard. He took both of the dryads out quickly and moved on to other dryads that were finally reaching them. He looked back at the dark one for only a moment, wishing that he hadn't killed her and that he could have known her under a different circumstance. She was a rare beauty.

Flipsy didn't even have the chance to battle with any of the dryads, nor did he want one. Most of them stayed their distance from him. However, some dryads would get brave and venture his way. When they approached he would just simply blow fire all over them. He started making a game out of each one, seeing how far he could spurt fire from each nostril. He lay there watching the battle, giving little hints to each of the Misfits as they fought. Only when it looked like one of the Misfits was in serious trouble, would he bother to ignite the dryad that they were fighting, catching her on fire. This annoyed Elsfur. He glanced back at Flipsy. The dragon was lying on his back as if he were at a picnic, popping the charred dryads into his mouth like grapes.

"You know," he yelled at Flipsy, while trying to defend himself from a dryad that had shaggy blue hair all over her body, "You *could* help."

"Yes, I could," his voice layered with a touch of English accent. He pushed his glasses up higher on his nose. "But, you look as though you are having a really good time. I wouldn't want to deprive you of it."

"You won't have to, master dragon," boomed a very deep voice. "We are here to kill the vicious beasts for you."

❦

Haylee flew as fast as she could toward the Dark Lands. The rain pelted her in the face, as lightning flashed all around. Gladdy lay limply over her back. She had tried talking to her, but Gladdy was unresponsive. Haylee was worried. She knew that she needed to get back to the Misfits, but how could she leave Gladdy in such a vulnerable state?

She could see the Dark Lands clearly now and picked out the tallest tree she could find. Maybe if she left Gladdy in a tall tree, she would be safe from predators and Shadow People. She found the perfect tree. It was in view of the castle and also of the plains. She landed in the tree and found a very wide limb. Gladdy crawled off Haylee's back and clung to the tree.

"Thank you, Haylee. Go back to the others. They will need you."

"I don't think I can leave you like this. You're so weak and you are shaking all over."

"I'll be fine. Go."

"Okay, but I will be back for you soon." Haylee nuzzled the elf and looked deep into her eyes. "I'll be back."

Gladdy nodded and slid down, trying to find a comfortable place to sit. Haylee glanced one more time at Gladdy and then jumped. The tree swayed violently to and fro, almost pitching Gladdy off the limb. She regained her seat and then waved at the little dragon reassuringly.

&ep;

Snollygob and Elsfur looked at Timmynog. He just shrugged and then watched as the dryad he was fighting fell to her knees and then face down in the dirt.

"Who did that?" shrieked Timmynog. He searched, but found no one but the Misfits and dryads. One by one the dryads fell where they stood. Some even panicked and ran away until there were no more dryads left to fight. Timmynog, Elsfur and Snollygob ran to each other and placed their backs together, so that no one could get behind them. Flipsy jumped to his feet and began to roar.

"Hush, Flipsy, I can't hear myself think when you are doing that. Show yourself, you invisible demon!" demanded Elsfur.

"Not until I have your word that you will not harm us," said the voice in the air.

Elsfur looked at the others and signaled for them to lower their swords.

"Us?" Snollygob said. "How many of you are there?"

"Just two."

Two people appeared right in front of the Misfits. They were identical twins. Both of the twins were dressed in all black, including capes that hung from their backs and big, heavy boots on their feet. They had black bandanas wrapped around their faces. What little skin the Misfits could see was covered in something green and furry. They had a peculiar and unpleasant earthy smell to them. Not far from where they stood was a cart full of unusual plants. It too was giving off a nasty smell.

"We were passing this way and saw that you might need help. So we thought we would assist. We are not fans of the dryads," said one of the twins. "My name is Mold," he pointed to the man standing next to him, "and this is my brother Fungus. We are herbalists from the Land of the Fitful."

"Thank you for the much needed help," said Elsfur, bowing. "I am Elsfur. This is Snollygob of the Killmoulis race, Timmynog from the Land of the Fitful, and Flipsy." Elsfur pointed out each creature as he introduced him.

"No thanks is necessary," said the other twin Fungus, in a raspy voice. "It is our goal in life to rid the land of useless dryads. They hog the forests to themselves and won't let others in. The forests are so vital to our line of work."

"I can see where they might get in the way," Timmynog said. "They are very protective of their forests."

"I wouldn't call the forest theirs. The forests are put on the earth for everyone to use."

"Yes...well," Elsfur said as silence fell through the group. He smiled when he thought of Grandmother Muckernut and what she might say on the subject. "So, how is it that you can become invisible?"

"We make potions from the plants that we gather," said Mold. "We have modified them to the point that we can control when we want to be invisible and when we are visible."

"That would be a nice tool to have," muttered Snollygob.

"Very nice indeed, master Killmoulis," sneered Fungus. "It helps us to sneak around and acquire articles for our trade, that might not normally be possible."

Snollygob looked at the twins with disdain. He didn't like thieves.

"It keeps us away from them as well," the twin said, pointing to the Shadow People. "They cannot smell us because of our particular scent, nor can they see us, so they leave us be. The tricky part is not letting them touch you. I wouldn't come in contact with those nasty beasts if I were you. We have seen what they can do, and it is not pretty."

"That is one of our goals," retorted Flipsy. "To stay as far away as possible from the Shadow People." Something about the twins made him uneasy. "What brings you to this part of the country?"

"Our search for rare plants is taking us toward the forest that surrounds the Crystal Sea Palace," said Mold.

"Why the forest by the Crystal Sea Palace?" Elsfur asked, curiously.

The twins smiled and looked knowingly at one another.

"We were told of the riches that grow in that forest. We could make such wonderful medicines and potions from the plants, trees and animals that reproduce there. We plan to open an herbal shop. If you are ever that way, stop by."

"I'll think about that," said Elsfur. "Um...I know the king and queen of the Crystal Sea Palace. They have told me there are creatures living in that forest you wouldn't want in your worst nightmare. King Renauldee grew that forest to protect the kingdom that the forest surrounds. He then brought the creatures from the sea to live in that forest. They are loyal to him and will kill you without any thought."

"We know what lives in that forest, kind elf," said Mold, laughing and snorting. "The sea is a treasure trove in itself. The creatures harbor a lot of minerals from the sea, since that is where they were born. We will be very rich indeed from our work. Our cousin said there was a cabin just waiting for us to occupy, close to the road that leads to the castle. We will begin our business there. Other herbalists are going to tell stories about us for years to come."

"They'll talk about how you died being stupid," retorted Flipsy. He laughed at his own joke. He snorted so hard, flames shot out of his mouth, barely missing Timmynog.

"Hey, watch it!" yelled Timmynog, as he brushed at the sleeve of his shirt. "You almost caught my shirt on fire."

"Sorry, Timmynog," said Flipsy, still laughing.

"Well, it has been fun," Fungus said, staring at the dragon like he was a chest full of treasure. "Dragons have many wonderful qualities as well. You wouldn't want to sell your dragon to us, would you?"

"What!" the Misfits bellowed, outraged.

"Flipsy is a Filligrim Dragon and the princeling of King Granite. I don't have to tell you what the consequences would be to sell him for your enterprise," Elsfur said sternly. "He is a prince. In fact, he is the dragon that is bound to Prince Andrew, Prince Becken's first born and heir to the throne of Filligrim. You should get down on your knees and apologize."

Mold and Fungus looked at one another in surprise.

"There is no mark of royalty upon this dragon," Mold said, inspecting Flipsy.

Flipsy stood up tall and stuck out his chest. A thin line began moving across Flipsy's chest, slowly drawing the pattern of the Filligrim crest upon it.

"Is that proof enough for you, slime?" asked Elsfur, with contempt. "He doesn't wear his mark for fear of capture."

Both of the twins looked outraged by the tone of Elsfur's voice. Their faces grew cold. However, they both went to their knees.

"Our apologies, my prince," said Mold, bowing his head. "Please ignore our stupidity."

Everyone looked at Flipsy. His mouth was hanging open. No one had ever got on his knees in respect to him.

"Uh...well, I—I," he stammered. "I'll let it pass this time. But watch what you say if you are ever around me again."

The Misfits watched as the twins got to their feet, walked over to the waiting cart and began pulling it toward the Misfits, stopping it right in front of them.

"We want to give you a gift. It is our way of saying we are sorry, my prince," said Fungus. "It is an honor to be in your presence, and you may need these to help you and your friends stay safe." He dug into the heaps of plants in the cart and brought out a beautiful red flower with five petals on it. On each petal were long, thin yellow stripes. He presented it to Flipsy and bowed. Flipsy took the flower and examined it. "If you eat this flower as you are dying, your life will be restored. But, make sure you are dying or nasty things will happen to you." The man pulled his bandana from his face. The Misfits flinched at the sight. He was rotten and decaying. "My brother and I were forced to eat this flower once. Our captor was a very unpleasant man in the Far West. We managed to escape from him, but we were never the same. We belonged to an army that had battled years ago. In that battle we served a man named Prince Becken. He was from Filligrim and we were from another country. Our armies joined forces and we were assigned to Prince Becken. His general betrayed him and sold us out for gold. He told our captor of our battle strategies and how the evil man could go about capturing us. We have lived in our captor's castle until a few years ago. Someone left a key to our dungeon door inside a loaf of bread. It was a miracle. Thirty of us managed to escape the dungeon without so much as an alarm being set off or a guard in our way.

"Prince Becken?" Elsfur said. "Are you sure it was Prince Becken?"

"Yes. After being in battle with him, I would have served under no other man. He was a mighty and fierce warrior. It was such a tragedy when he was killed."

"So, he really is dead?"

"Yes," said Mold. "I saw him killed with my own eyes. Now, we have two more gifts that will serve you well." He held out a plain green plant with delicate silver flowers on it to Timmynog. This is very rare. It is the binoculus flower."

"Ahhh," said Timmynog. He looked at the men with reverence. "Those grow in the mountains around the stone giants' homeland. You two have undeniably been on a very far journey."

"Indeed we have," Mold said. "For it was on

the other side of the giant country that we were held captive. Those particular flowers will come in handy if you need to see long distance. Eat two of the petals and you will be able to see like a bird. The last plant I give you is rare, as well. I only hope that one day I will be able to find another. It is called a Dophina Root." He handed them a dried up root that was oblong in shape and yellow in color. "Stick this in the ground and it will grow into an enormous tree right before your eyes. Then a door in the trunk will open up to you, allowing you to hide inside. It expands to fit however many people that are in need of hiding, even a dragon. When you are through using it, pull a leaf from a limb and it will shrink back into the root. You can also use it for lodging. It might come in handy for what lies ahead of you."

Everyone turned and looked at the Shadow People that were continuously hitting the barrier. Silence fell between the herbalists and the Misfits.

"We will be on our way," Fungus finally said. "Like I said, if you are ever in the forest around the Crystal Sea Palace, come and see us."

"Once again," Elsfur said, "thank you for helping us. Also, thank you for the gifts."

They nodded. The Misfits remained quiet until the twins were far away.

"What if Prince Becken is alive?" Timmynog said.

"You heard what those nasty men said," Snollygob replied angrily. "They saw Prince Becken die."

"Still..." Timmynog watched the retreating

backs of Mold and Fungus. "What if?"

Elsfur smiled at Timmynog. They all knew what a gift it would be for their queen to have her king by her side, restoring Prince Andy and Prince Kwagar's father.

Flipsy spread out his wing and looked at the hole. It was already a lot smaller. The thin membrane always healed faster than any part on his body.

"I think I can fly," he said.

"I don't know, Flipsy. I don't think you can carry all three of us," said Snollygob.

"We need to go now," said Timmynog. He was pointing in the direction of the twins. They had disappeared.

"Get behind me," Flipsy growled. The Misfits did as they were told. Flipsy blew fire, swinging his head back and forth, just in case the twins had come back. Nothing happened. "Maybe they have gone on their way."

"Maybe they have," said Timmynog. "But, I think we need to leave now, just in case."

"I don't think they are a threat to us. Besides, what about Haylee?" Elsfur asked, staring in the direction where the twins had been. "She will be coming back here to find us. If we are gone...."

"I will find her in the sky or in the Dark Lands," said Flipsy, confidently. "Get on."

Just as he said this, Haylee hit the earth in front of them. The impact knocked Timmynog, Snollygob and Elsfur onto their backsides. She looked at the three lying on the ground, grinned and asked, "Anyone need a ride?"

THE MEMORY

Gladdy tightened her grip on the branch and watched as Haylee landed back in the tree. Flipsy hovered overhead and waited for Gladdy to get back on the small dragon. Everyone was soaking wet, and it didn't look as though the rain was going to quit anytime soon.

As soon as Haylee was in the air, Flipsy roared over the wind, "I smell something familiar."

"What is it, Flipsy?" asked Elsfur.

"Andy. But, there…there is something else that is confusing me." He inhaled deeply, causing his abdomen to expand greatly, pushing his riders' legs out until they felt like they were doing the splits. Then he let out his breath and cried, "It's Kwagar."

"What!" everyone yelled in unison.

"I smell Kwagar."

"How can that be?" boomed Timmynog. "Kwagar is in Hamamelis Prison."

"I do have royal nostrils, you know."

"Oh, excuse us," laughed Snollygob. "I didn't realize that royal nostrils could smell better than people who are not royal."

"Very funny. I just know what I smell, and it's Kwagar. I can also smell King Foxglove, Shade, Meadow, Shimmer, Grandmother Muckernut, and Daisy. Oh, and something that is so revolting." Flipsy blew fire, clearing out his snout, and then he roared loudly in anger.

"Will you stop roaring so loudly," Elsfur said, chastising Flipsy. "You'll give away our position if we need to sneak up on any enemy."

"I don't smell anything," Haylee said. "Are you sure you're feeling okay, Flipsy?"

"Sorry, Elsfur. I feel fine, Haylee, and I know what I smell. However, I could do without that gross, pungent odor."

"What pungent odor are you talking about?" asked Haylee, sniffing the wind.

"It's a gargoyle," Flipsy said, roaring again.

"Now I know he's gone mad," Snollygob said. "Everyone knows that gargoyles live only at the goblin prison and the Luna Peelo Caves in the Dingy Mountains. That's thousands of leagues from here."

৵৽

"Boy, this is a popular place. We are about to have visitors," the gargoyle whispered to Andy.

His breath gagged Andy. Andy blinked the rain out of his eyes and looked around cautiously.

"Who? I don't see anyone."

The gargoyle pointed to the sky. "Dragons. You have two of them coming this way."

"There are two dragons right next to you," said Andy, shaking his head and pointing at Hannah and Flopsy.

"Didn't we just go through this?" A low warning rumbled deep in the gargoyle's chest. "When I say that there are dragons coming this way, *that* is what I mean." The gargoyle looked up again and smiled, exposing his fangs. "See."

Andy looked in the direction the gargoyle was looking. There was no mistake about it. There in the dark rain clouds was Flipsy, accompanied by another dragon and several riders.

Panic went through his bones. He had to get to Lady Apricot before the other dragons got there, or all was lost. He wiped his wet face with the sleeve of his shirt and then drew his sword. He motioned for everyone to stay put, nodded at Grandmother Muckernut and then took off running with the gargoyle and Grandmother Muckernut right on his heels.

"Do you have a plan?" Grandmother Muckernut asked.

"Kill Lady Apricot and anyone else who gets in our way."

"Well, you're not going to do it without us," said Shimmer. She and Thane had just caught up with them.

"Lady Apricot is mine," said Grandmother Muckernut. "Andy, you get to the stone. Thane, Shimmer and the gargoyle, you take out as many dryads as possible."

Andy saw movement in the woods not far from them. It was Kwagar, King Foxglove, Shade, and Meadow. They were coming to help. He could also feel the rumbling of extremely heavy feet. The dragons had given them just enough time to make it as close to the dryads as possible and then they followed, bringing Theodius and Daisy with them.

The dryads looked up when they felt the vibrations of the dragons. They saw all of the Misfits running toward them. Lady Apricot was the most surprised. She had obviously thought that Andy would be with Queen Estonia. Grandmother Muckernut kicked in an extra burst of speed as she pulled her sword from its sheath, leaped into the air and somersaulted over Lady Apricot. She landed facing the orange-colored dryad and the fight was on. The other dryads were so awestruck by the fighting that they didn't notice the gargoyle. He launched himself on several dryads at once. The bone crunching echoed around the still woods.

Andy commenced his own fight with a scarlet-colored dryad. She was really fast and very strong. After several minutes of fighting, she knocked Andy to the ground. She stood over him and readied her blade, with a taunting smile. Just as she was about to plunge it into his heart, Daisy flew into her face with a blinding light. Andy grabbed his sword and stabbed the dryad in the stomach. She fell on top of Andy, dead.

"Thanks, Daisy," he said, heaving the dead dryad off of him. She nodded.

Andy began his search for the place where he

buried the jewel, but found no traces.

It's become a tree, said a voice in his head. Startled, Andy looked around. Everyone was fighting and no one was looking at him. He shook his head and started looking once more. Then he heard the voice again. It sounded like Kwagar. *I hid it behind a dense bush over to your left.* Andy looked astounded at his brother. Kwagar smiled back. *We are twins, brother. Linked. And since I can converse with nature, I can communicate with you.*

Andy smiled and nodded at his brother. Then he began searching for the bush that Kwagar described and saw a little tree with golden fruit. Its beauty took his breath away. He wanted to reach out, pick one of the fruits and take a huge bite of it. Before he knew what was happening, Andy had wrapped his hand around one of the golden fruits.

Stop! Andy heard in his head. *Andy, the fruit is what caused the plague. Leave it be.*

Alarmed, Andy let go of the fruit and looked to where Kwagar was fighting a silver-colored dryad, and then looked back at the tree. How could something so beautiful, be so evil? He dropped to his knees and began digging with the tip of his sword at the base of the tree. The jewel had to be in the roots. He dug as fast as he could, while fighting broke out all around him. He didn't have to dig far. When Andy uncovered the last bit of earth from around the jewel, he could clearly see what had happened to it. Roots had sprouted from the edges of the jewel, as though it was some sort of weird, little, black bean with red stripes that had been planted in the ground. The birdcage necklace was fused to the jewel and the chains were tangled in the roots.

Andy cut the roots from the jewel and the birdcage necklace. Just as he wrapped his hand around the jewel, something weird happened. Grandmother Muckernut charged Lady Apricot, knocking her to the ground. Grandmother Muckernut grabbed Lady Apricot's face. In that instant all three of them were transported back in time.

అ•అ

Andy looked around. He was no longer standing in the Dark Lands. He was standing in a very dark place and couldn't move any parts of his body, except his eyes.

All he could see was Grandmother Muckernut holding Lady Apricot down with her forearm across the dryad's neck, while her other hand pressed on Lady Apricot's forehead. Not far from them was a single beam of light shining down on what looked like a meadow.

Where had everyone else gone? He could hear Lady Apricot mumbling something, a teasing whisper. It sounded like she was saying, "Remember the dead council. Remember the dead council. It's *all* here in my memory."

This bewildered Andy. Was he in Lady Apricot's memory? The scene in the meadow started to play out. Creatures materialized. They were standing by a tree, each one with a look of grief. To Andy, it was like being in a pitch-black movie theater, watching a bad movie....

❧❧

Light filtered through the domed trees that covered a meadow tucked away in a very old forest, giving just enough light for the creatures that lived there, to see by. A very tall hedge ran the complete border of the meadow, making it secure from the outside world. A single mockernut tree, a very large toadstool and five expectant beings stood in the very middle of the meadow. The beings were of different races: an elf, a dwarf, a human, a unicorn, and a goblin. A small wooden door in the hedge at the far end of the meadow creaked open causing a quick intake of breath from some of the beings, and whimpers from others.

A beautiful dryad came through the door. Her stride and posture were perfect as she walked purposefully toward the center of the meadow. Her tawny-colored skin glinted in the patches of light that seeped through the trees above, coming to rest on the dark green grass below her feet. Her ginger colored eyes took in the group, and then came to rest on the tree.

"I'm here, Grandmother Muckernut, with news." Her voice was very soothing to the ears, like a slow-running stream.

All eyes turned toward the tree and watched as it transformed into a beautiful, rainbow-colored dryad. Leaves from the tree limbs slid over her body, fashioning an unusual dress. She sat down on the toadstool and looked up at the other dryad.

"What is it, Apricot?" she asked calmly.

"Acorn the dormer was here. He confirmed what you had guessed about the other part of the council. They are all dead!" Everyone in the group gasped and some began to cry. Apricot went on, "One was still alive when he got there. It was Thangus the ogre. He said that they managed to hide the jewel, but were overrun on the way back by a dark shadow, and then Thangus died. He also managed to give Acorn this just before he gave up his last breath." Apricot handed Grandmother Muckernut a chain with a little birdcage dangling from it. Apricot bowed her head in sorrow. "I'm sorry, my lady."

"At least you got this necklace back. It unlocks the box that holds the crown. This is most dreadful!" Grandmother Muckernut said, looking at the group standing in front of her. Her eyes glinted with tears as they came to rest on a lady elf by the name of Hendrel. Hendrel nodded in agreement. The rest of the group looked at the beautiful raven-haired elf. Her leaf-green eyes looked back at the group. They all knew what had to be done. It had already been agreed upon by all of the council, and the agreement could not be broken.

"From this day forward, Hendrel will be the legend keeper. She will pass down what has happened to the crown and the races, to every daughter born from this day forward in her family. Also, my sanctuary will need protection and secrecy, for I alone know the whereabouts of the jewel, which will mean that the rest of you will be wiped of mind, so that no one will know where the crown is hidden."

"You will not wipe my mind, Muckernut!" shouted Ragan the dwarf. As he raised his fist toward the dryad, Apricot stepped in between them.

"Your mind will be wiped," she said in a tone of authority. Her eyes turned black as she lowered her voice to almost a growl. "Or you will be killed! Take your pick."

Ragan stepped back, hearing noises around him. He looked around. Dryads were coming out of the hedges with spears in their hands.

He pulled himself up to his full height and said in a not-so-brave voice, "How do we know that you and your dryads won't take the jewel, find the crown, and become the leader of the races?"

Grandmother Muckernut stood up and Apricot stepped aside. Towering over the dwarf, she defiantly said, "I am Grandmother Muckernut, Leader of the Dryads of Hemlock Forest, noblest of my entire kinsman. How dare you insinuate that I am a traitor to the races! It was I who was chosen to make that jewel! It was I who warned the people of its evil! Now you dare stand there and accuse me of this!"

"No, no, no," the dwarf whimpered. "I take it all back, your ladyship. I'm sorry for what I said. I apologize with all of my heart."

Grandmother Muckernut wiped a tear from her face and bent down to his level. "I don't believe you," she snarled. "Take him out and wipe his mind. If he gives you any problems, you have my permission to kill him, and anyone else that has a problem with the process."

The dryads surrounded the dwarf with spears, as well as the remaining three that were to be mind-wiped, and began escorting them out of the meadow. As they left, Apricot looked back at Grandmother Muckernut, her eyes coming to rest on the necklace in Grandmother Muckernut's hand. Greed glinted in her eyes, for the briefest of moments, in the knowledge of what the necklace was made for. Then her eyes caught Grandmother Muckernut looking at her with a confused expression. She smiled, bowed her head and then turned and left Hendrel and Grandmother Muckernut in silence. Grandmother Muckernut looked down at the necklace, pondering Apricot's actions for a moment. What had she seen in Apricot's eyes? Grandmother Muckernut thought perhaps that she was being overly cautious. Apricot was her most trusted servant. These were troubling times, when paranoia can run rampant, if not held in check. Maybe she was making too much of Apricot's smile. But the feeling it gave her was overwhelming.

She had always been able to sense things about others. Could Apricot know more than she was letting on about the council? Grandmother Muckernut knew there would be no way to prove it. However, she would be watching Apricot a little more closely from now on. She turned to Hendrel.

"What will become of them after they have had their minds wiped?" Hendrel asked, still staring at the door after it had closed.

"They will be taken back and left at the edge of

their lands to wander until they are found by loved ones. It is harsh, but it's what has to be done in order for the jewel to be safe. I will also have to send dormers to find out if the crown is completely safe. I can only hope that our friends who were attacked didn't give information as to the whereabouts of the crown before they were killed."

"I guess I am to travel back to my lands alone?" Hendrel said quietly.

"No. I will have one of the Filligrim Castle dragons take you home in the morning. I will send word with one of my dryads to fetch one for you." Grandmother Muckernut sat back down on the toadstool. "Now, I will ring for Buttercup to bring us some coneflower tea, and you and I will discuss the legend in detail. I also think I should draw you a map for your future generations, just in case something happens and they have to find me."

"I will be glad when all of the troubles of this world are at an end." Hendrel's shoulders slumped and her hair fell over her face. Tears trickled down her rosy cheeks and onto her dress. She wept for her friends that she had known for so long. How could someone have taken her friends' lives so easily? Did this horrible person ever stop to consider that her friends had families and loved ones? How could all of the dreams of all the different races have come to this?

Grandmother Muckernut sighed really hard and closed her eyes. "I believe peace is coming and will last for a very long time. You should weep for your friends. They were very true, the best of all the races in the different kingdoms. Such a waste!" She paused and let Hendrel grieve for a moment. Then she slapped her hands together and tried to smile, her eyes glistening from her own tears.

"Now, I know this will be hard for us to concentrate on, but we have to go on. There is so much to do if we are to protect what's left. So let's get down to business, shall we?"

❧

The scene faded with a scream. Andy blinked and looked around. He found that he was back in the Dark Lands, still holding the jewel and it was still raining. He looked at the jewel in confusion and then at Grandmother Muckernut. Everyone had stopped fighting and was looking at the pair of dryads. Apricot had a sword sticking out of her stomach.

Grandmother Muckernut backed away and pointed a shaky, accusatory finger at the dying dryad.

"*You* had a part in those council members' deaths, didn't you? I can't believe that I forgot about that day. If you knew about the necklace, you traitor, why did you bother to give it back to me?"

Lady Apricot cackled. "I only suspected—what the necklace did," she gasped. Had I known before, I—would have never given it back to you. Several times—after that day—I almost had it within my grasp, but I—failed my master. Then you—went and gave it to *him*," Apricot pointed in Andy's direction, "which left me no way of finding it."

"Then it seems I did the right thing,"

Grandmother Muckernut said, with satisfaction. She looked at Andy and saw that he was holding the jewel. "Andy, get back to Queen Estonia, before it's too late." Then she pulled her sword out of Lady Apricot's stomach and stabbed her one more time. This time it was in the heart. Lady Apricot reached her hand toward Grandmother Muckernut and then opened her mouth as if to say something else, only it didn't come. Her breath rattled and a single tear slid down her face—then all was silent.

Just as Andy turned to run, two dragons fell from the sky, knocking several people off their feet. Andy turned to greet them, but stopped, noticing that standing just a distance away was a whole horde of goblins, the Shadow Man and what Andy could only assume was a stone giant. One of the goblins was wearing a crown on his head. The Shadow Man was just like Andy's Aunt Estonia, only he was a very big man that kept fading in and out with movement, like a badly drawn, black and gray cartoon that had been animated.

Andy grabbed his head in pain. Kwagar was screaming inside Andy's head. As it faded, he heard Kwagar shout out loud at the goblin. "You will die by my blade, Mosaic!"

At first the goblin looked bewildered at Kwagar. Then he smiled and drew his sword. "I don't think so, my little escapee. You will die and then I will eat you," Prince Mosaic laughed. He looked at his little minions. "Anyone for Prince Kwagar stew?"

"No one threatens my brother and gets away

with it!" Andy bellowed, drawing his sword.

Prince Mosaic looked to see who was speaking to him. He sized up the boy, with his eyes coming to rest on the jewel in Andy's hand. Astonished, his heart leaped. The Jewel of the Races was so close to him. All he had to do was reach out and take it. But with the Shadow Man standing right next to him, he had no chance. So much power in one little stone. He had to get rid of the Shadow Man. Of course the Shadow Man wasn't the only creature he had to eliminate. His eyes darted around, looking at all of the dragons and Misfits that were in his way, not to mention the stone giant standing behind him. It might be a little challenging, but it was a risk he was willing to take.

TAKING DOWN A SHADOW MAN AND THE STONE GIANT TOO

Seeing the Shadow Man and Prince Mosaic, the gargoyle howled with rage. "Dryad isn't the only thing I'm having for dinner today." He raised one of his razor sharp claws and pointed it. A single drop of liquid fell from its point. Andy could only imagine the poison that was contained within that single drop.

"Gargoyle," Andy said. "I need you to take out as many goblins and dryads as possible. Leave Mosaic and Shadow Man to the others. Is that clear? If something happens to me, Grandmother Muckernut is in charge of you."

The gargoyle glared at Andy for a moment as if trying to make up his mind and then he shook his head. He turned around and looked at the dryads that had regrouped and were now standing close to the goblins. He grinned, as he let out a long, low gassy sound. Everyone within smelling distance was literally gagging.

"Everyone, remember what Queen Estonia said right before we left her," Andy said in a low voice to those around him. "No magic. Don't let the enemy know. If you are by a newcomer, then let them know as well. I don't want any dead Misfits on my hands."

Andy looked at his Aunt Gladdy. He couldn't believe the transformation she had gone through. She was utterly beautiful. Gladdy looked back at Andy and smiled at him. She was so glad to see him alive. Her lip quivered, seeing Theodius. But she knew her hellos would have to wait. There was a certain Shadow Man that had to be taken down. She pulled the sword out of its sheath that Caleb had given her. Then she raised her hand toward the sky. A bolt of lightning flashed down and hit her on the head. Andy thought she was dead for sure, but she just stood there with electricity flickering all over her body. Her eyes turned a bright yellow. It was magic.

"Aunt Gladdy, no!" Andy shouted. But it was too late. The earth began moving. Roots whipped up out of the ground. Gladdy fought off, striking with bolts of electricity. Andy ran forward to help her and just as he did, the Shadow Man raised his arm and a bright burst of light flew from his hand.

It was heading straight at Andy. Flopsy leaped into the path of the light and was struck down. Flipsy, Haylee and Hannah roared in anger. It was so loud that everyone had to cover their ears. Hannah took off running full speed, knocking over dryads and goblins, to get at the Shadow Man. She too was hit with a bolt of light, but not before she knocked him into a tree.

"Haylee, you and Shimmer get Andy back to the castle. The only way to stop this is for that stone to be destroyed," Grandmother Muckernut shouted.

Shimmer ran and jumped upon the little dragon. Haylee bit at dryads as she worked her way over to Andy. He was busy fighting the roots, trying to help his Aunt Gladdy.

"Andy, we must go," Haylee begged.

"Are you crazy? I can't leave my aunt here to battle this alone."

"Andy, we have to get to the castle. You heard Grandmother Muckernut. We need to go now!" Shimmer said. When Andy didn't move, Shimmer said, "Grab him."

The little dragon snapped her jaws gently around Andy and flew off with him. A bolt of light shot past her, barely missing Haylee's head. She flipped Andy up in the air and caught him in her claw. Then she looked back at the ground. They were being pursued by a bunch of goblins and dryads and the stone giant. She had to get to the castle before they did, with plenty of time to spare.

With her spare claw, she started hitting tree after tree, knocking them to the ground. She could take out several of the creatures at once with this method, but it was slowing her down. She turned, inhaled deeply and blew fire all over the forest floor. Everything ignited and started burning. The dryads and goblins stopped, trying to figure out how to get around the burning timbers. But the giant just leaped over and through the fire and kept pursuing the little dragon. Once it had jumped so high, that he touched her tail with his fingers.

Haylee began flying as fast as she could. Relief filled her when the castle came into view.

"Your name is Haylee, right?" Andy yelled over the rushing wind in his ears.

"Yes."

"Haylee, you need to take me back. I have to help them."

"No."

"Are you capable of saying more than one word at a time?" he asked in frustration.

"Yes. But I'm a little busy trying to stay ahead of the enormously huge boulder-man that is chasing after us right now."

৯৽৵

Queen Estonia's breathing quickened. Claude held her hand, as his black tears slid silently down his face. He wished that Andy and Theodius would hurry and get back to the castle. He just knew they would be able to help his mistress.

"I'm losing my grip. Something has happened. Magic was used."

"Can you stop it?" Claude asked, knowing full

well what would happen to an outsider if they used magic in the Dark Lands."

"I'm trying, but I'm...so weak. Claude," whispered Queen Estonia, "when—when I die...."

"Don't talk like that, my lady. Theodius and Andy will make it all better. They can heal you with the stone. I just know they can."

"I want to—to die, Claude. It has to happen."

"No! No!" he said angrily. "You must live and keep on ruling this land. What will happen to all the Shadow People if you die?"

"I'm hoping—they won't be shadows anymore, that—that *you* won't be a shadow anymore. The reason this all—started was because of that stone and I mean to see it destroyed before—I die."

"I won't let you die," Claude cried harder. "What will I do without you?"

"That's what I want—to tell you," she breathed. "This—this castle will be—your home. I want you and—your family to have it."

Claude looked at her with disbelief in his eyes. She had always been kind to him, but never in his wildest dreams did he imagine her leaving him this wonderful castle. He got up from the bed and looked out the window. The Dark Lands and town lay before him, its silence a constant companion. It was a dreary world to live in, but Claude had adjusted to it, just like all of the other Shadow People had. Would the Dark Lands return to normal if the Shadow Queen were dead and the Jewel of the Races destroyed? For that matter, would he really be as he once was, a normal man, living a normal life? As he looked at the queen, now a very pale gray, his attitude began to change as he listened to her labored breathing. Now, he willed Andy to return with the jewel and quickly. But not to heal the queen, but to take her life, so that he could have his back. He felt ashamed, knowing how cruel his thoughts were, and he wished he had never thought them. He walked back to her side and slid his hand in hers, lending her his strength.

"Try to make the land stop the attack. You've got to help them just a little bit longer."

Queen Estonia smiled at her friend, nodded her head and closed her eyes in concentration.

$\approx \infty$

Grandmother Muckernut was tiring as she fought hard against a massive mole goblin. As she killed him, she looked around at the fighting taking place. Flipsy was holding his own, as he battled the Shadow Man. King Foxglove and Kwagar were fighting a nimble Prince Mosaic. Meadow lay on the ground unconscious, in a pool of blood. Shade, Thane and Theodius were trying to help Gladdy battle the roots that were now tightly wrapped around her body. The gargoyle had a dryad's detached arm in his mouth like a chicken leg, while he battled with another dryad and a goblin. Many goblins and dryads were dead and the battle was slowing. Elsfur, Timmynog and Snollygob were fighting what remained of the dryads. Most of them had gone after Haylee, Shimmer and Andy.

Hearing sounds behind her, Grandmother

Muckernut turned to face a new enemy. Blood drained from her face as she spotted Shadow People quite a distance away.

"Elsfur," she yelled, pointing in the direction of the Shadow People. "We have to get out of here."

He looked to where she was pointing and nodded. They had to find a way to free Gladdy from the roots or she would be dead soon. Her electricity was fading along with her strength. As Elsfur ran to help Kwagar, he heard a loud scream. Flipsy had engulfed the Shadow Man in flames. Elsfur changed course and hurried toward the Shadow Man. He would kill him, just as he had dreamed of ever since the day that Andy had disappeared. Just as Elsfur reached him, however, the Shadow Man vanished in a puff of smoke. Elsfur and Flipsy stared in amazement. Elsfur's heart leaped and laughter escaped his lips. Could this be true? Had Flipsy killed the Shadow Man?

Distracted by the Shadow Man's scream and Elsfur's laugh, King Foxglove and Kwagar turned briefly to see what was being celebrated. Mosaic seized this opportunity and stabbed King Foxglove. Kwagar's hatred for the goblin heightened and he lashed out at the goblin, stabbing him in the shoulder. The goblin grabbed his shoulder and smiled at Kwagar, as he pulled his blade out of King Foxglove. Kwagar dropped his sword and caught the elf king as he began to fall to the ground. Mosaic bowed to the king and Kwagar, and then disappeared into the forest.

Timmynog and Snollygob killed the last of the dryads and then came to Gladdy's aide. The ground, however, suddenly stopped its attack. Everyone looked around, bewildered by its sudden cease in attack, and came to only one conclusion. Queen Estonia must have regained control of her power over the land, or…she was dead.

Gladdy fell into the arms of Theodius, broken and gasping for air. Everyone stood around her, looking concerned.

"We must leave this place and find help for Gladdy, or it's about to get real interesting around here," Grandmother Muckernut said.

"Define interesting," said Snollygob, spraying slobber from both mouths.

"Oh my goodness, we're about to die!" Grandmother Muckernut said, dramatically.

"That's a pretty good definition," said Thane dryly. "Do you really think we'll make it out alive?" He stared in the direction of the nasty Shadow People.

"I have every intention of making it out alive, thank you," snorted Snollygob. "I have an herb garden that needs tending for the market in Filligrim."

Thane stared at him blankly, then said, "We have nasty, green Shadow People coming, intent on killing us, and all you can think of is your herb garden!"

Before Snollygob could answer, Flipsy thundered over to where everyone was gathered. "Elsfur, the dophina root. Hurry up and place it in the ground. We may just have a chance to escape the Shadow People. Also, give one of the red petals to Kwagar, so that he can place it in King

Foxglove's mouth."

Timmynog took the flower petal from Elsfur
and handed it to Kwagar. Elsfur kneeled down with
his dagger and began digging a hole in the now
muddy ground. He placed the root in and covered
it. He had just finished, when the ground began to
vibrate. Out popped a stem that quickly grew into a
young sapling. It only took twenty more seconds
for it to become a full-grown tree. They all stood
back in amazement. Most of them jumped back
when a door popped open.

"Hurry," said Flipsy. "Get everyone inside. I'll
get Flopsy and Hannah."

"I'm going to go and help Andy," the gargoyle
said. Something had changed in the huge beast. A
warm spot was growing in the very center of his
heart, a warm spot for Andy. He didn't need to be
told to go and help Andy, he just wanted to. "He
may need my help up at the castle. We don't know
for sure that the Shadow Man is dead. Wouldn't it
be nice if I could add him as my main course, after
those delicious dryad drumsticks?"

Everyone looked a little horrified, as the
gargoyle did his best to smile. It wasn't pleasant,
not to mention the gas that he was passing. They
were also confused by the beast's loyalty to Andy.
Gargoyles were usually only loyal to their own
kind.

"I'm sure Shimmer will be pleased to see you
again," said Grandmother Muckernut, holding her
nose.

"Please," Gladdy pleaded, while gasping for
breath. "Help Andy all you can."

Fire glinted in his eyes as he nodded at Gladdy. Then he shot into the air like a bullet, flying as fast as he could toward the castle. As fast as he was flying, he would probably beat Haylee, Andy and Shimmer to the castle.

ॐॐ

"How do you kill a stone giant?" Shimmer yelled over the wind in her ears. Haylee was flying as fast as she could, while carrying two people.

"I have no clue. Fire doesn't seem to have an effect on them," said Haylee.

Andy looked at the jewel in his hand. He could feel the power pulsing in it. Then, as if the jewel knew that he needed help, he heard a voice in his head. At first he thought it was Kwagar, but the voice was deeper and sounded very ancient.

Use me, it whispered in Andy's mind. *Put me in the dragon's mouth. I will cause the dragon to blow ice-fire. Then you can destroy the giant with your sword.*

Andy thought about this for a moment. Could that really work? Would Haylee's fire come out as ice instead of boiling flames? Should he trust that which he was about to destroy? Yes, was the answer in Andy's heart. It was worth a try.

"Haylee," Andy yelled. "I need you to put the jewel in your mouth."

"Andy, did you hit your head? Because you sound barmy."

"I don't know what barmy is, but you need to listen to me. The jewel will turn your fire to ice.

We can freeze the stone giant and then I can kill it with my sword. Trust me."

"Andy, that jewel is the whole reason we are having so much trouble."

"Trust me," Andy said one more time, pleadingly.

Andy held out his hand and looked imploringly into the huge eye looking back at him. She looked at him for a long time, then grinned and opened her jaws. Andy tossed the jewel into her mouth. She placed it under her tongue and waited for a moment. A cooling sensation trickled down her throat and into her belly. Suddenly, she felt she could take out the whole forest, with just one puff of ice-fire breath. She took in a deep breath, expanding her enormous abdomen. She whirled around and hovered in mid-air, waiting for the stone giant to get closer. When he was within range, she exhaled a shower of ice-fire all over the stone giant, covering him from head to toe. The stone giant slowed more and more as he got closer. He finally stopped, frozen stiff, right underneath the little dragon. Haylee knew exactly what to do next.

"Bombs away," she yelled.

She opened her claw and released Andy. Andy pulled out his sword as he fell and held it downward with both hands. He landed on his feet, right on top of the stone giant's shoulders, ramming the sword straight down into its skull. The giant's head cracked. At first just a little, and then all over. Andy jumped off the giant, just as it crumbled into millions of tiny pieces. Andy jumped up yelling and laughing. Haylee landed just on the other side of the giant. Shimmer started laughing as Andy began dancing a weird little dance, but stopped as a black-cloaked man appeared a few feet behind Andy: the Shadow Man.

"Give me the jewel," he quietly commanded.

"I'll give you nothing," Andy said, whirling around to face his enemy. "You are the reason this whole mess got started, Saber." Andy spit the man's name out like it was poison.

"Temper, temper," the Shadow Man said, coolly. The Shadow Man picked at his fingernails with the dagger in his hand. He smiled at Andy and said, "You know, I could use someone like you to head my armies once I become ruler of every land in existence."

"What would you need armies for, if you are the ruler of every land in existence? There will be no one left to fight." Andy was trying to think of what to do, to stall for time. How could he outsmart the Shadow Man? He glanced at Haylee, who was trying to get his attention. She was gesturing with her eyes, skyward, and acting like she could smell something. Andy knew that could only mean one thing: the gargoyle was headed this way.

"Oh, you are very clever, Andy. Just what I like, an intelligent human. I have examined your mind. It's superior to other human minds. Of course, you're not totally human, are you? You have a nice mixture in you: elf, Asrai and human, but mostly human. My parents were foolish as well. But I didn't turn out so nice. Most kids with parents of two different races don't start becoming shadows until they are in their teens. I, on the other hand, was born this way. Isn't that strange? I was born while the jewel was being created and I matured a lot faster than most kids. I was almost an adult by the time the jewel came out of Grandmother Muckernut. I didn't know at the time what an impact the jewel had made on my life. But I knew that I was different. I had a lust for power and a thirst for blood that couldn't be quenched. Then one day, I was in a forest watching a bunch of dormers during planting season. I was thinking of killing one just for the pleasure of it, when I found this beautiful dryad walking alone. I befriended her. Wooed her. She would have done anything for me. I was in search of power and I needed a following. She gave me just that. She knew of different creatures with the same goal in mind, the domination of the different lands. After a while, I had amassed quite a following.

Then one night, she told me about the jewel and the crown and how it was about to be hidden. We devised a plan to kill all of the council and take the crown and jewel for ourselves. We spied on the council. That was when I found out that my own parents were on the council." Saber laughed hysterically. "I heard the council and my parents talking about other children with the same problem that I had. Can you believe that?" Saber became very serious. "There were others like me, a whole new race of people. I confronted my parents and they acted like they had done nothing wrong. This infuriated me and I killed them. Then I told Apricot to get ready, because I was going to set things straight. But something went wrong. She got cold feet. She told me that she couldn't hurt Grandmother Muckernut, that her Grandmother Muckernut was very special to her people. I looked at her and I laughed. She was a weak and pathetic fool. Of course I had to punish Apricot for messing everything up. Letting the jewel and crown slip through our fingers was tragic."

"The tragedy was the killing of innocent lives," Andy yelled. "How can you be so calloused? How can you just stand there and talk about those creatures' deaths as if you were talking about the weather?"

"Because, they made me who I am! The ignorance of those races is why there is a Dark Lands and a Shadow People. Do you think the people of this land like being what they are?"

"I don't think they like being what they are," Andy said in frustration, "but taking the crown and the jewel and becoming the ruler of everyone will not make it right. The rulers didn't know this would happen. How could *anyone* have known this would happen? They just wanted to have everyone under the same banner, to have a happy, peaceful nation. They didn't do this on purpose."

"Andy," the Shadow Man said calmly, "I am what I am and that is evil. Evil runs in my veins, my heart and soul. Can you not see that I'm dark and sinister? I don't care what has happened in the past. I only know what my future is and I see myself as ruler of everyone. Everyone will bow down to me!"

"Not me! I will never bow down to you

because I will destroy you first. It may not be today, but you can bet, in the future you will become worm dirt."

"Bold words, little man. Are you that ready to meet your death?" laughed Saber. "You know, you're not looking yourself these days. It looks as though your little vacation here in the Dark Lands has done you some good. Becoming a shadow of your former self?"

"Speaking of someone not looking like himself. How is it that you and Theodius the Cat are the same being?"

"Haven't you figured it out?" laughed Saber. "And here I thought you were intelligent. I had to have a part of me that could look out for my interests. Most Shadow People have twins. One good. One evil. Just like our fair queen in the castle. However, Thor, my twin, didn't turn out so nice. He became like me. Evil. Though, we didn't get that nice magic power that the queen inherited."

"No, you just got a black heart!"

"Andy, you can try to insult me all you like, but it doesn't affect me. I rather like the fact that my heart is black. It goes well with the rest of me, don't you think?"

"Yes, it does. So tell me, how did your brother become a cat if you two have no magic?" asked Andy, sick of the Shadow Man's mentality.

"Your friend Theodius is the one that turned my brother into a cat. It was when Theodius first came to the Dark Lands. He was there to counsel with Queen Estonia on the matters of war. My brother Thor likes to mess with people and do practical jokes. He antagonized Theodius so much, that Theodius turned him into a cat. I captured Theodius as he left the Dark Lands and tortured him severely for what he had done to my brother. I was going to make him turn my brother back. But my brother came up with a better plan. We would take over as rulers of all lands and Filligrim would be our first victory."

"Bet you didn't count on the Misfits ruining your world domination plan, did you?" Andy laughed.

"That's okay. There is still time. I know my brother, and he will never give up."

"Well, I guess that I'll just have to take care of Thor as well. We can't have both of you running around trying to rule the world, now can we?"

Saber just grinned at Andy. He stood there staring at him so long, that Andy got impatient. He gripped the handle of his sword tighter and closed the gap a little between himself and Saber.

"I'm guessing you are determined to try and kill me?" Saber said at last. "Well, if that is the case, then bring it on." Saber threw the little dagger at Andy. He knocked it off course with his sword. The Shadow Man laughed and drew his sword.

Andy spun the handle of his sword around and then gripped it tighter. He and the Shadow Man began circling each other.

Saber laughed again at Andy. "Do you even know how to use that sword?"

"You bet I do," Andy said. Then he lunged at Saber, their swords connecting in the air. The Shadow Man was strong and Andy knew it was going to be the fight of his life. The silent forest air was filled with the sound of clashing swords. They each fought hard. Andy fought for the destruction of the crown. The Shadow Man fought for total domination.

Shimmer couldn't stand the thought of losing Andy again. She silently got down off of Haylee and drew her sword. She was not about to let Andy die at the hands of the Shadow Man. She started inching her way toward the huge man. Just as she got close enough, Saber threw a bolt of lightning at her chest and knocked her into a tree. Haylee jumped in between Shimmer and Saber, just in case he threw another blast Shimmer's way. Andy watched Shimmer fall, unconscious. He screamed and rushed at the Shadow Man, swinging his blade as fast as he could. But Saber was faster. He cut Andy's arm and pushed him to the ground. But as Andy fell, he managed to slice a large gash in Saber's leg. Saber staggered, and then held his sword to Andy's throat. Andy watched as black blood poured from the Shadow Man's leg.

"Give me that jewel or you die now!" he said, wincing. He faded in and out more and more, like a light turning on and off.

"I don't think so, Saber. As I told you, I will be the one to destroy you."

Saber raised his sword and just as he was about to strike, the gargoyle swooped down out of the sky and caught Saber with his claws, slicing a large wound in his side, spinning him around and knocking him to the ground. Andy stood up and picked up his sword and positioned himself over

Saber, the Shadow Man. He stared at the Shadow Man for a moment. Saber took this hesitation as fear.

"You can't do it, can you? I don't think you have it in you to kill me."

"I haven't killed you because I think the gargoyle has already killed you. I hear those talons can be pretty deadly. Oh look, here he comes," Andy said, grinning. Andy saw fear flash in Saber's jet black eyes, just briefly.

"Just know one thing, Andy," Saber said through gritted teeth. "I will always be a thorn in your side."

"I don't think so," Andy said. But in the back of his mind, he somehow knew that this would not be the end that he had hoped for.

The gargoyle lumbered over to where Andy stood and looked down at the Shadow Man.

"You and the goblins have kept my kind as slaves far too long. As soon as I watch Prince Andrew finish you off, I'm going to go and find Prince Mosaic and munch on him. Then when I'm done with him, I'm going to free my kin from that prison and take them home." The rumble in the growl of these last words made the hair on Andy's skin stand on end.

Saber began laughing. His laughed turned to a cough and his color began to turn an ash gray, but he still kept that sneering smile. He looked at Andy, then at the gargoyle, raised his hand and suddenly a burst of light shot out of it. Andy knocked the huge gargoyle out of the way and caught the blast right in the chest. The gargoyle jumped back up and readied for the attack, but Saber had disappeared.

Stunned, Andy shook his head and got to his feet, still reeling a little from the blast.

"Where did he go?" Andy asked, looking around.

The gargoyle shook his head in disgust. "He just vanished into thin air. I should have killed him, instead of talking so much."

"It's okay," Andy said, patting the huge beast on the arm. He ran over to where Haylee was standing guard over Shimmer.

"Shimmer, are you all right?" he said, cradling her head in his hands. When her eyes didn't open he said, "It's okay. Saber has vanished."

"Food," she mumbled.

"What? I didn't understand what you said."

"I said, FOOD!" Her piercing blue eyes blinked open. "I need lots of food. I haven't eaten in a long time. I'm an Asrai warrior girl you know. I need a lot of food for my growing body."

"It doesn't sound like you're hurt too badly, if all you can think about is food," Andy said grinning. "Come on, maybe I can find you something up at the castle. I might even be able to find some groodle berries."

"Yeah, that's what I'm talking about!" Shimmer said, beaming at Andy. But then she turned serious. "Oh, Andy, you know what this means don't you? Your aunt is going to die."

"Yes, I know. But it's her wish to die. She wants to save her people. Estonia has had a very long life." He helped Shimmer up and then looked at Haylee. "Well, little dragon, are you ready to carry us to our destination?"

Haylee beamed at him. "You bet I am."

Andy held out his hand and watched as Haylee spit out the black jewel, with loads of dragon spit.

"Ewww, thanks for the extra gift. Just what I've always wanted, lots of dragon slobber."

"Hey, I'll have you know that dragon slobber has healing qualities."

"I'll keep that in mind," Andy said, as he wiped the slobber on his robes. Andy looked at the gargoyle. "You coming with us, or are you going to find Prince Mosaic?"

"How can I leave you now, after you just saved my life? No, I'm coming with you." As he said this, a long, loud tooting sound came out his backside. "Well, that felt good! Nothing better than a dryad meal, with a few goblins thrown in for good measure."

"Do you have to keep doing that?" Shimmer said, holding her nose. "Enough already. I really don't like hearing your bodily functions or smelling them either."

Gargoyle looked at her blankly, like he didn't know what all the fuss was about, and then at Andy. "By the way, when I left your friends, most of them were still intact. I think only one was messed up."

Andy felt the blood drain from his face. The gargoyle laughed.

"Don't be alarmed. It was just an elf and he was moving around when I took off."

Relief washed over Andy. He helped Shimmer

mount Haylee and then he crawled up behind her. A beast of his own roared to life in his chest, as he put his arms around her waist. He was so glad to be back with her.

"Okay, Haylee, let's go."

Haylee smiled at the gargoyle. "Wanna see who can fly faster?" Then she leaped into the air, almost knocking Shimmer and Andy off, and took off toward the castle, with the gargoyle following close behind.

ONE STRIPE DOWN
TWO TO GO

aylee landed in front of the castle steps, with the gargoyle right next to her.

"Looks like I win, stinky boy," she said, beaming. "Later we'll go two out of three."

Andy and Shimmer hopped down and ran up the steps to the door. It opened easily, as if it had been waiting for their return. Dread crept into Andy's very being. Every step he took toward Queen Estonia took all of his effort. Something or someone didn't want him to go near her. Shimmer had to keep stopping, so that Andy could catch up.

"What's the matter with you? I thought you were all for this."

"It's not me. I can barely move. I feel like I have on cement shoes," Andy said, looking at his feet. Then a tingle ran from his hand, up his arm and then to his mind.

Andy, it said. *Don't do this to me. Please don't kill me.*

Andy looked down at the jewel in his hand.

"Uh, Shimmer...."

"Yes," Shimmer said, looking confused.

"Nothing. Let's keep going."

When they reached Andy's room where Queen Estonia lay, they could see that her breathing was very shallow. Andy took a step toward the bed and stopped. The jewel began burning like a red-hot coal in Andy's hand. Andy dropped it on the floor.

"What are you doing?" Shimmer asked. "Give it to the queen, before it's too late."

"It burned me. I felt like I had just picked up a burning ember out of the fire." Andy looked at his hand. It was already blistering and very red. "I don't think it wants to die."

"Nonsense," said Claude. "It's a jewel, not a living being."

"Really? Because, it has been talking to me. It told me how to kill the stone giant and just now it told me not to kill it."

Shimmer looked at the jewel incredulously. It was bright red. She went to the bathroom and took some towels, put them in the sink and turned on the cold water. After wringing out the towels, she took them and placed them over the jewel. She looked at Andy.

"Pick it up now, Andy. The towels will protect you."

"I can't put that burning hot stone in my aunt's hand. How cruel is that!"

"Andy," Queen Estonia said, weakly. "I don't

care if it burns a hole right though my hand. I'm almost gone. Please...."

Andy looked into her pleading eyes. They were dull now. Her life was ebbing away. He bent over and wrapped the jewel into the cool, wet towels. The minute that he was holding it again, it spoke:

Andy, if you do this, you will lose so much. I can make you the most powerful being in every land in existence. Creatures will bow to you. Your name will be honored forever. Songs will be sung about you throughout the lands. Take me as your jewel. Fit me to the crown and put me on your head. I will transform you into the most beautiful creature ever born. Let me show you what I can do.

Andy stared at the towels. Suddenly his blistered hand began feeling better. He looked at it in amazement, as right before his eyes the redness, swelling and blisters disappeared. Shimmer and Claude gasped, shocked by what they were seeing.

"Andy," Queen Estonia called. She made her voice as strong as she possibly could and then said, "Listen to me. I can hear every word the jewel is speaking to you. The magic in that jewel is evil. It will eventually destroy you. Look what it has done to the Shadow People. Look at what it has done to the Dark Lands. The people of this land are afflicted because of the evil in that jewel. Please don't listen to it. Give the stone to me, so that I may undo the wrong that the Shadow People have suffered. My death will give life. Hurry!"

Andy looked at her. He was confused. What would it mean to have so much power? To be loved by everyone in the land? Would Shimmer love him if he were the most handsome creature ever born? Would she love him if he were the most powerful man alive? He looked at Shimmer. Was Elsfur still the one she loved? He looked deep into her eyes. There was love there, love that was for him, not Elsfur. Could it be that she was falling in love with Andy? Andy's heart started beating faster and sweat beaded on his brow. He didn't need a jewel to know what or who he was. He was Prince Andrew Misfit, son of Queen Noor and Prince Becken, heir to the throne of Filligrim in the Valley of the Misfits and he was in love with the most beautiful girl in the world.

Andy's heart was so full of love, that it felt like it could burst inside his chest. Shimmer smiled at him, as if she knew all of his thoughts and agreed with them. He moved closer to Shimmer, memorizing every inch of her face. He touched her face, and was a little surprised when she didn't flinch.

Love and courage filled him as he strode toward his aunt and dropped the now black jewel into her hand. Her fingers tightened around it, gripping it so hard, it cut into her skin. Her face changed. Queen Estonia's eyes were so full of fear, fear of the unknown. Andy began stroking her hair, trying to calm her.

"I'm so glad I got to meet you, Aunt Estonia. I will always treasure the time I had here in your castle. It's not every day that a guy gets to meet his great, great, shadow aunt." Andy laughed at his little joke.

"I—," was all she could say.

"Shh...it's okay," Andy reassured her, as he held her hand. "Goodbye, Aunt Estonia."

She smiled at him and tears flowed down her cheeks. Her breathing became erratic and she desperately gasped for air. Finally, a calm spread over her face...and then peace, as she breathed her last breath. As Andy closed her eyes, her body began to transform. The shadow melted away from her skin. She was now the young girl she had been, before her life had changed. She was no longer a shadow.

Andy looked up at Shimmer. She smiled at him, astonished to see his aunt looking like a normal girl. Estonia looked so peaceful in her death that one could have thought that she was only sleeping. They both were shaken from their transfixed awe, as Claude cried out.

"Look at me!" he said, as he began to dance. "Look at me!" Claude had also changed back into his normal self, only he was young. He took Shimmer and Andy's hands and they all three began dancing around the room. Even the room had changed. It was colorful and no longer drab.

"It worked!" said Shimmer. "Even the darkness that had started to take over your appearance is gone, Andy. I wonder if it has worked for the plagued Shadow People as well?"

"Only one way to find out," said Andy. "Let's go find some."

Claude looked at the young girl lying on the bed. Tears of happiness flowed from his eyes. "Thank you," he said, "for everything."

"You will see to it that she has a proper queen

burial?" Andy asked, his voice thick with emotion.

"Yes. Her people will remember her for always. She gave us a home, when no one else wanted us."

Andy stood there looking at the queen and then thought of something that the Shadow Man had said.

"Claude, are you a twin?"

"Yes, yes I am. How did you know that?"

"Saber told me that most Shadow People have twins and that there is always a good twin and an evil twin."

"Not all of us have twins. And as for the good and evil thing, that is simply not true. He is evil, I can tell you that. I tried to warn her majesty about him, but she wouldn't listen. She said that he was trying to do what was right for our kingdom. You see where that got her."

"Yes," Andy said. "But she is at peace now. No more worries about her kingdom."

"We better get a move on, Andy. Maybe we can still help the others," Shimmer said.

Andy nodded, a little sad to leave the queen and her castle.

Andy, Shimmer and Claude were about to leave the room when Shimmer said, "Andy, you better get the jewel. Even though it doesn't work anymore, you don't need to leave it lying around."

"Oh yeah, that wouldn't be good, would it." Andy bent over and started to pick up the jewel and then he stopped. The jewel had changed. It was lighter in color and it had only two red stripes on it, instead of three. "You have got to be kidding me!"

he said, as he picked up the jewel.

That's right, Andy, the jewel said weakly. *I'm not the jewel I was, but I still have power. You'll have to do a lot more than a dead queen to kill me off.*

"It's not dead."

"What do you mean it's not dead?" Shimmer asked.

"It just told me that I would have to do a lot more than just have a queen die, to kill it."

"Well, what do we do now?" Shimmer asked in frustration.

"We find out how to get rid of it, that's what!"

"Just as long as you don't bury it in the Dark Lands. Please take it as far from here as possible," said Claude.

"What will you do now, Claude?" Andy asked.

"Queen Estonia gave this castle to me and my family. She was such a wonderful woman. So good to her people."

Andy smiled at Claude. He was actually going to miss him. He shook his hand.

"That's great. At least you have a place to live and it's fit for a king. Claude, in the library there are symbols. There is a passageway on the other side of those symbols that goes to the castle in Filligrim. If you ever need anything, go through that passageway and come to me. I will help you in any way I can. Also, there is a tunnel in the cell that Theodius and I occupied. You might want to seal it up if you are going to use it to store prisoners." Andy smiled and winked.

"Thank you, Andy. Good luck getting rid of

that evil thing," said Claude, pointing to the jewel."

"No matter what, if it's within my power, this jewel will be destroyed," Andy said, with conviction in every word.

DEPARTING THE DARK LANDS

Haylee and the gargoyle circled above the area where the Misfits, dryads and goblins had been fighting. There were plenty of dead bodies and lots of people Andy didn't recognize, but there were no Misfits.

"Look at all of the people," shouted Shimmer. "They're rejoicing. They have been saved. Let's land and see if they know where the Misfits are."

They landed in a clearing. The sun was now up and the rain had cleared. It was as if the rain had washed away the sickness of the land. Everything was more vibrant. Color had returned to the land. The dark magic that had infected the land was gone.

The people were dancing and singing as Andy and Shimmer got off of Haylee. Their happiness was contagious. Andy and Shimmer laughed and danced around with the people until they ran out of breath.

Andy asked one of the young men if they had seen any elves or dryads, but he just shook his head and said no.

"Where could they have gone?" Shimmer asked.

"I don't know," Andy said, perplexed. Then he got an idea. "Gargoyle, do you smell any of my friends?"

The gargoyle stuck his nose up in the air and took in a large breath. Then he began following his nose, sniffing deeply at every other step. Andy and Shimmer followed behind him. He came to a dead-end about one hundred yards from where he started. He was standing in front of an enormous tree. He walked around the tree, going in several directions, only to come back to the tree every time. He even flew up to the top most part of the tree and then came back down. His face looked mystified.

"I smell them right here." He pointed to where they were standing. "But I don't see them anywhere. I can't smell them in any direction going off from this tree. It's like they have disappeared."

"Are you sure?" Andy asked. He was as bewildered as the gargoyle.

"Maybe they are inside the tree," laughed the gargoyle. "Crazier things have happened."

"I have heard of such trees. When I was a little girl, my mother told me about roots that you plant in the ground and they become trees that you can hide in. I would have loved to have had one when I was a little girl. It would have made a great playhouse," Shimmer said, wistfully.

"I could knock and see if anyone answers back." The gargoyle's stomach rumbled as he looked in the direction of the Shadow People."

Andy thought about this for a moment. Could this be a tree that you can hide in? It made sense. If the Misfits thought they were in danger from the Shadow People, this would have been a good solution.

"Okay. Sure, give it a try. Knock as loud as you can," Andy said. "And stop looking at those Shadow People. They are not on the menu."

"Some people are grumpy. I wasn't even thinking of Shadow People. They are standing close to all of those dead dryads. I'm thinking that I could go for seconds after we find your friends."

"Is that all you two think about, is your stomach?" He looked back and forth between Shimmer and the gargoyle.

"Hey, you promised me I would get something up at the castle. I haven't got any food yet!" Shimmer said, stamping her foot.

"Yeah, and you promised me a dryad dinner and I haven't got my fill yet."

"Enough!" Andy shouted. "Let's find the Misfits and then you both can eat."

The gargoyle grinned at Andy and then turned to face the tree. He curled up his long talons into a fist and began pounding on the tree. Hearing a sound, the four of them backed up and looked at the tree. A small door opened about five feet up from the bottom of the tree. A humongous eyeball came into view on the other side. Haylee began snorting with laughter.

"It's Flipsy," she said. "Hey Flipsy, how did you fit in that tree? You're huge!"

His eyeball disappeared. Shimmer, Andy, Haylee and the gargoyle could hear arguing going on inside of the tree. Then another eyeball appeared.

"Would you look at that," said the muffled voice of Theodius. "It's Andy, Shimmer, Haylee and that stinky gargoyle."

"Hey!" roared the gargoyle. "I don't stink that bad."

Andy, Shimmer and Haylee all looked at each other and then shook their heads.

"Yes, you do!" They all said in unison and then they began to laugh. It felt so good to Andy to laugh with his friends. They had regained the jewel and even lessened its power. They had temporarily gotten rid of the Shadow Man and they had saved all of the Shadow People from the epidemic. But the biggest achievement of all was that Shimmer now belonged to Andy.

The door in the tree opened, allowing Andy, Shimmer, the gargoyle and Haylee, to see inside. Their mouths dropped open, in awe of what they were seeing. The room inside the tree was gigantic. Not only were the Misfits inside, but there were three dragons as well.

That evening they had a feast. Everyone in the Dark Lands came. Someone brought hogs and roasted them over a spit, while others brought vegetables from their gardens. Claude had sent food, tables and chairs from the castle for everyone. Morgan, who was feeling much better thanks to the care of Theodius and Shade, had gone to his farm and brought back homemade stores from his pantry. The gargoyle carried cots out of the large tree and set them up so that Gladdy, King Foxglove and Meadow could enjoy the festivities as well.

Some of the Shadow People who knew how to play instruments gathered and played. Everyone danced and sang. Large bonfires kept everyone warm as they partied through the night. It was the best party Andy had ever gone to. He knew exactly what the Shadow People were feeling. His heart was light and blissfully happy as he danced with Shimmer.

"Well, someone has changed a lot since I saw him last," said Gladdy, as Andy sat down next to her cot. They both sat in silence for a moment, watching everyone dance and laugh.

"I guess I have changed a lot. Being a prisoner will do that to you," Andy finally said.

"I wasn't just talking about the growing up change. I'm talking about the falling in love change."

Andy blushed. He watched Shimmer dance with Snollygob.

"You can't imagine how happy I am right at this moment, Aunt Gladdy."

"Oh, yes I can. I have Theodius back, remember. I couldn't believe it when I saw him standing there when we arrived in the Dark Lands. It was like I had never been away. Time has been cruel to us both, but the love is still there. I'm so glad that he had you in that nasty dungeon. He told me how you and he have become such good friends and that you wouldn't leave him in that dungeon. His memory has almost completely returned."

She reached over and took Andy's hand and squeezed it. She was so glad to have him back.

"Speaking of change," Andy beamed. "Look at you. You have changed so much that I hardly recognize you. Just imagine, this whole time I was being raised by an elf! And a very beautiful one, at that."

Now it was Gladdy's turn to blush. Andy examined her face. Even though she had nearly died, she glowed with happiness.

As the night wore on, everyone partied and feasted. One by one the Shadow People left for their homes. Some talked about staying in the Dark Lands and making a fine kingdom that people would want to come and visit. Others talked about going home to where they were born and finding their families that they had been forced to leave.

When all was quiet and just the Misfits were sitting around the fire, they talked about their adventures and the disappearance of the Shadow Man. Andy told them about the conversation that he and Saber had, and how the gargoyle had saved him. He told them about the jewel and how it was still alive and how brave Queen Estonia had been, accepting her fate. He also told how Theodius the Cat was Saber's twin brother and how the real Theodius turned him into a cat.

"Saber said that his brother's name was Thor.

He also said that Thor would never give up."

"That's funny," said Grandmother Muckernut. "The cat said his name was Saber."

"I guess we will never really know who they are," said Elsfur. "I just know that we will constantly have to watch our backs. The sooner we get rid of that jewel and crown, the better."

"But how are we to do that?" asked Snollygob. "Is there any way to get rid of that blasted jewel?"

"I think we should leave in the morning for Crystal Sea Palace. Queen Noor has taken refuge there and I know that King Renauldee and Queen Arianna would like to meet their grandson," said Gladdy, beaming at Andy. "Who knows, King Renauldee may have some answers."

"Don't forget, we have to take Marcella the Sheely with us," said Daisy. "If we don't, she might eat me."

"No one is going to eat you, Daisy," said Andy. "Not if I can help it."

Morgan cleared his throat. He had been quiet all evening, watching everyone have a good time. His feeling of guilt was overwhelming. He knew that it was the jewel that had started the plague, but he couldn't help feeling bad knowing that he had been the one to eat the fruit.

"Could I say something?" he asked, shyly. Andy nodded in approval and Morgan timidly continued. "I just want to thank each and every one of you for what you have done for this land and my people. If you hadn't helped, there is no telling how many creatures would have died."

"It was the sacrifice of your queen that did it,"

said Andy. "Queen Estonia was a brave woman. Remember her. Write songs about her. Help her legend to live on."

"I will, Prince Andrew. You can count on me."

Hearing his formal name, Andy didn't quite know what to say. So he just bowed his head.

"Well, since we have such a long way to go, we better get a good night's sleep," said Elsfur. He eyed Shimmer sitting next to Andy. His heart was breaking on the inside, knowing that he had lost her. His heart didn't want to admit his defeat. Could there be a way of winning her back?

Andy laid his head on the pillow a while later, listening to the wind blowing through the tree. It was a very calming sound. He smiled in the dark at the thought of meeting his mother and grandparents. He couldn't believe that just a few months ago he was thinking about his mother as well, except they were anxious and fearful thoughts. Back then he hadn't wanted to hurt his Aunt Gladdy. Now he knew where he stood with her. She would always be his mother and nothing would ever change that. He would also have the support of good friends when he met his birth mother. There was so much catching up to do with not only Queen Noor, but Kwagar as well.

Andy drifted into a blissful sleep. He didn't have his normal dreams of the glittery blue girl and baseball games. This time he had a dreamed of a handsome man, riding a tall horse, battling against enormous creatures. The dream ended with one face floating in a blue, swirling light. But it wasn't the face of the girl that he loved; it was the face of a woman with long-flowing red hair and bright green eyes. Her skin glowed so bright it hurt his eyes just to look at her. Accompanying the woman was a huge wolf with eyes like globes.

Troubling times are ahead, Andy, the woman said, her voice tinkling like bells. *Beware of the disappearing little ones and the creatures beyond the Land of the Fitful.*

Andy awoke suddenly. He looked around the still dark room and at the creatures that were sleeping. He shivered. Would life ever be normal again? He lay his head back down and went back to sleep.

The next morning the gargoyle and Daisy flew down to the Golden River to pick up Marcella the Sheely. The Sheely was not keen on the idea of having to ride on a gargoyle and the gargoyle was not happy that a wet, slimy, green woman with fish bones in her long black hair was going to be riding on his back.

"She smells," he complained to Andy, when he got back to the camp. Elsfur was just about to pull the leaf from the tree to make it into a root again, when he heard what the gargoyle said.

"Ha! You're one to talk. Because of the lack of better places to sleep, I had to sleep by you last night. Ugh, I thought I was going to die from asphyxiation. You, Mr. Gargoyle, are the disgusting one!" Elsfur said, as he pulled the leaf.

The gargoyle watched the tree turn back into a root and then whispered to Andy, "Just look at her. She's all slimy and gross. You expect me to fly a thousand leagues with that on my back. Have you seen her nails? They're all black and look decayed."

"Oh please!" said Elsfur, in disgust.

"How could he hear me? I was whispering."

"I have excellent hearing. I *am* an elf, if you haven't noticed." Elsfur pointed at his ears as proof.

"I have noticed and there is something else that I have noticed. You like to stick your abnormally large ears into other people's business. Now BUTT OUT!" The gargoyle's growl was so deep it reverberated in Andy's chest. He felt like he was standing in front of a bass amplifier, turned up all the way.

"Enough!" Andy shouted. "If I put a blanket on your back, so that she is not touching your skin, will that make you feel better?"

The gargoyle frowned and then looked at Marcella and then back at Andy. He did this several times, trying to make up his mind if the blanket would be good enough. Finally he relented and slinked off to pout.

When everyone was ready, the dragons and gargoyle took off with their passengers. King Foxglove, Shade and Meadow stood on the ground with Morgan, waving goodbye. Andy wondered when he would get to see any of them again. Thane decided to travel on to the sea, rather than go home. He had his sister Gladdy back and he wanted to spend as much time with her as possible.

Andy had Flipsy circle the castle before they headed to Crystal Sea Palace. A lump rose in his throat as he looked at the stone building. He couldn't figure why he was feeling so emotional. It could have been because the castle had been his home for a while and he would miss it. It could have been that he knew that his aunt would be buried without any of her family there to say goodbye. Andy knew that Claude would give her a good burial and that she would be in good hands. He made himself a promise that when the jewel and crown were destroyed, he would come back and plant a garden around Estonia's grave, just like the ones at Filligrim Castle.

"Let's go Flipsy," Andy said, taking one last look.

TALLULAH P. BRIAR

Andy had been able to smell the sea for quite some time. The large yellow moon was guiding them now. They had taken only a few breaks so that the dragons and gargoyle could rest. Toward the end of the day, seagulls had flown alongside them. Flopsy kept plucking the birds out of the air, until Gladdy forbid him to eat any more.

"It's bad enough that we're flying up and down and side to side. My stomach feels as if it's been on one of those roller coasters from the other world. And then to have to watch you eat those poor birds and hear all those bones crunching, and feathers and blood flying everywhere, is just too much," she protested.

Everyone except for the other dragons and the gargoyle, had agreed.

"I don't know what you're fussing about. At least your skin isn't drying out and cracking like a desert. If I don't get back in the water soon, I won't be able to hold my head up as the most beautiful Sheely in the land anymore. I will be shamed by my kind and have to live in a hovel to hide my ugliness."

"Ha! The most beautiful," mumbled gargoyle. "What does she think she was living in back in the Dark Lands, a palace?"

"I'll have you know, I had no choice but to live in that drain pipe, creature! The goblins wanted me for my talent."

"And what is that, having the most fish bones in your hair?" he shot back.

"No, I'm an alchemist. I can change metal into gold." This piece of news made the entire group of Misfits stare with a little respect at the nasty green woman.

But Andy rolled his eyes. Everyone had been grumbling for the last few hours and he couldn't wait until they arrived at the castle.

"Look!" shouted Daisy, excitedly. "It's the ocean. I have never seen the ocean."

"Well, you are in for a treat," said an unusually happy Kwagar. "I love coming here. When I was little, I would go down and swim with the mermaids. It was so much fun."

"Sounds like it," said Daisy, as she wondered how she might swim without getting her wings wet.

"Look, there is our grandfather's castle," Kwagar said to Andy. Andy looked to where he was pointing. He couldn't tell much about it in the moonlight, but it reminded him of the castle people made out of sand on the beaches back in the other world.

Bells rang out, announcing the approach of the dragons. Guards ran out into the courtyard and stood at attention.

Nervousness and excitement filled Andy's heart as the dragons circled the castle and then landed in the courtyard. Some of the guards stepped back, trying to avoid the massive creatures' tails. As they dismounted, a man, joined by a woman, came out of the castle doors. Andy was a little surprised by the appearance of the king and queen. Both of them had fish scales on their faces and their eyes were rounder than normal human eyes. Kwagar ran to greet them, as everyone else bowed.

"Grandmother! Grandfather!" he said, joyously. "How good it is to see you again."

Both of his grandparents stared in shock and horror at their grandson. He was emaciated and filthy.

"Kwagar," said Queen Arianna, as she embraced her grandson. "What have those filthy goblins done to my boy?"

"I'm fine. I could use some of Cook's good food though."

"How about a bath as well," boomed King Renauldee, as he let go of Kwagar. "We'll have you looking like your old self in no time." He looked at everyone and gasped as he spotted Andy. Tears welled in his eyes. "Prince Andrew, welcome to your grandparents' home."

Andy smiled and didn't quite know what to do with himself. Both the king and the queen came forward and embraced Andy. Andy closed his eyes, feeling the warmth and love, and when he opened them, he found himself staring at a very beautiful woman. He knew her face at once. It had been the face he had seen on the battlefield in the Black Mountains. Only she had been unconscious and tied to a pole.

Andy let go of his grandparents and ran to embrace his mother. Tears streamed down her face and she hugged him like she would never let him go again...*Her child*...It had been sixteen years since she had last held him. She finally looked him in the eyes, and smiled.

"Hello, Mother," Andy said. "I didn't think this day would ever come."

"Neither did I, Andrew. I thought I had lost you forever. Now you stand before me, a grown man. I have missed your whole life."

"Well, you have me now and you can watch me as I go through the rest of my life."

"I would be honored to be around as your mother, for the rest of your life." She looked at Kwagar and held her hand out to him. As he joined them she said, "For the rest of both of your lives. We are a complete family now."

King Renauldee looked at all of the Misfits, Thane and the dragons, and said, "I owe each of you a debt of gratitude for bringing our grandchildren to us safely. My guards will feed the dragons all they want. They will have the finest stables. The rest of you come and dine with us at our table. I will have my servants show you to our finest guest rooms where you can freshen up. New clothes will be assembled for you and a feast prepared."

"Um, Grandfather," Andy said, the word feeling weird on his tongue. "The gargoyle is my friend and loyal companion. He is also a great warrior. I couldn't have done what I did without him. Also, Marcella the Sheely helped us as well. Could you see to it that she gets home to her family?"

"I will have my personal guard take her straight away. Also, the gargoyle will be honored, along with the dragons. Guards, take them to the stable and give them whatever they want and need and see to it that Marcella gets home." Then King Renauldee clapped his hands and servants ushered everyone where they would be lodging. Andy went over to where Flipsy was.

"I will come visit you after I have rested. Thank you for flying us all the way here. You're an awesome dragon. I'm very proud of you."

"Thank you, Andy. Go rest and I will see you later." Andy watched as the dragons and gargoyle flew off to the back of the castle.

After Andy had bathed, one of the servants came in to give him some clothes. She was pretty with long, flowing blonde hair that curled at the ends and blue eyes that were shaped like cat eyes. Her pupils looked like slits, rather than round like human eyes. On both cheeks were pale pink and white scales, in the shape of an ocean wave.

The clothes she gave to Andy were made of a

very shiny material and were colored much like the inside of a large seashell, all mottled with different hues of greens, yellows and pale pinks. Andy was thankful that there wasn't much pink in the coloring.

"What is your name?" Andy asked, as the girl helped him put on his tunic.

"My name is Lauren. I am Queen Arianna's handmaiden and future bride of your brother."

Andy did a double take at the girl, and then asked, "What did you say?"

"I said I'm hand—"

"No, the other part."

"Oh, I said that I'm betrothed to your brother, Kwagar."

"My brother has a fiancée?" Andy was astonished.

"Yes. Kwagar and I have loved each other for quite some time. We will marry when he turns eighteen. Didn't he tell you?"

"No. Um...we haven't had much time to talk. He was in prison and I was in prison...." Andy ended lamely, not knowing what to say. He couldn't believe what he was hearing. Kwagar was getting married.

"Would you like for me to show you where we will be dining?"

"Sure—yeah, okay," Andy said, still feeling awkward. Never in his wildest dreams would he have thought about getting married until he was out of college and working at a steady job for a while. That was the mentality of the other world. This world never failed to surprise him. Would it still be that way, even after he had been here for years?

He followed Lauren through the halls. They reminded Andy of walking through a giant snail shell. The walls were pearly in color and shone like the northern lights of the other world. Torches made of long seashells held small flickering flames in them, brightening the halls.

Trying to fill in a lulled conversation, Andy said, "So, how did you and Kwagar meet?"

"I am your cousin. My father is King Renauldee's first cousin. When Kwagar declared love for me, Queen Arianna wanted to get to know me more like a daughter. So I became her handmaiden."

"That sounds more like a servant, than a daughter," Andy said.

Lauren laughed. "Actually, I'm training to be Kwagar's wife. Queen Arianna is teaching me how to be a proper lady for when I become queen."

"Oh, so you're like in a queen-in-training program."

"I guess you could call it that," Lauren smiled. "It is a great honor among my people to be tutored by the queen herself. For centuries, a future queen was to have a male tutor and was kept away from family and friends so that she could put her full attention into it. Queen Arianna thought it was a ridiculous rule, and had it abolished so that she could tutor me herself. Now, I don't have to be away from my family. I can see them anytime I want."

"That was nice of my grandmother." Andy was beginning to like his grandparents more and more.

They finally came to a stop in front of double doors made from giant clamshells with pearls for handles. Two guards opened the doors for them.

King Renauldee stood waiting for Andy. "I would like to speak with you privately in my chambers after dinner. There are some matters I wish to discuss with you. I'm so glad to have you here, Andy. You and Kwagar have made Queen Arianna and me so happy. In fact, we are going to have a huge celebration for our new prince. It will be bigger than the festival we just had. I have already made preparations. Come and eat. You will love the food in my kingdom. I have the finest chef in the land. We call him Cook," King Renauldee boasted.

After one of the finest meals Andy had enjoyed in a long time, Andy, Kwagar and King Renauldee left to go to the king's study. He had Andy and Kwagar recount their individual tales of being captured, imprisoned, their escape, the battle that was fought in the Dark Lands and the demise of the Dark Queen.

King Renauldee sat quietly for a few moments, reflecting on all he had just heard. Then he looked at Andy and said, "May I see the jewel?"

Andy looked at Kwagar and then looked back at his grandfather. King Renauldee was holding out his hand. Andy felt hesitant about who should see the jewel. The jewel was still powerful and he didn't know how much influence it might have over the king.

"I haven't let anyone hold it except Haylee. It could be very dangerous. The jewel is extremely powerful."

"I understand, Andy." The king began chewing his bottom lip, as if trying to make up his mind. "I am going to tell both of you a secret. The only other people that know of this secret are the dead kings that lived before me. My ancestor was on the council that had the jewel and crown made. After the crown was hidden, my ancestor had been mind-wiped so that he wouldn't remember where the crown had been hidden. However, he did remember bits and pieces of all that went on. One of the pieces of information that he wrote down concerned a scepter."

"Do you mean that the council not only made a crown and jewel, they made a scepter?" Andy said, trying to wrap his brain around this piece of information.

"I'm afraid so," King Renauldee said. "That's not all. Not long after my ancestor recovered, a note was sent to him by an anonymous person. It said that the crown had been hidden in his kingdom."

"You mean the crown is hidden here?" Kwagar practically shouted.

"Keep your voice down, Kwagar." King Renauldee chided. "Even my castle has its spies." He looked at Andy. "I would like to help you destroy the crown. It has been in my care far too long and I don't like having the responsibility."

Andy reached for the pouch in his pocket. He took out the jewel and handed it to his grandfather.

"The bottom stripe is missing," King Renauldee said.

"Yes. Is that a problem?" Andy asked.

"It's just that, you would think that the topmost stripe would have disappeared. According to my ancestor, the stripes had meanings. I think if you find out the meanings, you will find out how to destroy it."

Andy's mood fell. Here was another undertaking to add on top of an already mounting pile of tasks. While his mission had not been simple, there had been only two on the list: destroy the crown and the jewel. Now, he had to figure out what the stripes were and destroy a scepter as well. His grandfather handed him back the jewel.

"Keep the jewel hidden and on your person at all times, until you can figure out how to destroy it. I will help you if I can. In the journal right next to the word scepter, my ancestor wrote the word, *Eldfjall.*"

"King Granite's realm," said Kwagar, in almost a whisper.

"Yes. I'm guessing this mystery is going to be taking you to the top of the world, to the realm of the dragons. You would think that the top of the world would be very cold, but it is just the opposite. King Granite's realm is in a volcano in the Morcrim Mountains. It isn't going to be easy, even if you have dragons taking you there. It is a very perilous place. But enough about going on a journey. You will stay and we will learn more about each other," King Renauldee said, smiling. "I'm sure Kwagar is anxious to visit with his bride to be, and your grandmother would love to pamper you with lavish gifts. But first, before she gets ahold of you, I would like to take you somewhere. Somewhere I think you would really enjoy." King Renauldee paused for effect before saying, "Would you like to see the crown?"

"What crown? You mean 'the crown'? You actually know where the crown is hidden?" Andy asked, very surprised by his grandfather's question.

"Yes. In fact, I had to rehide it, after your father showed your mother where it was hidden, the little imp."

"That would be great!" Andy said, hardly able to contain his enthusiasm. "But—but, I started this journey with my friends and I think they should be able to come as well."

"Very well. If you think that is wise, they may come."

King Renauldee led the large group down past the dungeons and into the deepest parts of the castle. Shimmer's grip on Andy's hand tightened as they passed rats and large spider webs. Finally, after traveling down long halls and many flights of stairs, they came to a dead end. The wall was solid steel. To the far right side of the wall hung a small lit torch. King Renauldee placed his hand on the wall and then looked at everyone.

"Could all of you turn around? I have a secret way of opening the door and I don't want anyone to know. Just as a precaution." He watched as the group turned around. When he felt no one would see, he spat in his hand and rubbed it on the wall. The wall shimmered at first and then disappeared. "Okay, let's proceed."

Andy stood in awe of the hall that he was

facing. It was a long tube of glass and it was sitting on the ocean floor! Tiles made of seashells made up the flooring and starfish-shaped torches lit the way. Andy could have stood and watched the sea life for hours.

"It's just beautiful," he told King Renauldee. "If I were you, I would come here all the time. I would have a bed brought here, so that I could lie and watch the fish swimming above me."

"I'm glad you like it. But we need to keep moving. There are safeguards that keep the crown safe, and one of them is a sea beast that is capable of breaking through this glass and eating you. Come along."

At the end of the glass tunnel was a very large, round door made of solid gold. In the center was a silver combination wheel. It reminded Andy of the wheel that steers a ship. Andy's heart pounded in anticipation of seeing the room that held the crown. He knew that the room that held the jewel had been very beautiful and wondered if his grandfather had built this one to be as beautiful.

King Renauldee asked everyone to turn around again as he spun out the combination on the wheel. Andy heard the lock click and the door swing open. He turned to see a bright shining light. The walls were made of alternate stripes of mother of pearl, gold, silver, and jade. Hanging from the ceiling was a chandelier made of diamonds and crystals. There was only one item in the room and it was a giant clam made of solid gold. Etched in the clam were different scenes, depicting mermaids swimming in the sea. Andy could hardly breathe, the room was so stunning. He couldn't believe that someone would take the time to build such a beautiful room, for just a crown. King Renauldee walked over to the clam.

"I had this made for the crown box. I felt that since the crown was in a mermaid realm, it should reflect the creatures that guard it." Everyone watched as he passed his hand over his mouth and then placed it on the clam. After a short moment, something clicked and the clam slowly opened. Inside was a crystal box with red velvet lining the bottom and a little keyhole in the shape of a bird.

Everyone gasped. Instead of a beautiful crown, there was a yellowed piece of paper. All eyes rested upon King Renauldee. He stood there, dumbfounded.

"No! No! This cannot be! Where is the crown?" he asked, outraged.

Andy took out the birdcage necklace from his little pouch, and opened the birdcage. The little bird inside sprang to life and then flew out of the cage and into the hole in the crystal box. The lock clicked. Andy opened the lid and reached in, taking out the yellowed piece of paper. Everyone watched as he read aloud the words. Words that were so disheartening to hear:

> *My ancestor was murdered for the*
> *sake of her race.*
> *So I have stolen the crown from its*
> *glass case.*
> *You will find me in a hollow, with no*
> *direction,*

While I keep the crown in my
protection.
No map or compass will point the way.
Which leaves me with one more thing
to say.
If you come looking for me, be
prepared to fight.
For I will protect the crown, with all
of my might.
                    ~Tallulah P. Briar

"You have got to be kidding me!" Andy said, fuming, and throwing up his hands. "Who in the world is Tallulah P. Briar?"

"My question would be, how on earth did she get into this room?" roared King Renauldee.

Andy looked around at everyone. All of them were shaking their heads in disbelief. It was one more mystery they would have to solve.

CAST OF CHARACTERS

Misfits

Andy~ Prince of Filligrim, son of Queen Noor and Prince Becken and raised by Gladiola Misfit in our world. He is the future king of Filligrim.

Daisy~ Andy's pixie and best friend.

Gladdy~ A lady elf from the Land of Chaldeon. Andy's aunt who raised him in our world to protect him from his evil grandfather.

Kwagar~ Andy's twin brother. He inherited his father's Asrai powers, and can move earth and objects with his mind.

Queen Noor~ Queen of Filligrim Castle and mother to Andy and Kwagar.

Prince Becken~ He was the father of Andy and Kwagar. He went missing during a battle with creatures beyond the Land of the Fitful. He was declared dead.

Mystic~ An Asrai that was banished from the Land of the Misfits. She is also grandmother to Andy and Kwagar. She can control all forms of nature.

Elsfur~ An elf from River Birch Forest, betrothed to King Foxglove's daughter and leader of the Special Guard at Filligrim Castle.

Shimmer~ An Asrai Warrior girl that can turn into a blue mist. She is also the head of the Weapons Department.

Timmynog~ A Stone Giant from the Land of the Fitful. He is also Kwagar's protector.

Snollygob~ He is a Killmoulis and part of the Special Guard. He eats through his nose and talks through his ears.

Portumus~ Captain of the Filligrim Guard.

Spongy~ A sponge magically created by Gladdy to be a bathroom helper.

Mrs. Plumthistle~ Filligrim Castle's cook.

Amanda~ One of Queen Noor's handmaidens; twin sister to Taylor and sister to Caleb the stable boy.

Taylor~ One of Queen Noor's handmaidens; twin sister to Amanda and sister to Caleb the stable boy.

Caleb~ The stable boy for Filligrim Castle. Brother to twin sisters, Amanda and Taylor.

Windsor~ Leader of the unicorns.

Dragons

Flipsy~ Andy's dragon and twin brother to Flopsy.

Flopsy~ Kwagar's dragon and twin brother to Flipsy.

Hannah~ A dragon from the Land of Chaldeon.

Haylee~ A dragon from the Land of Chaldeon and Hannah's little sister.

Elves of River Birch Forest

King Foxglove~ King of the elves in River Birch Forest and father to Wisteria.

Shade~ One of King Foxglove's loyal servants and bodyguards.

Meadow~ One of King Foxglove's loyal servants and bodyguards.

The Goblins of Goblin City and the Dingy Mountains

King Vulgaree~ King of the Goblins and father of Prince Mosaic.

Prince Mosaic~ Son of King Vulgaree. Started the war in the Black Mountains hoping to win and rule the Land of the Misfits. Allies himself with the Shadow Man.

Mucous~ Servant of Prince Mosaic.

Dryads of Hemlock Forest

Grandmother Muckernut~ Leader of the dryads and close friend of Gladdy.

Apricot~ Grandmother Muckernut's servant. She is also next in line as leader of the dryads. She allies herself with Prince Mosaic and the Shadow Man to gain power.

Elves of Mulberry Forest

King Silverthorne~ King of the elves of Mulberry Forest and uncle to Gladdy and Thane.

Thane~ Nephew of King Silverthorne and brother to Gladdy.

Paowyn and Thornthistle~ Guards of the Arch of Mutador, the entrance to Mulberry Forest.

People of the Dark Lands

Queen Estonia~ Queen of the Dark Lands and Andy's great, great aunt.

Morgan~ An elf that turned into a shadow and was sent to the Dark Lands.

Claude~ A Shadow Person that lives in Charlock Castle and personal servant to Queen Estonia.

Shadow Man/Theodius the Cat~ A Shadow Person that intends to harness the Crown of the Races' power to soothe his own lust for greed and total domination of the races.

Book One:
Prince Andy and the
Misfits: Shadow Man
Paperback: 356 pages
Publisher: Tate
Publishing &
Enterprises (January 4,
2011)
Language: English
ISBN-10: 161663619X
ISBN-13: 978-
1616636197
*Available everywhere fine
books are sold online, in
print and eBook*

Also, watch for the next
installment of *Prince Andy and the
Misfits* with book three: *Loombria,*
coming soon! Follow the author at
www.karengammons.com for
exciting news!

12031885R00227

Made in the USA
Charleston, SC
06 April 2012